I0565023

*It was the sincere final wish of my father, Harold Knoll, that this book be
dedicated to the loving memory of his wife, my mother,
Winnie Knoll, and his daughter, my sister, Margaret Knoll.
We gotcha covered, dad.*

A Special Thanks to:

*To the hard working staff at Young Films and Publishing
that made this book and my father's dream possible.*

...Daniel Knoll

HAROLD KNOLL

Cover and interior designs by Young Films & Publishing LLC
Editing by:
Jackie L. Young &
Amber Young

Printed in the United States of America

ISBN 0-9774328-8-2

FRATELLI

By Harold Knoll

CHAPTER I

Angelo Panettorio swung the black Cadillac Fleetwood Brougham off I94 at 80 mph onto a snow-covered county road, rounded a corner, and hit ABS brakes. He stopped before an approaching open Model T Touring car with three Keystone Kops in front leading a marching band playing "Hail, Hail, the Gang's All Here!"

The Model T braked and skidded into the ditch as the band bunched up blaring wildly and a black Lincoln Town Car screeched to a stop behind the Cadillac.

Glancing in his rearview mirror at two men in the Lincoln, Angelo spat out a shredded toothpick. He reached to the seat beside him for a 9 mm Beretta, hesitated and wrapped it in *The Wall Street Journal*. This he topped with a paperback of *How To Win Friends and Influence People* leaving the package on the seat.

He got out into the early spring sunshine, smoothed his black silk turtleneck shirt, flicked lint off his black silk slacks, smiled and raised his hands. The smile changed to a frown at the shoulder of the road when slush soaked his new crocodile tasseled loafers.

As the Model T was pushed out of the ditch by two laughing Keystone Kops, the Lincoln began to back away. But a jolly Kop wearing a large tin CHIEF badge flexed his floppy nightstick and ordered the pair out. They complied, raising their hands after adjusting black fedoras and smoothing lapels on black suits.

The musicians reassembled in their green elf hats, pink pointy ears, brown jerkins, red hose and black pointy shoes. Two shivering girls in scanty cheerleader's costume straightened their Trollville High School banner and winked when Angelo bowed.

Restarting the Model T, the Kops escorted the three visitors to the rear seat, made a U-turn and drove slowly to a nearby hamlet followed by the band playing "Go, Tell It on the Mountain." The procession was halted by a stout troll wearing a red MAYOR sash who flung his arms wide and cried:"God dag! Velkommen to Trollville!"

Jammed in the rear seat between the two gentlemen from the Lincoln, the unarmed Angelo could feel they were packing and looked back wistfully at his Cadillac.

After the Model T parked at a rickety reviewing stand, the mayor escorted the trio to a scaffold where he pinned blue PARTICIPANT ribbons on them, remnants of last year's elementary school field day. In the nearby village park a sign said, "Trollville: Where It's Always Halloween." Idlers in parkas and boots watched the band march away in numbing cold playing "The Sidewalks of New York." Angelo felt alone.

"Which one of you three strangers is the official representative Senator Somaro sent from Washington to stand in for him at this historic occasion?" the mayor said.

The trio eyed each other and Angelo immediately said, "Jack Smith at your service, Mayor. Senator Somaro is sorry he ain't here because he got bit by a caucus."

"And these two?"

"Secret Service. See them tight lips? When the senator travels they even follow him into the john where one shakes the last three drops off the senator's eight-inch banana while the other hums 'Good-night, Ladies.'"

"But the senator isn't here now," said the police chief, "and the citizens got all dressed up in their Norwegian troll costumes in his honor."

"You mean you don't dress like this all the time? Well, that's the feds for you. Did you ever hear they done anything right? Maybe you and your men stick close to them agents in case we got another terrorist attack like the one the senator had last year."

"We never heard nothing about a terrorist attack against our senator," the mayor said.

Angelo jerked a thumb at his two companions. "Classified information. But just ask them guys. They'll tell you the senator was touring Sicily when he made the mistake of calling the locals Italians. Them two guys saved his ass that time. Just answer with the head, boys."

The pair nodded glumly as the mayor blew a whistle and cried, "Everybody in your places! Start the grand parade!"

"But the band has already gone back to the high school," the police chief said.

"Remind me to tell the school board to fire that knucklehead of a band director even though he is my brother-in-law."

Angelo drove his Cadillac in the lead after trolls slapped taped signs to the front doors proclaiming, "Vote for Senator Somaro."

The Lincoln followed with the two men in front and two Keystone Kops in back.

"You have the candy?" said the mayor sitting beside Angelo as they rolled past a few natives on the windswept street.

"What candy?"

"Senator Somaro always throws out candy to the kids watching the grand parade."

"The senator is worried about the kids gettin' cavities so he told me to bring this instead."

Angelo reached to the floor and produced a bulging cloth coin sack bearing the name of a Brooklyn bank, scene of a recently unauthorized withdrawal. "You throw them shiny quarters out your side and I'll throw them out mine," Angelo said turning the heater up because frigid air was pouring into the open windows.

The mayor wiggled in his seat and reached under himself for the items Angelo had left. "Hope I haven't messed up your *Wall Street Journal* and book. Your newspaper sure feels heavy."

"If you wanna run an organization today you gotta plow through that heavy stuff even though the bulls is fulla bullshit and the bears is bare-assed."

"And the book?"

"When the fox is chased by the rabbits instead of vice versa he gotta change his MO."

Since Main Street was only three blocks long the parade ended abruptly.

"I gotta go, Mayor. We're damn busy in Washington buildin' consensuses."

"Young fella, please thank the senator for looking out for our kids' dental health. And I just have one question: If you and the Secret Service came here from Washington, how come your cars have New York plates?"

Angelo put a finger to his lips.

"Mayor, that question involves national security. But I'm gonna pass along a tip that will enhance your net worth like we say on Wall Street."

The mayor leaned close, quarters jingling in his pocket.

"Them two punks in the car behind us ain't really Secret Service. They're Middle Eastern terrorists which is why I asked for two cops to sit behind them. You just give your police chief the high sign and order him to toss them two jokers into the slammer. Next get on the horn to the Secret Service and tell them Senator Somaro certifies you're entitled to the $10,000 reward and to be in the photo pop with the president handin' you the check while Senator Somaro kibitzes. -But be careful. Them terrorists is packin'."

The mayor studied the rear view mirror. "They are kind of dark complected."

"Notice that squint from too much sun? Put a turban and a bedsheet on them sons of the desert and they'll hitch a ride on the first two-seater camel they see and ream your ass."

"Ten thousand you say?"

"Why fart around waitin' for the state lottery when you can get what's comin' to you now? Like *la puttana* told the worried bishop in bed, 'You can always say the rosary some other time and this is after all a missionary position.'"

The mayor leaned out of the passenger window, beckoned the police chief and whispered. Soon the suspects felt gun muzzles in their backs while outside the Lincoln the police chief waved frantically to the editor of the village weekly who carried an ancient Speed Graphic. The editor posed the suspects flanked by the mayor and police chief and had them all say cheese. Before jailing the suspects, the Keystone Kops doffed their costumes disclosing their real uniforms, which were nearly identical.

"How come your editor takes pictures with his lens cap on?" Angelo asked the mayor.

"Shoot! No wonder they always come out so dark."

"And how come this big deal about trolls? I seen troll booths comin' up here from Chicago but nobody organized no parade."

"It's our annual troll festival because the village is 100 percent Norwegian. Come and be my guest at the village hall and you'll eat your fill of lutefisk."

"Sorry Mayor, but the senator got me booked at South Madison where I'm gonna represent him at a basketball game."

"Who's playing?"

"Southside Royal Rockets versus Ku Klux Klan Knights."

"Well *uff-da* to you."

"Up yours too, Mayor."

As Angelo drove the Cadillac along the county road toward I94 he stopped on the shoulder, tossed Senator Somaro's signs into the ditch, removed the Cadillac's stolen plates, tossed them after the signs and installed another set of stolen plates. He took I94 west toward Madison and pulled into the first rest stop. When he left the men's room, he saw a little old lady sitting on a bench and eating a bagel with cream cheese and lox.

"You got a good nosh there with that three-ounce deli size."

She stopped in mid-bite and scrutinized him. "*Sephardic?*"

"Siciliano. When I was a kid in Brooklyn I worked for Reilly's Bagels."

"A dago and a mick in bagels?"

"Today things ain't what they seem. *Scusi* but I gotta call my grandma."

As he dropped new quarters into the pay phone, she said, "I knew you were a *mensh.*"

CHAPTER II

Don Topo Scempio held a cherry-sized fruit in an early morning sunbeam that had sneaked through the dusty front windows of his old attached Brooklyn home. Between his bony thumb and forefinger he rotated the tiny red globe, felt its firmness, admired its unblemished skin and murmured, "*Il Marte in piccolo*"—a miniature Mars.

He had retrieved the fallen fruit from a lush array of Jerusalem Cherry houseplants crowding a front window shelf. The don called his plants his little orchard and delighted in observing the green fruits ripen through yellow, orange and red.

As he relaxed in a Goodwill recliner in his living room, he laid the fruit on an end table and rubbed his thin hands together producing little warmth. Then he glanced glumly at a corner where an aphid-ravaged plant languished in quarantine on an old wooden beer crate despite an insecticidal soap shampoo.

"*I frutti e la verdura!*" he exclaimed, gritting his teeth.

He swore by fruit and vegetables after his confessor had warned blasphemy was the open manhole to hell. Rolling a shriveled leaf in his fingers, he muttered, "Bugs better not fuck with Don Topo."

He reached for the ancient black rotary phone, the only one in the house, and called his nephew.

"Professore, the don wants for you to get down here

immediatamente and whack them aphids off his Jerusalem Cherry."

"But *zio mio,* with all due respect I know nothing about horticulture. My discipline is etymology, not entomology. In fact I'd gladly provide assistance with your syntax-"

But the don pounded the phone on the dented top of the rickety end table. "What's this crapola about sin taxes? The don hears enough about that from Washington. You a bug expert so drag your ass down here or maybe the don sends an adjuster to refurbish your recollection who makes your mortgage payments. Bring your best bug killer and a spray gun that don't miss. The don wants this hit done right."

Don Topo hung up grumbling about the perfidy of nephews and underbosses.

In the bowels of the drafty house the ancient furnace wheezed as he shivered. He rose with a groan and stroked the wrinkled lapels of his shiny double-breasted blue serge suit. Complementing this was a Christmas gift from his wife, a gray silk clip-on bowtie accented by a red blob of pasta sauce.

Then he inspected his healthy plants bearing a bountiful crop of plump red fruit. The don plucked a ripe handful, which he deposited in a cut glass bowl on a scarred mahogany coffee table. Taped to the bowl was a scrap of paper with the warning *"NON TOCCARE!"* It reminded his grandchildren to keep away because the misnamed fruits were not cherries but an inedible relative of the tomato.

Withered *Signora* Maria Scempio, coarse gray hair in a bun, brought him the *New York Daily News.* It had been delivered to the front door by a third grader who rang the bell, removed his Yankee baseball cap, rubbed his shoes on the doormat, bowed, said *"Buon giorno"* and pedaled off on his bicycle.

His other clients had to retrieve their newspaper from the sidewalk. Last year this merchant, an altar boy at the

Church of Our Irrepressible Lady, told Maria he was an involuntary pedestrian because his bicycle had been stolen. The don's associates informed the neighborhood that the thief would not be punished if he returned the bicycle to La Santa Spogliarellista Fraternal and Benevolent Club and apologized to the don which was done forthwith.

Now the don nodded as Maria retired to her espresso in the kitchen. With moving lips, he slowly read a one-paragraph story headed "2 suspects jailed in Wisconsin." Don Topo shook his head and murmured, *"La buffonesco."*

But he had already received this news yesterday and had reacted by immediately dispatching a colleague to Madison.

His wife returned to help him into a worn black overcoat as he groaned. Around his neck, she wound a scratchy gray woolen scarf she had crocheted the previous Christmas. While he tucked the folded *Daily News* into his coat pocket, she presented matching gloves crocheted the Christmas before that. When she presented a pair of fuzzy black earmuffs, he waved them off with a trembling hand.

"But you always shake in the cold," she said.

"Better shake than rattle and roll in the gutter with two in the head because the don didn't hear the car behind him. "

Finally, she placed an old black fedora on his head tilting the brim to the left as he frowned. When she returned to the kitchen, he tilted the brim to the right in the front hall mirror and pulled up a red cock's feather hidden in the hatband. Then he called to his wife, "When the Hebe urology doctor phones tell him to phone the don at the club."

"He no phone."

"Hah?"

"I hear from my cousin at Mass all the doctors in the clinic afraid to cut off your prostrate because if knife slips and they cut off wrong thing they get the knife themself."

As the don shrugged and reached for the loose glass knob on the front door the phone rang. *"Presto!"* Maria answered.

Since the caller's voice was familiar she handed the phone to the don who listened to a few cryptic words, said "*La società* 10 minutes" and hung up.

He gave his hat brim a final right tilt in the hall mirror and left for the five-block walk to La Santa Spogliarellista Fraternal and Benevolent Club. An arthritic, the don plodded, nodding when women passersby greeted him and men tipped their hats at him.

But he tipped his hat only to *il capo di tutti capi* as he passed the Church of Our Irrepressible Lady. There he presided over the parish council and in his reserved front center pew attended Mass faithfully every Easter Sunday As the old *soldato* walked he faced rigidly ahead but his eyes flicked between the street and his reflection in the plate glass windows of the mom-and-pop stores. He did not look over his shoulder and disdained a bodyguard.

However, when someone behind him touched his shoulder, Don Topo clutched his chest. He stopped and turned to confront a bearded little man in baker's whites and white yarmulke whose apron was lettered Reilly's Bagels.

"Don Topo, with all due respect how come Angelo hasn't come in to get his bagels this morning?"

The don looked up at a weathered gold-painted life preserver oscillating on a rusty chain directly overhead. The sign said, "FRESH BAGELS UPSTAIRS." He frowned, shrugged, sidestepped and continued walking.

At his storefront club all curb parking spaces legal and illegal were occupied, all parking meters had expired and cars were double-parked at the fire hydrant. On the broad sidewalk directly in front of the club was the don's gleaming black Lincoln Town Car bearing this sticker on the front bumper: "I am Pro-Life." None of these vehicles had been ticketed.

Across the street at an unexpired meter was the only legally parked vehicle on the block, a battered white Aizilop Plumbing van. Its front bumper sticker said "Respect

Authority" while the rear bumper sticker said, "Support Your Local Police." The van displayed U.S. Government plates.

Dutifully feeding coins into the meter was the van driver, the only visible occupant. He wore an immaculate white coverall with cuffs and glossy black wingtips.

During the weeks, the plumbing van had been there, its purpose was debated by Don Topo and *Consigliere* Alessandro Z. Savio a.k.a. Iron Al. There was already a plumbing shop on the block operated by a Sicilian, who enjoyed all the neighborhood's patronage.

And what was the significance of the large dark window in the van's side? Iron Al dubbed it *il malocchio,* the evil eye. However, one day the don noted the driver was wearing a baseball cap displaying FEDS in gold.

"Maybe that's speedy delivery service for plumbing supplies," the don told the *consigliere* who scratched his chin and asked: "Then how come the only time the driver goes anywhere is to walk to the luncheonette to get two coffees?"

"*La Provvidenza.*"

The club's burly doorman, the don's nephew, once crossed the street and taunted the driver: "When you gonna come fix our leaky toilet?"

But Don Topo was not amused.

"We gotta show respect because they gotta do what they gotta do and us likewise and vice versa."

On the feast day of Santa Spogliarellista, the don dispatched the doorman to the van. He carried a covered basket containing a quart thermos of espresso, pastries from a Sicilian bakery operated by the don's cousin and two linen napkins.

Now having completed his walk the don rapped twice on the locked club door, frowning at the dusty window on which his fingertip traced a radiant sun face as he shivered. He also noted the parched aspidistra within was drooping for all passersby to see. When the doorman helped him off with his hat and coat, the don said, "Pasquale, how you gonna tell if some guy at the door is an official club member if you can't see through the glass? And you gotta water that plant regular even if you just take a leak in it. You the only papa and mamma that orphan plant got. I don't like to see things die."

"*Si padrone.*"

"And clean out that crap too."

The don pointed to the plant's tub littered with cigarette butts dropped by arriving members. He had banned smoking in the club blaming this vice for his coughing and eye irritation. After kicking the habit he chewed sugarless bubblegum, engaging in bubble-blowing contests with his grandchildren who visited the club after school for a can of pop and a handful of raisins. Out of respect for *il nonno,* they permitted him to win.

This morning he nodded to pinochle players in the club's anteroom. It had rickety card tables, an espresso machine, faded Sicilian travel posters on the cracked plaster walls and in a corner a life-size plaster statue of the virginal Santa Spogliarellista, her right thumb down, her left index finger beckoning.

In the anteroom, Pasquale opened the door to the sanctum sanctorum, bowed and closed the door after the don.

Awaiting the don was a middle-aged gentleman at the don's desk, a card table, on which sat an old black rotary dial phone, small notepad and pencil stub. Beside the table was a new paper shredder whose manufacturer's label displayed the American flag.

He wore an old but neatly pressed blue serge suit complemented by a flag lapel pin, faded blue shirt and blue polyester tie bearing red asterisks of pasta sauce. His black shoes were cracked but shined.

Don Topo sat at the table and accepted a nod from *Consigliere* Iron Al, heir apparent, who had phoned the don at home for the appointment.

Iron Al fetched two espressos as an overweight black and silver German shepherd dozing in a corner awoke, yawned and shook his glossy coat. His leather collar tinkled with veterinary medallions, ID disc and a Saint Francis of Assisi medal. He ambled to the table and with a languid tail wag accepted a head pat from the don. But when the *consigliere* essayed this greeting the dog growled, retired to his post, eyed the *consigliere,* growled again and fell asleep.

"I think maybe, if you agree, Garibaldi is bored here," the *consigliere* said.

The don sipped espresso and shrugged.

"How many times the don gotta remind you what his grandfather in Palermo used to say: 'Use a spade to dig up potatoes but don't use a potato to dig up spades.'"

But *il verme* finally turned slightly. The *consigliere,* who had frequently suffered recitations of that proverb, countered not with his customary shrug but with a non sequitur of his own:

"Like *il padre* said when he farted in the confessional, 'The penitent who holds his nose can still see the road to heaven.'"

The don set his espresso cup down firmly and scowled. "You stop your silly *sillogismo.* First, you say Garibaldi's bored. Then you say *il padre* farted. That dog I picked out myself when he was guardin' that warehouse."

The don's voice sank to a whisper, which he delivered in his cupped hands, pointing with a pinky to the center of the card table.

"He was happier then too," Iron Al whispered. "I think maybe he wants more excitement than he gets here."

"Whaddya want me to do—fly him to Vegas? He ain't interested in pussy. He was fixed."

"Then maybe I rent a Rin Tin Tin video he can watch so he got like they say a role model."

But shaking his head, the don indicated a black-and-white TV set where a vintage Western depicted white hats pursuing black hats. He raised his voice, addressing the center of the card table:

"We all a bunch of patriotic U.S. of A. citizens hangin'

out in this club just bullshittin' and watchin' John Wayne restore law and order. If he's a true-blue role model for us then he's okay for our dog."

Under the table top was a bug installed during a clandestine midnight visit by the two FBI agents from across the street. The buggers had suborned Garibaldi with his favorite snack—marshmallows.

Although Garibaldi had cordially welcomed the agents, he gave the game away next morning by sniffing under the table at what he thought was an hors d'oeuvre. The grateful don left the bug in place and engaged only in chitchat there.

From that bug the plumbers in the van diligently recorded hours of inadmissible trivia:
• Why does canine Garibaldi circle before retiring?
• Why did patriot Garibaldi abandon his dog Castore on fleeing to America for political asylum?
• Why does Catania claim the best *cassata* dessert when only a moron would deny Palermo's superiority?
• Why won't the Dodgers repent and return to Brooklyn?

All this coupled with the don's proverbs and Garibaldi's occasional growls inflicted ennui and varicose veins on the sedentary eavesdroppers.

However, actionable matters were discussed on a secure but creaky plywood bench along the wall that sat under a fading photo of the club's championship bocce team. The don had captained the team until arthritis deprived him of playing with his cherished balls.

"We got a problem," Don Topo whispered when he and Iron Al had adjourned to the bench. Then parking his bubblegum under the bench, the don explained, "This the don does because when he was a little *ladro* in Palermo boosting oranges and lemons, his mamma always said, 'A man cannot balance two eggplants in one hand or two ideas in his mind at the same time.'"

However *il verme* turned again:

"But suppose the eggplants is small and the guy's hand is big?"

The don retrieved his gum, chewed vigorously, blew an enormous bubble, which burst, picked the remains from his mustache, reparked the wad and handed down his opinion from the bench. "And suppose the guy who asks the don that kinda irrespectable question got a head as big as that bubble inside which is a peanut brain?"

Iron Al both shrugged and frowned finally leading Don Topo back to the agenda.

"Angelo's slippery like an eel," the *consigliere* said.

"But you can't catch an eel in a bear trap. Even that *Yid* Reilly was askin' the don about Angelo who got his fuckin' Jew bagels there. An underboss should go to the bakery of the don's cousin for *pasticceria* like any decent siciliano. "

"Reilly ain't a Jew name."

"Tell the don somethin' he don't know. The don also knows Reilly changed his name from Flynn."

"But Flynn ain't a Jew name neither."

"Before that it was Cohen but after he changed it to Flynn he figured he'd change it again. You know how connivin' them people is. He changed it from Flynn to Reilly so when people asked him he'd be able to say what his name was before he changed it." The don raised his voice and addressed the card table: "Just don't let the don catch any son of a bitch eatin' Jew bagels in this club and the don don't give a shit who hears it!" His voice dropped to a whisper again: "Now where was the don?"

"Discussin' eels for which I got a good recipe," the *consigliere* whispered.

The don shook his head sadly. "*Il padrone* sends two senior adjusters after Angelo and they get busted while them shitkickin' cops grabs *il padrone's* Lincoln for their staff car without dubious process."

"That's why you made Angelo underboss. He's smart."

The don clenched his bony fists. "He's *un traditore.* Why couldn't Angelo wait for the don's retirement party steada tryin' to outplace the don with a bullet? That ain't good business. Now the don gotta put off goin' to St. Petersburg. The don gotta take time to whack that rat fink and move you up from first base to home plate."

"What was Angelo doin' in Wisconsin?"

"When Angelo was a kid he worked for Reilly. Then when Angelo's folks passes away he goes to Wisconsin to live with his *nonna*. When Angelo grows up, he comes back to Brooklyn to work for the don. But on Easter, Thanksgivin' and Christmas Angelo always goes to see her to pay respect."

"But it ain't Easter yet."

"*Asino*! Shut up the mouth and listen. When them two jokers come back from shitkickers' land the don transfers them to his pizzeria on Staten Island. But the don don't wait. He already sent out *un esperto* to Madison where the don knows the little old *nonna* lives. You know who the don means. This *goombah* never misses and the cops never find the corpus delirious. In his wallet, he carries a picture of Jimmy Hoffa and when the don asks how come, *il esperto* just smiles. He is *semper fedele* to the don just like Garibaldi."

Hearing his name, the dozing German shepherd shook his head, growled and returned to canine cloud-cuckoo-land,

But the *consigliere* was troubled and he scratched his head with one hand and his chin with the other. "I never seen little old ladies get whacked in Mafia movies. That don't show respect."

"Who says whacked? *Il esperto* gonna motivate her to say where Angelo is. And if she dunno then we got somebody else to motivate in Wisconsin—Angelo's cousin Claudio. They was buddies in the neighborhood just like Damon and Pizza."

"I ain't seen Claudio around for a long time."

"Sure because Claudio left years ago to be a priest or somethin' at a monastery in the Wisconsin boonies. If Angelo's in Wisconsin he'll also see Claudio. *Il esperto* will pay respect to Claudio too."

Iron Al stroked his mustache, his signal for deep thought. "But suppose *il esperto* is just good at puttin' daylight through people instead of motivatin' a certain little old lady and a certain priest to be rat finks. You know like Murray's Law."

Don Topo blew his biggest *bolla gigantesca* until it popped with a bang that brought doorman Pasquale running with drawn Beretta, only to be waved off. As the don picked gum fragments off his nose, he said, "If *il esperto* fucks up his inhuman relations then the don takes care of all three of them personal. After this last ha-ha the don retires to St. Petersburg with the wife and girlfriend because he showed them young punks around here he ain't no Mustache Pete."

HAROLD KNOLL

CHAPTER III

As *la Signora* Serafina Panettorio lifted her rose-decorated bone china espresso cup, a deafening roar shook the kitchen in her little frame house near Madison's Dane County Regional Airport. *"Merda!* Here it comes again!"

The cup jiggled in her tiny hand sloshing espresso over her frilly pink housecoat and fuzzy bunny bedroom slippers, a gift from her only grandchild Angelo. She clamped her lips on an unlit cigarette, braced her back against the sink and glared at the cracked plaster ceiling where a light fixture danced on a chain.

In the corner, a three-foot painted plaster statue of Saint Anthony of Padua began to slide on an apple box.

"Rock but no roll!" she cried, dropping the cup, a wedding gift.

Serafina ran to the shrine and hugged the saint who hugged the Christ child on his arm. When quiet returned she picked the shattered cup off the linoleum floor, clasped one hand to her palpitating chest, shook a freckled fist at the ceiling and cried, *"Va all'inferno* you motherfuckers!"

She lit a votive candle at the shrine and genuflected. Next she adjusted last year's Palm Sunday frond behind the framed photo on the wall of her mustachioed husband Pietro, a wiseguy with the Milwaukee *famiglia* who had died in bed. Then she donned a baggy black dress, black cloth coat, black knit cap, and trendy high black leather boots, another gift from Angelo. Finally she jabbed the off switch on a black and white television touting an airline vacation in Acapulco and stamped out the front door.

Serafina chewed on her unlit cigarette and flipped it into the gutter toward a car parked across the street at a fire hydrant. From her kitchen window, she had observed the driver staring for hours at her house. Serafina recalled Pietro's dictum, "If the car got more than one antenna it's the cops or FBI. If it got only one antenna then it's none of the above. If the guy is white and wears a dark suit, white shirt and dark tie, he's FBI no matter how many antennas he got. But no matter what he's wearin', if he's in a new or late model black Thunderbird and he's parked at a fireplug across the street and is starin' at the house, then you got a wiseguy with a contract."

She nodded. It was a late model black Thunderbird all right. She fanned her hand under her chin at the driver, walked around the corner and climbed the icy steps of the rectory of the Church of La Madonna della Confusione, murmuring as she gripped the shaky rail, "No salty sand for a little old lady."

Preoccupied she threw open the door of the pastor's study without knocking.

"*Per amor del cielo!*" cried Padre Lascivo as he zipped up his fly, the door to his adjoining bedroom slamming behind him. "How many times I gotta tell you I do counseling here. A troubled *moglie* whose husband beat her up don't wanna be interrupted. You gotta make appointment."

"I don't see no *moglie* unless you counsel her *orizzontalamente* somewheres else."

Padre Lascivo glanced at the closed bedroom door, slipped on his black jacket that had been lying on the carpet near the door, rubbed his hand over his forehead, sat behind his desk, laid out a pad and pen and said, "You already been to confession Saturday."

"No. I wanna talk about *i aeroplani* upstairs."

The pastor, doodling a nude Hercules, laid down his

pen. "I'm a priest, not a head doctor."

"So who you know got *il malocchio*?" she said rapidly blinking.

Padre Lascivo tugged his sweaty collar and looked at the wall where a painting depicted a gridiron hero, the well done Saint Lawrence of Rome.

"Pay attention," Serafina said.

Padre Lascivo resumed doodling Hercules strafed by a Fokker D. VII observed by a malevolent eye. But he stopped and shook his head. "No understand."

Serafina pointed to the ceiling and began to sway, arms outstretched like wings.

"*I aeroplani* go baroom baroom back and forth to airport. I got the shakes. I wanna say *una maledizione* so they crash boom in big fire. But everybody get killed, no, even people on ground?"

The priest sighed with relief. "Ah, you worry about mortal sin because you imagine you whacked them, no?"

"*Sì.*"

"And you wanna hire somebody with evil eye to do the contract instead of you, no?"

"*Sì.*"

He shook his head and drew a big X through his doodling, "Evil eye is also a mortal sin." He tapped his chest. "I feel your pain, *Signora* Panettorio. This morning at Mass you heard the big plane come over and saw how the chalice shook so much I nearly spilled the wine."

"Then the priest just talks and will not help a poor little old lady? Pietro *mio* who you yourself sent to heaven from this church—Pietro used to say his Brass Rule: 'If somebody tries to screw you, screw the fucker back twice as hard.'"

The priest nodded. "In Palermo papa once told me, 'When the front door is locked go through a window.'"

"I remember him. He was a good burglar."

"So for a faithful soul the church is happy to make an arrangement acceptable to both *il Dio* and *Cesare.* Pray to

Santo Antonio di Padova who you respect that all the airlines that fly over your house will lose so much money in Madison that they gotta fly somewhere else. You hit *i bastardi* in *il portafoglio* and at the worst, you commit a teeny-weeny venial sin to which I close one eye. Go in peace, *figlia mia.*"

For the first time that day, she smiled. She kissed his hand.

"Anything else the church can help you with?" he said.

She shook her head. "Just a *goombah* parked across the street got a contract on me but I take care of him myself."

When she left, the priest locked his study door and went to the bedroom. A bespectacled young man in a cassock was sitting on the bed reading the diocesan newspaper.

"Next week same time," the priest said.

As Serafina entered her house, the phone was ringing.

CHAPTER IV

"*Nipotino mio!*" Serafina exclaimed after she had untangled the cord of the kitchen wall phone. "I worry so much for you, Angelino. Yesterday when I call Brooklyn the operator says you disconnected. Where are you? Did you eat? Did you find *una moglie* so I get visits from your bambini?"

"Grandma, I'll be over in about an hour. I'm callin' from the freeway. We talk then."

She jigged and dropped the phone.

"*Grazie*, Santo Antonio di Padova!" she told her corner shrine, picking up the phone and struggling with the cord again.

"You okay, Grandma?"

"*Si.* "

"Any visitors?"

"Just a gorilla parked across the street watchin' the house."

"What's he drivin'?"

"New Thunderbird. Color black."

"Benny Deuce. He got muscles between the ears and sits on his brains. Supposed to be *un esperto.*"

She parted lacy pink curtains over the kitchen sink. "He's gettin' out and comin' over here."

"Grandma, you can't keep him out and we can't call the cops. So listen good to what I tell you to do till I get there."

Meanwhile at the supercharged Thunderbird, Benedetto Orso, *caporegime* of the Scempio *famiglia,* wiggled out of the black leather seat and for the hundredth time bumped his balding pate on the closed sunroof.

He wallowed across the street shivering in his white Italian silk suit, hunched against the early spring chill, his size 14 tennies slipping on ice. He alternately patted his hit kit on his right side and his .22 Beretta on his left, ready to motivate a frightened little old lady.

The curtains no longer fluttered in the kitchen window. He imagined grandma cowering under her bed while *il orco* of the fairy tale broke down her door and gobbled her up. And yet cocky as he was he glanced back at the Thunderbird and wished he could drive himself and his dark secret forthwith back to Brooklyn.

Nevertheless he shrugged and banged both fists on the flimsy front door. When there was no response, he drew back and hurled himself over the BENVENUTO mat as the door flew open an instant before.

Just inside, Serafina stuck out one foot. Benny Deuce tripped and plunged onto the frayed living room carpet, stunned and gasping, a beached whale. He looked up at the little old lady who giggled as she waltzed around him singing a Sicilian lullaby in a screeching falsetto, a song he recalled from childhood.

But he shuddered when she sidled to the door and fastened two sliding bolts and a security chain. Cupping a wrinkled hand around her left eye, she peered down at him. Then waving her thin arms she leaned over him and chanted: "Giovannino, you are prisoner in *il castello mio* and I am *la strega* who will eat you for supper."

Her eyes rolled and her stringy hair, coiffed for his benefit, seemed a den of snakes. She pressed a broad tip marker to his forehead and wrote something as he lurched to his feet. Recalling his grandmother's tales of *la Gorgone,* he confronted the little old lady in housecoat and slippers:

"With all due respect are you *Signora* Serafina Panettorio?"

"Non, Giovannino. I am her sister Francesca."

"Then where the fuck is Serafina?"

"I buried her in the cellar and I go for soap to wash out your mouth, you bad little boy. Then I eat you and bury your bones next to her."

She ran into the bathroom, seized a bar of bath soap, brandished it and flew at him crying, "Bad boy! I make you blow bubbles and then I eat you with my own recipe pasta sauce like I ate Serafina!"

He began to edge toward the door as she whirled and said, "But first we dance *la tarantella* because *il ragno* wrapped his eight legs around me and bit me so I must dance."

He staggered to the door, frantically slid the bolts and undid the chain as she clawed his back and drooled on his neck. He threw open the door, tripped on the BENVENUTO mat, slid over the icy sidewalk, lumbered across the street and was almost compacted by a honking dumpster.

"La stregoneria!" he cried lunging behind the wheel of his Thunderbird, again banging his head on the sun roof.

Benny Deuce blessed himself to ward off the old lady's witchcraft but looked up in horror at the rearview mirror which displayed in reverse 999 scrawled across his forehead. It was the unlucky number on which he had once lost $5,000 playing the numbers and quit gambling.

"How did you know that?" he cried, unaware Serafina had written 666 upside down.

He spat into a rag and erased the number fortunately written in watercolor.

Dreading the wrath of Don Topo, Benny Deuce jockeyed his Thunderbird from a tight parking space by bashing cars fore and aft.

At the kitchen window Serafina threw the curtains wide open and bade him farewell by cocking her right arm and clamping her left hand on her biceps. From her housecoat pocket, she removed a bequest from Pietro, his Smith & Wesson .38 Chief's Special Airweight with a two-inch barrel.

"For *la motivazione* a little old lady first uses this," she said tapping an index finger on the side of her head, "before using this."

Then she replaced the revolver in a cupboard.

CHAPTER V

"You ever wonder what the fuckin' phone company done with our old phone booth?" Don Topo Scempio asked *Consigliere* Iron Al.

The pair shivered at the windiest corner in Brooklyn near La Santa Spogliarellista Fraternal and Benevolent Club. The don was leaning into a new open air pay telephone stand while Iron Al, who was dodging a capricious north wind, circled it.

"Last year when the don was in Palermo to visit *la mamma* what do you think he sees in the fruit and vegetable market?" the don said.

Iron Al, weary of verbal reruns, shrugged as the don said "It's a fuckin' old phone booth from New York. He swears it was ours but now it's fulla lemons peddled by *un paesano.* A guy could stay warm in that old booth. Sure the bums would come in and take a leak or a dump but Iron Al, after you scrubbed it out every week it smelled just like the clubhouse."

"What do you think we oughta do about it?" Iron Al said.

Don Topo turned his coat collar up and leaned into the stand. "The don will make an arrangement," he said. "Now what time you got?"

The *consigliere* reluctantly pulled down a heavy glove and bared his wrist to consult a new gold Rolex liberated from a Fifth Avenue jeweler. "Eleven-05."

Don Topo huddled deeper into his overcoat, coughed and put out a gloved hand. "Hit the don."

The *consigliere* presented a Smith Brothers licorice cough drop which the don sucked noisily.

"You think them brothers is really named Trade and Mark like is printed here?" the don said.

"Which brothers?"

The don jabbed a finger at the cough drop box. "Them brothers. Now everybody knows Santo Marco but did you ever hear of Santo Trade?" Before the *consigliere* could shrug the don said, "Now what the fuck's keepin' Benedetto? When he phones the house, the don says, 'Call back 11 sharp. You know where.' Now what time you got?"

"Eleven-07."

"Your watch is wrong."

The *consigliere* frowned. "It's a Rolex."

"You ain't never heard of Hong Kong crooks imitating U.S. of A. products? You can't trust nobody today."

"You can trust me."

"When the blacksmith loads an anvil on the donkey, the blacksmith says, 'Trust me it ain't heavy,' but the donkey says, 'Heehaw'"

The *consigliere* shrugged, the don coughed and the phone rang. But although the don was shivering, he waited for the second ring to grab the receiver.

"Don Topo—" Benny Deuce began.

"Benedetto, how many times the don gotta tell you no names even on a pay phone?"

"*Scusi.*"

"Now what's the problem? The don is freezin' his ass off on this corner. You seen Serafina?"

"Maybe yes, maybe no."

"Watch your fuckin' syntax. Why can't you talk *logicamente* like the don?"

"I think Serafina wasn't there. Just some old nutty sister tried to put *il malocchio* on me."

The don's forehead furrowed as he parked his cough drop in his cheek to assure good syntax. "The sister got a name?"

"Francesca."

"What she look like?"

Benny Deuce painted a vivid portrait.

"You describin' Serafina. She ain't got a sister. You the one should be put away, not her."

"Whaddaya mean 'put away'?"

"The don means wearin' one of them double-breasted one-size-fits-all nuthouse blazers and stashed in a rubber room, that's what."

There was a long pause at the other end as Benny Deuce cogitated.

"You fall into a haystack?"

"Huh? No, I mean yeah. I'm still here."

"Then drag your ass back to Serafina *presto* and if she don't appreciate bein' treated with respect you can motivate her some more and even whack her if you got to. But first find out where the hell Angelo is and phone the don same time same place tomorrow mornin'."

"But she's a poor little old lady."

"Does the don hear *il esperto* talkin'? You forgettin' you put a big dent in the Brooklyn census?"

"Can I go back first thing tomorrow mornin', Don Topo? I'm bent outa shape right now. I gotta see a chiropractor and rest up overnight in a motel."

He explained Serafina's welcome.

"*I frutti e la verdura!*" the don exclaimed and hung up. "Let's get back to the club," he told the shivering *consigliere*. "The don thunk he got his first hard-on in a month but when he felt his dick it's solid ice."

On the return stroll to the club they encountered Reilly the bagel baker outside his shop, paper bag in hand, the wind whipping his baker's whites.

"Don Topo, could I take just a minute of your valuable time, please?"

The don paused, frowned and nodded as did Iron Al.

"Angelo still hasn't stopped by for his bagels. Could he be taking a winter vacation soaking in a nice hot tub somewhere?"

The don nodded.

"We're cold here but the don thinks they make it hot for that rat fink where he is at."

Don Topo nervously eyed the golden lifesaver sign oscillating above him. He started to leave but the bakery bag was pressed into his hand.

"Some warm bagels fresh today for you, Don Topo. Angelo's like a son to me and I hope you locate him soon."

"Likewise," the don said passing the bag to Iron Al as they left.

"What should I do with them bagels?" Iron Al said.

"Save them for when Garibaldi runs out of puppy biscuits. "

"Maybe we sent the wrong motivator after Angelo," Iron Al said, prudently using the plural pronoun.

But the don shook his head. "For years the don never wanted to give Benedetto the button. Like you know he dresses good but wears tennies with Velcro tops even when we all got on tuxes and patent leather shoes for our annual blowout payin' respect to Santa Spogliarellista on her feast day. It's because he never learned to tie his shoelaces. You look at him for the first time you say, 'Here comes *il Signor Buffone.*"

Iron Al shrugged and said, *"Possibilmente."*

"But Maria keeps sayin', 'We're his godparents and you don't show respect to his mamma when you make him POPO.'"

"POPO?"

"Whatsamatta? You don't know your syntax neither? POPO— Pissed On and Passed Over."

The *consigliere* stroked his nose with his index finger, a meditative gesture often rehearsed in his bathroom mirror.

As they passed the Church of Our Irrepressible Lady,

Don Topo tipped his hat and asked, "Now what was the don sayin'?"

"POPO."

"Yeah. So the don gives Benedetto the button and you know what happens?"

"He's no more *il Signor Buffone?*"

"Wrong! Benedetto is still *il Signor Buffone* but with a difference. He becomes the best hitman *la famiglia* ever got. You make out a contract with him the party of the first part and you never see the party of the second part again. Benedetto works alone, he works fast and only he knows where them other parties is buried which is okay by the don. He's boosted the productivity of our *famiglia* and he can wear whatever he wants so long it ain't a wire."

As they neared La Santa Spogliarellista Fraternal and Benevolent Club the *consigliere* slowed, glanced over each shoulder and whispered, "One question, Don Topo, with all due respect."

"Shoot."

"He's your best hitman, he's *un caporegime* getting half of what his crew makes and yet he always needs dough. You think maybe he's doin' drugs or gamblin'?"

The don scowled. "Watch how you talk about the don's godson. Benedetto never does drugs. He stopped gamblin' after he dropped a bundle on 999 in the numbers because the fix that was supposed to be in wasn't."

"So maybe he sends it all to *la mamma* in Palermo?"

"He's a good boy who helps *la mamma* but he don't send her all he makes."

"So?"

They were outside the club now and Don Topo nodded to his nephew Pasquale who bowed and flung open the door.

"So the don lets the squirrels bury nuts in his back yard. They got their secrets and the don got his. But if the fuckers dig out front in his petunia bed he'll cut their balls off. *Capisca?*"

At midnight a telephone company van borrowed from the firm's garage pulled away from the pay phone on the corner. At the wheel, was a retired telephone plant foreman, the don's cousin, accompanied by two other retired plant employees.

Inside the van was the new outdoor pay phone stand that had stood briefly at the corner. Installed hastily but expertly in its place was an old enclosed pay phone booth rescued from a junkyard.

The driver jerked a thumb toward the van's interior. "Did you tape on the sign the don made?"

His colleagues nodded. The crudely lettered cardboard said: "CHEEP SHIT."

CHAPTER VI

Too proud for reading glasses, Serafina squinted at the New York Stock Exchange listings in *The Wall Street Journal*.

"I got it for you like you asked, Grandma," Angelo said at the kitchen table over a breakfast of scrambled eggs, sausage, bacon and toast. "I hadda learn to read this paper because *un capo* should be a man of business and not a Mustache Pete like Don Topo. He learned to make change of a buck behind a fruit and vegetable pushcart."

"Just tell if their stocks go up, down or just fartin' around," she said ticking off the major airlines serving the Dane County Regional Airport.

"Down," Angelo said at the first name and repeated this for the others.

Serafina clapped her hands and knelt at her corner shrine, "Santo Antonio di Padova, you have answered prayers of a little old lady. Their stocks go down the toilet like you promised." She was about to hang up on her celestial phone call when the house rumbled as jet engines roared overhead. "But Santo Antonio, I just got one question: How come you let *i bastardi* still fly over my house?"

At the table, she sipped espresso from a plastic cup since her wedding cups had been dropped and shattered.

"Don't worry about the noise here, Grandma. I'm takin' you somewhere quiet and safe."

"Where we goin'?"

"When I got gas at the convenience store this morning I asked the manager if he knows where Claudio's monastery is at. He gave me general directions. All I know it's somewheres off I94 between here and Milwaukee. The manager says it's the Penitentiary Brothers of Saint Peccato. I heard of that goombah. Carlo Peccato was a made soldier with Uncle Pietro's Milwaukee *famiglia* until Carlo got religion. He took off for the monastery without his don's okay so the don put out a contract on him."

Serafina refilled Angelo's espresso cup.

"Now take a card."

She offered him a pack of saints' prayer cards with the top card extended. He turned the card over and studied the serene portrait of Saint Carlo Peccato with a thumbnail description of the order of brothers he had founded.

"You see it ain't Penitentiary Brothers," she said. "It's Penitential."

Angelo shrugged as he studied the tinted portrait. "Same difference etymologically," he said.

"I'm happy for *cugino* Claudio that he went to right monastery," she said. "Santo Peccato is my Number 2 saint in the deck after Santo Antonio."

He returned the card to Serafina, who buried it in the deck, shuffled deftly, rapped the deck on the table and said, "Pick a card."

When Angelo laid the card face down on the table, she turned the card over—Saint Peccato again.

"With all due respect, Grandma, you stacked the deck."

She shook her head, tossed the cards fanwise on the table, flipped them along her arm, rapped the deck on the table and said:

"Sometimes we gotta help a saint make a miracle. I got 52 saints in the deck and Santo Peccato jumps out now to say he needs us at his monastery."

"What for?"

"Pietro *mio* told me the Pope took away Carlo Peccato's

saint button claiming Carlo wasn't dead enough to be a saint. The Pope also took away church button from monastery chapel makin' all them brothers *protestanti*. We gotta go there to help get them buttons back before them brothers go *all'inferno*."

From the cupboard Serafina fetched a small pasteboard box and handed this to Angelo.

"Round, pointy both ends, not the cheap flat kind—corretto?"

Angelo smiled and selected a toothpick, which he chewed.

"My favorite, Grandma. *Tante grazie.* Now I think better so I ask: How come Holy Carlo's don whacks him just for goin' AWOL? A good blackjack massage woulda been enough motivation for Carlo to stay a team player like we say in management."

Serafina nodded and put a finger to her lips.

"Pietro *mio* say Santo Peccato done somethin' else that the don felt is not kosher. When I ask Pietro what is it he say *omertà* but that someday Santo Peccato himself will explain."

"But Pietro always lost playin' the horses so how come he could predict the future?"

Serafina blessed herself and looked up at the ceiling. "Pietro *mio* is upstairs in the same club with Santo Peccato."

"But Pietro said that before he went upstairs."

"You gotta have *la fede.* When was the last time you went to Mass?"

Angelo glanced at the kitchen clock, helped her on with her coat and presented a gift-wrapped box. *"D' Italia* to keep you warm in the miserable winters they got in Wisconsin."

She unwrapped a bright red woolen scarf, wound it about her neck and hugged her grandson. "You pay respect, Angelino. You good boy."

She went to her cupboard, fetched her Smith & Wesson .38 and put it in her purse together with the saints' cards.

"Grandma, are you playin' with a full deck?"

"Now you don't show respect."

"Aw Grandma, I mean you got 52 saints in the pack but do you have jokers?"

"Sure—four Popes. Now before we go I say that Claudio's monastery would be a good *famiglia* for you, Angelino."

"I don't wanna be a priest. I'm gonna be *il padrone modesto* after I go back to Brooklyn and whack Don Topo who talks of himself like *il Dio*. He promised me his chair after he goes to St. Petersburg but the rat fink reneged."

"From what I hear about that monastery you don't gotta be priest. Maybe you run *famiglia* business there like in Brooklyn and still be *il capo* with *una moglie* and *i bambini*. Take me to monastery where I help you."

Angelo chewed furiously on his toothpick, deposited the shreds in a wastebasket and said, "When we get there I talk to Claudio and make an arrangement for *nonna mia*."

She hugged him and they got into his Cadillac after first checking the street.

"The gorilla ain't here," Serafina said.

"Benny Deuce is a late sleeper. We cruise around the neighborhood. You got an ice cream shop here?"

"Is too cold for *il gelato*."

"Not for Benny Deuce. He gotta have a triple scoop cone after breakfast."

Angelo drove slowly past the first shop but there was no Thunderbird parked in front. As they drove toward the second Serafina said, "This one is better. Bigger scoops."

"For a little old lady you got all your marbles, Grandma."

Serafina tapped the bulge in her purse and smiled.

Meanwhile at the second ice cream shop, the sole customer was frowning at a three-dip ice cream cone he held in his paw. The top dip was chocolate, the center New York and the bottom pistachio.

"How come," he asked the cringing proprietor, "in New

York we call it vanilla and here in fag city you call vanilla New York which us in New York never heard about?"

"I hold a Ph.D. in philosophy from the University of Wisconsin—Madison and I term that a metaphysical question."

Benny Deuce shrugged. Since pistachio was his favorite he began licking the towering cone at its base while the proprietor observed the destabilization.

"Vanilla is vanilla is vanilla," Benny Deuce said.

"I'm not an aficionado of Stein."

"You better watch your syntax. Now I got another question. Where the fuck is the monastery at?"

"I'm not into Thomism either. But I suggest you phone the reference department at the Madison Public Library."

The proprietor dialed the number and handed him the phone.

"Where's the monastery at?" Benny Deuce asked the librarian.

"Sir, can you be more explicit?"

"Don't fuck with me. You're supposed to give answers, not questions. Monastery is monastery is monastery."

"Sir, only Alice B. Toklas could help you."

"Then put her the fuck on even if you gotta get her outa the can."

"Sir, that would indeed be a long distance call for which we do not have her area code. Have a nice day."

Confronting the proprietor who was backed against the wall, Benny Deuce said, "And your pistachio stinks too."

His leaning tower of *gelato* nearly toppled in his hand when he stepped outside and saw a familiar black Cadillac approaching.

Precariously balancing the cone in one hand, he climbed behind the wheel of the Thunderbird, bumped his head on the sunroof, laid his .22 Beretta on the adjoining seat and roared down the side street onto Pennsylvania Avenue heading north with the Cadillac close behind.

"A contract is a contract is a contract," he said. "The

party of the second part ain't supposed to whack the party of the first part."

Licking furiously at ice cream dripping down his left hand, he steered with his right. The rearview mirror indicated Angelo was driving and beside him wearing a blood red scarf was Serafina of the evil eye. Suddenly the street signs said Packers Avenue.

"I hate Madison!" he said. "The streets change names. If the Packers is here already maybe I'm up in Green Bay."

The Cadillac drew alongside on the left slightly ahead, the passenger window slid down and Serafina squinted over her .38 as Angelo shouted. Benny Deuce, already doing 70, floored the accelerator. He reluctantly tossed his cone on the floor as a bullet punched through the windshield and tore through the sunroof.

"Good riddance!" he cried.

The Cadillac swerved wildly as Angelo tried to restrain Serafina.

"Grandma, *per favore,* let me take care of him!"

She reluctantly raised her window but would not hand over the revolver, replacing it in her purse instead.

Meanwhile Benny Deuce had gained a two-block lead and was trying to pass a school bus, which was changing lanes erratically. Children waved from the rear window as Benny Deuce brushed glass fragments out of his hair and glanced sadly at the puddle of ice cream on the floor.

With the Cadillac gaining on him again, Benny Deuce drew alongside the bus on the right and waved to the driver, a little old nun who smiled and waved back. The side of the bus was lettered SAINT ANALFABETA'S SCHOOL. He had never heard of Saint Analfabeta but shrugged and said, "A saint is a saint is a saint."

Risking a sideswipe from the meandering bus, Benny Deuce continued in tandem, correctly assuming his pursuers would not endanger the children by shooting. Without signaling, the bus swerved right onto International Lane as Benny obediently followed.

Before Angelo could follow, he heard a siren behind and saw in the rearview mirror a Madison police cruiser, lights flashing. The officer, who had been distributing "Just Say No to Drugs" bumper stickers, interrupted to respond to a speeding report.

As a journeyman getaway driver, Angelo turned sharply left in front of the cruiser. It swung left to avoid him but collided head-on with a semitrailer. Angelo darted ahead past the wreck and then sped left across opposing traffic. He raced down a side street with Serafina clutching her seat.

"Where we goin' now?" she said.

"Back to your place to get you packed."

"And then?"

"To Claudio's monastery where we take a breather."

"But the gorilla?"

"*La famiglia's* No. 1 hitman will come to us."

Benny Deuce craned his neck around the hole in his windshield as he followed the Saint Analfabeta School bus into the Dane County Regional Airport. It occurred to him that the damaged windshield might attract unwelcome attention and that prompt dumping of his beloved Thunderbird was indicated.

The bus headed for the parking meters in front of the terminal, climbing a curb and bashing three meters before the little old nun drove back on the pavement and parked at an upright meter. But Benny Deuce left the Thunderbird in the short-term parking lot as less conspicuous He stuck the Beretta in the waistband of his slacks, carefully buttoned his jacket, grabbed a duffel bag and hurried to the bus which disgorged noisy youngsters.

Vainly attempting to form a queue was the little old nun. She was swathed in a voluminous black habit and black knit shawl and brandished something that struck terror into Benny Deuce. It was an oak yardstick with a brass edge, which she flourished like a saber as she staggered along the ragged line, clutching a bulging black purse with her other hand.

He recalled Sister Sessualità at the School of Our Irrepressible Lady and her 24-inch ruler. She had warned she would hound wayward pupils to the ends of the earth.

Now he cautiously approached the frail nun who was inspecting the crumpled right front fender that had destroyed the meters. The youngsters cheered when they recognized him.

"Can I help you, Sister?"

She straightened up, held her back and blinked bleary eyes. "It's the devil's own job for a body shop and it's also my ass when Mother Superior finds out."

Benny Deuce checked the fender. "It's rubbin' on the tire is all."

He spat on his hands as the nun swung the yardstick over the heads of her charges. "Give the man some room!" she cried.

Benny Deuce gripped the heavy fender in both hands and jerked back. The fender emitted a resonating sound midway between twang and bong and snapped back into place as the children cheered.

The nun peered through her bifocals and cried, "Holy *merda!* You saved my ass with a miracle!"

Benny Deuce blushed and patted her arm. "It ain't nuttin', Sister. But you shouldn't be drivin' in your condition. You shoulda stood in bed."

"It's a side effect from the medication I'm on. And to boot at the convent last night we had Spanish rice for dinner which binds me real bad even though it was the favorite dish of Saint Ignatius of Loyola."

"They never told me that in parochial school."

"Well he was a greaser, wasn't he?"

Benny Deuce sneezed in alcoholic fumes.

"Gesundheit," she said. "There was nobody else available to drive Satan's little helpers down to the airport to sing for Mother Superior when she gets back from a pilgrimage. She'll need medication too because travel always constipates her."

Benny Deuce looked over his shoulder and whispered, "Sister, I need a favor." He reached into his hit kit and extracted five $100 bills, which he folded discreetly and pressed into her hand. "My car ain't safe to drive. If you borrow me your bus so I can get back to town and pick up another car I'll leave a note on the bus for somebody to call you to tell you where it's at."

The nun steadied herself on her yardstick, unfolded the wad, counted it, handed him the bus keys and said, "Bless you for your contribution, my son. But how are all of us here going to get back to school with Mother Superior?"

"There's enough in that wad to hire a dozen cabs and plenty left over for more medication."

He received mumbled directions to I94 eastbound toward Milwaukee for guidance after he found a car. Then a towheaded little girl pointed her lollipop at the terminal and cried, "Sister Ubriaco, Mother Superior's coming in shades!"

Grinning impishly, the nun opened her purse and produced a nearly empty 750 ml bottle. "Peach brandy always unbinds Mother and me."

"But Sister, the bottle's almost shot. What will Mother Superior say?"

Sister Ubriaco straightened and flourished her yardstick. "Oh, she'll really crap when she sees me!"

Bustling out of the terminal was a husky nun in dark glasses, a lei accenting her habit. In one hand she swung a tennis racket and in the other lugged a camera bag. Following was a porter pushing a hand truck loaded with luggage, skis over his shoulder.

Benny Deuce raced to the bus and began to drive off. The last he saw of Saint Analfabeta's group was Sister Ubriaco dropping her brandy bottle which shattered on the sidewalk while Mother Superior shook her tennis racket at the vagabond bus.

Driving south on Packers Avenue, Benny Deuce passed a wrecker hauling the police cruiser, an ambulance hauling the injured cop, and a dozen cops grilling the hapless truck driver.

Benny Deuce squinted at his gold Rolex trying to recall if the little hand indicated minutes and the big hand hours. He gave up and peeked at the throwaway digital watch on his other wrist. It was time to find a pay phone. Don Topo and *Consigliere* Iron Al would be waiting impatiently at the corner phone booth in Brooklyn for his call.

He passed Tenney Park on the right, continued on East Gorham Street, passed the Capitol, was confused again when Gorham changed to University Avenue and finally pulled into a gas station that had an outdoor phone.

Back in Brooklyn, Don Topo and Iron Al shivered at the old enclosed phone booth that had replaced the new model as arranged. But Iron Al shivered more than the don because Iron Al stood outside while the don sat inside.

An Aizilop Plumbing van passed. The driver wore an immaculate white coverall displaying his embroidered name Mordecai. The back of the coverall was boldly lettered AIZILOP PLUMBING. The driver slowed, adjusted rimless glasses which slipped down his nose, noted the two mafiosi and reported on intercom to his colleague in the van's rear:

"Special Agent Mordecai X. Sachel observes two subjects at corner pay telephone. Within the booth is Don Topo Scempio. Without is *Consigliere* Alessandro Savio."

He pronounced his own name SAY-chel.

Six feet behind the driver sat a similarly attired gentleman whose name was embroidered in full: "J. Edgar Haman." He was sitting in a green canvas director's chair surrounded by surveillance and communications equipment. Stenciled across the chair's back was FOR OFFICIAL BUNS ONLY. On a shelf above his small desk was a framed portrait of a jowly gentleman whose lips were twisted midway between a smile and a grimace. An engraved brass plate screwed to the frame said OUR FOUNDER.

After listening to a tape of Don Topo and Iron Al debating pasta recipes, the surveillance operative switched off the machine and reversed the portrait to a mood reflecting his own: The founder scowled, bushy eyebrows contorted.

Having kept Mordecai waiting, Haman finally said, "Supervising Special Agent J. Edgar Haman acknowledges receipt and directs Special Agent Satchel to park surveillance vehicle forthwith."

The driver gritted his teeth and proceeded to a metered parking spot across the street from La Santa Spogliarellista Fraternal and Benevolent Club.

Meanwhile at the windswept corner, Iron Al tapped the phone booth door with a numb knuckle for he had left his gloves in the club. The don jerked awake, raising his gray head from the phone, his dusty black fedora slipping over one ear.

Before the *consigliere* could inform his drowsy superior that they had been observed by the plumbing van driver, the phone rang. Don Topo jerked again as his hat tumbled to the grimy floor. He opened the door and peered with astonishment at his *consigliere.*

"How come you know to rap the don that *il telefono* he is about to ring and then *il telefono* he rings pronto?"

Iron Al shrugged.

The don had just punctuated his query with a snap of his bony fingers when the phone rang a second time. As the befuddled don languidly removed his gloves, the anxious *consigliere* seized the phone and thrust it into his leader's hand for Benny Deuce would have hung up on the third ring as agreed. Then he would not have called back for another hour necessitating another bone-chilling vigil at the booth.

Before addressing Benny Deuce, the don tapped his bare head with a forefinger, smiled at his *consigliere* and offered a rare compliment on Iron Al's supposed prescience

"*La saggezza.*"

"Thanks boss," said the distant voice of Benny Deuce.

The don frowned, aware he was bareheaded in the cold but unaware of his hat's location.

"Who speaks to the don?"

"Benny Deuce."

"*Deficiente*, ain't the don told you never give names over *il telefono*?"

"*Scusi*, Don Topo."

"*Bene*, Benedetto. Now what does *la Signora* Panettorio tell you about a certain underboss, no name, the party of the second part who we call A?"

Benny Deuce, shivering at an outdoor pay phone stand in Madison, said. "*La Signora* Panettorio didn't say nuttin' to me about A but I'm workin' on it."

Don Topo stamped his numb foot but made only a muffled sound because his hat was under his shoe. He reached for the battered fedora, clutched his back, adjusted the red cock's feather in the band and set the hat gingerly on his head as the *consigliere* stifled a giggle.

Benny Deuce's evasive reply irritated the don. He had disliked riddles ever since his young grandchildren egged him on with "What goes up white and comes down yellow?" Now he drummed his stiff fingers on the booth's sturdy oak shelf. You couldn't beat oak he thought slipping into reverie.

While he believed, rivals should be dispatched into the next world in a concrete shroud, he had selected for himself a copper-lined oak coffin. It featured a bulletproof glass viewing port complemented by solid brass handles, chrome tailfins and bumpers, and a front bumper sticker of gold foil proclaiming, "I Gave America the Business."

The don's last vehicle was recommended by his undertaker cousin as "The pallbearers' ball-buster guaranteed wormproof."

"Don Topo, with all due respect, is you still there?" Benny Deuce inquired.

"*I frutti e la verdura!*" the don exclaimed jolted back to reality. "Why not *la Signora* Panettorio said nothin' to you?"

"Because she was tailin' me stead of vice versa."

"Sure. That explains a whole bunch."

"Then it's okay, boss?"

"No, it ain't. And where was A?"

"Who?"

"Angelo, *deficiente.*"

"A was drivin' his *nonna.*"

"Ain't you ashamed, Benedetto? You our No. 1 motivator can't take care of a little old *nonna* and her *nipotino.*"

"For that little old *nonna* every day is Halloween and her *nipotino* got my two best *soldati* busted without pullin' his Beretta."

"While parrot talks, eagle flies and kills rabbit. Now get your ass in your car and take care of *la nonna* and *il nipotino.*"

"I can't now, boss. That little old *nonna* totaled my windshield. But as soon as I can find another supercharged Thunderbird I'll take another whack at it."

The don contemplated the booth's grimy ceiling, implored the intercession of Our Irrespressible Lady and stamped his fist on the shelf.

"You better take a look at your contract. It don't say, 'The party of the first part will *try* to take a whack at the party of the second part.' It says, 'The party of the first part *will* whack the party of the second part.' So the first thing is your syntax is fucked up again. The second thing is the contract says the party of the second part is Angelo and anybody else that gotta be whacked to help you ice that rat includin' his *nonna* even if she is a little old lady. And the third thing is you got consideration which means the don gave you moola or kernel of the realm and when you took that the don got you by the short hairs."

"With all due respect Don Topo, I never read any of them contracts you gave me because Sister Sessualità told me I should never try to read anythin' over second grade level."

The don opened the phone booth door, grabbed the *consigliere's* coat collar and hauled him in.

"You're gettin' a second opinion right from the horse's

bocca," the don shouted into the phone and handed it to the consigliere.

"We got an enforceable contract because *ignoramus illegal non excusa* which means even a dumb bunny gotta do what his don orders," the *consigliere* said.

Don Topo shoved the *consigliere* out of the booth and shut the door against the cold.

"Now you steal yourself a Yugo because a shitty Jap car is all you deserve. Call the don back tomorrow and if you still fartin' around we add you to the party of the second part, *Capisci?*"

Benny Deuce stared at the dead phone in his hand and with a sob hung up, slipped a note and a $20 bill under the school bus' windshield wiper and trudged west on University Avenue. The note said: "Fone Sistr Ubriaco."

His tennies slipped on the icy sidewalk as he bent into the wind pummeling his thin leather jacket. Hatless he clamped bare hands over burning ears and for the first time cursed his don.

A chorus of barks and wails greeted him as he passed an animal control van parked at a gas station. The cab was unoccupied. He banged his fist on the locked rear doors as the canine chorus swelled.

Benny Deuce stepped back and kicked at the doors, which flew open. Led by a belligerent toy poodle, the joyful escapees leaped out and galloped west on University.

"You made it!" he cried as he ran with them.

He gazed longingly at made-in-the-U.S. of A. Fords, Chevies and Chryslers. But he pressed on into the crowded parking lot of Hilldale Mall where he spied a Yugo parked near an entrance.

It was a rusty sardine can on wheels that had been repainted blotchy orange. As he casually approached, the idling engine coughed a plume of greasy white exhaust through the rattling tailpipe secured with a wire hanger to the rear bumper. The car was unoccupied.

He knelt near the driver's door supposedly to adjust

the Velcro straps on his tennies and noted the door was ajar. With the engine already running it was Auto Theft 101.

In a trice, he was behind the wheel, sinking into a decrepit seat. He rammed the balky stick shift into reverse and with gears grinding began to chug out of the parking lot.

Carefully checking the rearview mirror, he was dismayed to see both a little old lady and little old man shlepping a shopping bag between them. They staggered to the oily spot vacated by their Yugo, dropped the bag, brandished their canes and hopped with surprising agility. He inferred they were consigning him to a deserved place in hell for stealing their venerable clunker.

But his last glimpse of the couple as he headed north on Midvale Boulevard showed them performing a *pas de deux* as joyfully as their infirmities would permit. Then he saw taped to the sun visor a note crudely lettered with red marker: "THANK YOU!"

"Why them dirty little old crooks!" he cried. "They conned me into rippin' off their insurance company!"

HAROLD KNOLL

CHAPTER VII

As he climbed the winding snow-covered private road toward the Penitential Brothers of Saint Peccato Monastery, the man huddled against the cold in a hooded poncho cut from an old army blanket. The sodden skirt of his gray habit dragged on the crushed rock surface and he shuffled in torn black leather sandals patched with masking tape. His frayed woolen socks were soaked, one red, one blue.

A wisp of smoke ascended from his deep hood as he bent over an open journal held vertically in bare reddened hands. When he heard a car approaching behind him, he stuffed his *Playboy* inside his poncho and fetched a worn leather-covered breviary. On it he snuffed out a Royal Jamaica cigar which he tucked into a pocket. He began limping through grimy slush on the road shoulder.

The Cadillac Fleetwood Brougham stopped beside him, the front passenger window lowered and a little old lady beckoned. When he approached she held out a card deck.

"*Per favore* pick a card," she said sliding one forward off the top, which he accepted, glanced at and handed back.

She peered into the man's hood and compared his face with the portrait on the saint's card.

"It's a miracle!" she cried turning to Angelo at the wheel. "Santo Peccato has come down from *il cielo* to help a little old *nonna* and her *nipotino*."

But Angelo tossed a crumpled dollar bill at the man, raised the window and accelerated, splattering crushed rock and snow over him as the dollar bill lay at his feet.

"A holy panhandler is all," Angelo said. "Up in *il cielo* they closed the books long ago on saints and miracles."

Meanwhile the man pocketed the dollar, placed two fingers in his mouth and whistled. From dense woods a buck deer bounded onto the right side of the road. Proudly carrying 10-point antlers he bowed his head and accepted a pat on the nose steaming vapor.

This was witnessed by Angelo and Serafina in their rearview mirrors for at her insistence he had stopped some 50 yards up the road. What they couldn't see was the handful of shelled corn the man removed from his pocket and fed to this deer, a daily ration.

"Another miracle!" Serafina cried. "Another Santo Francesco who talks with animals. Turn back and give *il padre* a lift."

Because the road was narrow, Angelo proceeded uphill to a turnaround but parked when they looked downhill and saw the man and deer were gone.

They walked downhill and studied the deer's tracks. These led from the woods on the right uphill side of the road to the road surface where the tracks mingled with the man's.

From there the deer's tracks crossed the road to the left downhill shoulder and continued across a snow-covered field and into the woods beyond. The man's footprints were confined to the road.

Angelo scratched his head and was startled by a tap on the shoulder from Serafina. She held a few corn kernels she had picked from the snow and pointed to the deer tracks leading to the road and those departing. Then she nodded and said, "Aha."

"Aha what? We know where the deer went but where the hell did that guy go? I see his tracks on the road but he vanishes leaving no tracks off the road. Another miracle, Grandma?"

Serafina began to trudge back to the car as Angelo hurried after her.

"Is another miracle but not the kind you think. Trouble with you, Angelo, you hang around Brooklyn where is all sidewalks. In Sicilia we got country, we got donkeys, goats and chickens. We understand animals. God gave you eyes but you no see."

Angelo opened the passenger door and she buckled in smiling. When he got behind the wheel he was about to turn the ignition key but couldn't resist asking, "See what, Grandma?"

"See deer tracks different on each side of road. Tracks one kind when deer is coming and another kind when he is leaving."

Angelo tapped the wheel in frustration. "I don't get it. What's the deer got to do with a joker whose tracks end when he vanishes? You mean the angels took him up to *il cielo* like *la Beata Vergine*?"

"He is saint but still on earth waiting to help us as we climb to top of mountain to his monastery. Your weak eyes miss too much."

"Saints is supposed to be stiffs lookin' like their pictures on your holy cards. Deadbeat is all he looks like to me."

She handed him the man's worn breviary she had retrieved from the road. Carlo Francesco Peccato was scrawled in pencil on the inside front cover.

Angelo sniffed the breviary and returned it. "Smell it?" he said.

"I gotta the sinus."

"Grandma, another miracle I don't get is how come this poor ghost can smoke cigars—and they ain't stogies neither."

CHAPTER VIII

When Benny Deuce drove the protesting Yugo north on Midvale Boulevard to Madison's Beltline, he turned right instead of left, proceeded through west Madison, passed Middleton and found himself in the country on Highway 12 with no freeway. He coaxed the Yugo to a roadside tavern, keeping the engine running and enveloping the area in white smoke.

Before he could enter the tavern, the front door flew open and the bartender, girded in a big white apron and brandishing a large mug of beer, cried, "Where's the fire?"

"Just this Jap clunker fartin'. *Grazie* for the beer."

"Sorry but it's for a man with fire in his belly," said the bartender taking a swig.

"Where's the monastery at?"

The bartender drained the mug and carefully wiped each finger on his apron. "Why seek a monastery when I can provide that service over the bar?"

"You a priest?"

"No, I'm not interested in boys but I do hold a doctorate in psychology from the UW-Madison. It's a prerequisite for a bartender's position in this area. Come in and get your id and ego back in synch while I anesthetize your superego and square your frame of reference."

But Benny Deuce shook his head. "You're talkin' analysis but I'm talkin' business."

Contemplating the Yugo's exhaust, the bartender coughed and said, "I was just starting to free associate and was reminded of Dante."

"My cousin Dante Orso is in jail at Palermo."

"No, the other one, Dante Alighieri."

"Oh, my uncle on my mother's side. He's in jail at Messina."

The bartender steadied the empty mug on the Yugo's vibrating hood, cupped his hand under his chin and stared at the smoke. "I wonder if you might be referring to the Priory. But I should explain—"

However, Benny Deuce, fearing the don's wrath, hastened behind the wheel, leaned out of the driver's window and said, "Where?"

The bartender held the beer mug westward. "Two miles thataway at a hamlet yclept Tropical Corners. The food's superior but—"

The Yugo had disappeared in the smoke. A few minutes later Benny Deuce parked at a large white brick building with a spacious lawn and a sign proclaiming: "Shanghai Priory. All the Chinese Food U Can Eat $5.95."

Below that, another sign advertised a bowling alley. The parking lot was jammed with pickups and semitrailers. Benny Deuce readjusted the Beretta in his waistband, offered two Hail Marys that the Yugo would start again and shut it off.

His stomach growled at the aroma of burnt grease but he squared his shoulders and resolved to uphold his contractual obligation before dining. When he entered he noted the restaurant and bar were up front while the bowling alley occupied the rear with no sign of monastic life. He inferred he might be in the wrong place.

Benny Deuce looked down at a petite young lady holding a menu who gazed up at him and winked. He posed a test question, "Where do I go to confession?"

She had freckles, snub nose and eyes of robin's egg blue. Her smile displayed impressive orthodontia while her index finger traced circles on his massive shoulder.

"I'm a good listener, you big hunk, and I believe in situation ethics," she whispered. "Come back at 3 this afternoon when I get off work and I'll give you a special absolution with no penance although I do admire a man with a big penance."

His paw gently removed her finger. "Where in hell are the priests? Ain't this supposed to be a church? And if it ain't, then where's the Chinamen to dish out the chop suey?"

"It was a priory but 10 years ago the order that ran it moved out because what guy wants to be celibate today with gorgeous gals like me around? Two Hebes from the Bronx bought the place and turned it into a Chinese restaurant keeping Priory in the name because everybody knows it. When they couldn't get Chinese help they hired us locals."

But Benny Deuce grunted and turned to leave.

"Won't you stay for lunch? The food's awesome."

He started for the door and then recalling his objective said, "You know where there's a real monastery east of Madison where I just come from?"

Her pinky touched his arm. "I used to live near there. It's between Madison and Milwaukee but it isn't a real monastery anymore since the Pope pulled their license because their saint is a phony pepperoni. You've been heading west. You've got to turn around and go east on the Beltline."

She wrote directions and a phone number on the back of a menu.

"Is that the monastery's number?" he said.

"No, it's mine. Why enter a monastery when you can find celestial happiness with me?"

Benny Deuce rubbed his abdomen. "Just gimme a dozen egg rolls to go with hot mustard and sweet-and-sour sauce."

She watched his broad back disappear through the front doorway, hoping he'd turn and wave but he didn't.

"There's people waiting to be seated, Millie," the

manager said.

"Up your egg foo yung," she said, brushing away a tear,

Returning to Middleton, Benny Deuce tossed the empty restaurant container out of the Yugo's window, burped contentedly and faced his biggest challenge — thinking. As a loyal *soldato* he had complied with Don Topo's wishes and was doing penance for the delayed hit by driving the hated Yugo. However, when a 4-watt bulb flickered in his head he banged a hammy fist on the dashboard.

"Bongo!" he cried when bingo had been intended.

Since Don Topo had not defined the penitential period. Benny Deuce realized he was free to dump the Yugo as soon as he found another Thunderbird. So he turned off Highway 12 and entered University Avenue eastbound, scanning streets and parking lots for his favorite car.

He pulled into a strip mall, the Yugo's motor gasping exhaust into an ominous mushroom cloud. Benny Deuce slowed, passing Cadillacs, Chryslers and the unmentionable Japanese cars until he spied a new Thunderbird being parked. Although it was not supercharged and was red instead of venerable black, he murmured, "A Thunderbird is a Thunderbird is a Thunderbird."

He parked alongside, engine running, grabbed his duffel bag, jumped out and pounded the Thunderbird's window. The astonished driver wearing a fireman's uniform lowered the window and was enveloped in the Yugo's exhaust.

"Where's the fire?" he cried gasping.

"In your rear end!"

Exiting with a king-size fire extinguisher, the fireman ran toward the rear while Benny Deuce entered the Thunderbird whose keys were in the ignition. When he backed into the Yugo cloud he barely discerned the contorted face of the fireman who brandished his extinguisher and cried, "You'll burn in hell for this!"

Benny Deuce tooled happily along University Avenue

westbound, picked up Highway 12 again, entered the Beltline and proceeded east toward the freeway. The car was new and pending arrival of license plates bore a hand-lettered LAF (License Applied For) sign in the rear window.

"The laugh's on that *stupido* who don't know it's spelled with two F's," Benny Deuce said.

When he approached a "Y" at the freeway entrances, he stopped in the roadway because highway signs required perusal. The right entrance displayed eastbound Chicago signs, the left westbound Wisconsin Dells signs. He did not want to go west but east and anyway after the egg rolls he did not fancy deli. So amid a horn medley behind he recited "Eeny, meeny, miny, mo," Ending on the eastbound side he turned right.

Benny Deuce accelerated to 90 and sat back to watch the landscape whiz by. But after 20 minutes, he noticed the dashboard auto compass indicated south. "Jap crap," he said wrenching the foreign-made compass off its mount and shaking it.

When he remounted the compass, it rotated wildly. By this time he should have been nearing the monastery but it was located east, not south of Madison. A Pacifico sign flashed by too fast to peruse but he swung onto the exit ramp seeking further travel directions.

As he cruised, the town's unfamiliar streets, he entered a decrepit neighborhood whose black residents stared at his new car and white face. Idle young men in team jackets and caps clustered at street corners.

Approaching a church he was passed by a battered Chrysler jammed with black youths. One held a 9 mm pistol out of a car window and fired two shots at the church as the car accelerated and disappeared around a corner with screeching tires. The shooting was ignored by the locals with one exception:

Rushing out of the church was a middle-aged black man in a dented black hat and shabby black overcoat. When he brandished a corn broom he slipped on the icy landing and bounced down a dozen rickety wooden steps to the sidewalk still clutching his broom upright like a baton.

Benny Deuce's head jerked at each bump. The man lay on his back staring at the leaden sky, his grizzled head against dirty snow. Benny Deuce made a U-turn parking directly in front of the church along the yellow curb on which FUNERALS ONLY was painted in black.

The man's coat was open, buttons having popped off in the fall. He was wearing a rumpled black suit, black clipon bowtie and frayed white shirt.

Benny Deuce removed his thin black leather jacket, knelt beside the man, covered his face, said a Hail Mary and started to rise when the broom, still upright, twitched and a moan issued from under the jacket. A callused hand slowly lifted the jacket, the man blinked and through trembling lips said, "Elijah, is you come for me in your fiery chariot?"

"No, I'm Benedetto, Benny Deuce for short, and I dumped my fiery chariot for this Thunderbird."

He helped the man to his feet and wielded the broom to brush snow off his coat.

"Blessed are you, my son, for helping a doorkeeper in the house of the Lord to rise up."

"Don't thank me, Father. Thank Don Topo who put out the contract." Benny Deuce frowned at the man's tilted head "What them punks done was no way to treat a Father. You got yourself a busted neck."

"I ain't the Father and my neck ain't broke."

The man reversed the broom for a cane and staggered to the church's outdoor bulletin board where he shook his head. "Look what them two shots done just after I set up them letters."

The bullets had smashed the glass cover punching holes through the upcoming sermon topic, "Stay Cool with the Lord for 5 Minutes."

Viewing his reflection in the remaining glass, the man adjusted his hat to the angle of his neck tilted left. "Last year them no-good gangsters shot at the altar during services.

The church was lucky because the bullet missed the solid brass cross but I wasn't because I was nipped in the neck which put a crick in it."

"Does it hurt, Father?"

"Only when I laugh. I ain't the regular pastor but you can call me that because I am the actin' temporary pastor which I shall explain."

"*Per favore* first tell me what your sign means. You got instant air conditioning?"

"No way, Brother. I don't got much book learnin' so when I preaches I sit down when I don't have nothin' more to say which is usually five minutes. Now how can I help you?"

"I got a problem."

"You come to the right place. I could tell when you was Good Samaritin' me that inside was a soul in pain. But first we got to see you don't get a parkin' ticket while visitin' the house of the Lord. Them cops is fierce on parkin' tickets in this neighborhood. Also jaywalkin'."

From his pocket the man took a small cardboard sign and slipped it under the Thunderbird's windshield wiper.

The hand-lettered sign said FUNERAL.

"You won't be hassled now, but lock the doors on your nice new automobile. We got us a lot of criminal activity since some Chicago trash got dumped here."

The man limped up the front steps, his left hand clutching the small of his back, his right holding the broom baton. Shingles had fallen from the roof and paint peeled from the siding. Previous gunfire had shattered a stained glass window partially covered with warped plywood.

Benny Deuce looked at the street number above the sagging front door.

"You got bad luck with a 99 up there. It should be 711."

"But that number's already took by the funeral home six blocks away which is always busy."

"It figures. I can make an arrangement to motivate them to swap."

The man opened the front door as Benny Deuce followed him inside.

"You musta got hurt when you fell."

"Just a teeny ways north-northwest of the sacro Cadillac but if Brother Paul could abide the thorn in his flesh so can a sufferin' servant."

He flicked a switch dimly lighting the interior and sat beside Benny Deuce in a pew ancient but gleaming. After the man drew his buttonless coat close against the cold, he carefully removed his hat, rubbed the brim on his sleeve and placed the hat on the pew. He sighed and folded his hands.

"Is this a sin of the flesh you is confessin' like covetin' your neighbor's ass?"

Benny Deuce backed away.

"I ain't no fag. I'm strictly a P-U-S-S-E guy."

The man paused but pressed on. "Has you adulterated like puttin' tap water in bourbon whiskey?"

"I have a couple boilermakers now and then but I don't overdo it."

"Has you carved any graven images?"

"When I was a kid I used to whittle till my knife got stole."

"Has you ever forgot to honor your father and mother?"

"You ever seen my old man's razor strop? Don't ask."

"Has you ever committed murder?"

Benny Deuce looked over his shoulder and whispered, "In my profession, Father, nobody mentions that M word."

The man unfolded his hands and patted Benny Deuce's shoulder, "Brother, I ain't a reverend. I got my own confession. I'm the church janitor and I didn't want to interrupt your confession because I knew right off you is a soul that needs a tune-up."

"The janitor? Where's the head guy?"

The man bobbed his chin at the altar, "Up there."

"I don't see nobody."

The janitor clapped his hands. "It's Jesus Christ, your

Lord and Saviour, risen from the dead to save sinners like me and you from the fiery pit. Has you ever felt the heat of the flames?"

"When I fell asleep at Coney Island and woke up with a bad sunburn. But my cousin Carmine can really take the heat. He's a fireman in East Harlem. Now where's your *capo* really at?"

The janitor shook his head, wincing at the crick in his neck and cleared his throat. "We had us a fine pastor, a mighty fortress thumbing his nose at an evil host."

"The middle finger is better than the thumb for that."

"I speak in parables and like the gospel says you don't get my drift, Brother. Anyhow, it was two months ago one Sunday mornin' durin' the service in which our choir is all in angel white but wearin' these garments over their coats because our furnace is out. They raises their handbells in their gloved hands and is a-ringin' and a-singin' the praises of the Lord when the front door flies open. In pops the messenger of Satan, a stoned teenage gangster with a grocery bag over his head and two holes cut for his beady eyes."

Benny Deuce banged his fist in his leathery palm and patted his hit kit under his right armpit. "Wished I coulda been there to put him away permanent."

"Verily verily, Brother. He holds a deer rifle stole from the hardware store. He waves it around and cusses us out somethin' fierce, takin' the name of the Lord in vain."

"That's a goddamn shame."

"That's blasphemy."

"You're damn right. What was his beef?"

"Our pastor caught him the day before messin' with our poor box. The pastor smote him in the vestry, kicked him in the nave and tossed him out on a flyin' buttress."

Benny Deuce clutched his crotch. "I seen that hold on TV rasslin'."

"Now that Sunday our pastor stands foursquare in front of the choir proclaimin', 'In the name of the Lord I command thee, emissary of Satan, to begone and return to the fires of hell! But the gangster starts shootin' as everybody includin' me hits the floor except for the pastor, his arms stretched out like Jesus on the cross. Boom! goes the first shot and it's a pop fly bustin' our big stained glass window showin' Samson smitin' the Philistines hip and thigh with the slogan underneath, 'Love Thy Neighbor.' Boom! goes the second shot and it's another pop fly into the belfry and ding-dongin' our bell."

Benny Deuce shook his head. "Lousy shootin'."

"A crime indeed."

"Reckless use of firearms, Father. You wanna whack a guy do it like in the Mafia movies. You go right up to him with a .22 Beretta in a restaurant where he got a big gob of pasta hangin' outa his mouth. You give him two in the head is all and walk out casual. You don't go bangin' away with no deer rifle. Them high-powered rounds can fly a mile and whack a little old lady ain't even in the contract."

The janitor jumped up and wrestled with his broom. "Now fearin' for the congregation our pastor charges up the aisle and smites the demon who shoots again. Boom! goes the third shot but this time it's a home run and hits the pastor smack in the vestibule."

Benny Deuce clutched his crotch. "Ouch!"

"The messenger of Satan flees back to Babylon on Lake Michigan."

"Huh?"

"The home of the Cubs and the White Sox."

The janitor lifted his frayed coat sleeve to wipe a tear as Benny Deuce blew his nose on a tissue and tossed it under the pew.

"Where's your pastor at now?"

"He is cruising the heavenly highway to the golden tollbooth in the sky."

"Hope he got his change ready."

The janitor cocked his head slightly more to the left. "I can hear him singin' in the heavenly choir."

"If he got shot in the vestibule he's singin' soprano."

"Now Brother, what's the problem? You been wanderin' thirsty in the desert luggin' a big rock. Cast down that rock and I will smite it with my rod"—he flourished his broom—"and bring forth cool drink."

Benny Deuce cleared his throat. "I could sure use a frosty Heileman's Special Export right now. But my real problem is I gotta get to a monastery."

"Rejoice! This is the place!"

Benny Deuce scratched his chin stubble. "This is the place south of Madison that's supposed to be the monastery that's east?"

A sunbeam pierced a broken stained glass window radiating the pew. The janitor lifted his face and thumped his broom. "I see the light! Is that monastery the one got in trouble with the Pope for wheelin' and dealin'?"

"Yeah," said Benny Deuce dazzled.

"The one that don't got a preacher no more but got a gangster for a saint?"

"Yeah but in my profession we call him a *goombah.*"

"Brother, I can tell you explicitively and positatively down to the last jot and tittle just where that monastery is at. Them sinners need a preacher. They gotta hearken to the word of the Lord. I left school in the eighth grade to do janitorin' pushin' the cloth instead of wearin' it. Years ago when I was sellin' household products door-to-door I stopped at that monastery and asked if they would take me in as a brother but they said, 'We don't take your kind here.' I left with a heart heavy but not hardened. Even my own board of elders treats me like a hewer of wood and a drawer of water. But I still dream dreams of serving the Lord."

The janitor provided precise directions for the trip's first leg, the return to Madison on I90, and then continuing on I94 east to the monastery. Benny Deuce's eyes glazed while the janitor regarded him with concern.

"I'll also give you my official Wisconsin state road map with the picture of our governor flashin' his pearly whites. He comes down to visit us disadvantated multicultural folks just before election to promise how much he'll do for us after."

Benny Deuce opened the map upside down, frowned and shook his head. "Can't read no map. Too many squiggles and wiggles. Sometimes can't even read them road signs exceptin' GAS and EAT. "

The janitor took Benny Deuce's arm and led him outside where they stood at the top of the steps, the janitor watching his footing this time. Then the same battered Chrysler roared past filled with jeering youths as the janitor hit the deck but they didn't shoot. Benny Deuce stood watching until the car was out of sight. He helped the janitor to his feet and again wielded the broom to brush snow off his coat.

"You could smite them Philistines, couldn't you?"

"Sure, I could take care of that Philistine gang so you'd never see them again, but sometimes a guy gotta know when to be a wolf and when to be a fox. That's somethin' the Mustache Pete who runs my *famiglia* don't know. You ain't safe. I seen what happened to my old neighborhood in East New York and it's happened here. You got a famiglia?"

"A who?"

"A family."

"My wife was called upstairs."

Benny Deuce craned his neck at the steeple. "These days phones is jacked in all over."

"And my two boys is growed and gone. One is a minister in a big church in Kansas City and the other is in Leavenworth Penitentiary. I never hear from them. The elders give me a room rent free in the church basement. Here's my only family now."

A skinny tomcat with a dull gray coat climbed the steps with a mouse in his mouth, which he dropped at the janitor's feet. The cat scratched one ear whose tip had been chewed off.

"You done good, Jonah," the janitor said and the cat devoured the mouse.

"How ya doin', Pussy?" Benny Deuce said.

The cat growled and stood beside the janitor.

"He don't like for you to call him Pussy. He's a tomcat part angel, part sinner like us. I share my bread and beans with him but a tomcat needs meat which is why Jonah is the best mouser in Pacifico."

"So he should be satisfied."

"No he ain't. A professor in the congregation says Jonah wants self-actualization except I don't know what that means. Can't ask the professor for three years because he's in jail now for obfuscation except I don't know what that means neither."

Benny Deuce knelt and smiled at the cat who growled louder but did not back off.

"*Gattino mio,* you got *cojones.* If you pay *rispetto* to me then I do likewise and you get pasta with meat sauce plus lotsa self-aberration. *Capisci?*"

Jonah meowed and permitted Benny Deuce to take his paw briefly. Then Benny Deuce got up and told the janitor, "Maybe we talk about an arrangement."

"I'm listenin'."

"Since I got lost you're helpin' me find my way. You be my navigator and show me where that monastery's at. I gotta get there *presto* to do troubleshootin' for my *padrone* and if I don't he'll troubleshoot me. At the monastery we have a sitdown with them people to help you get in."

The janitor began to shiver and drew his coat tightly around him. "This troubleshootin' you do—how much is trouble and how much is shootin'?"

"I take care of everything. I got dough. I give you a good bonus for helpin' me. Just leave the church a note and pack a suitcase."

"What's your name again?"

"Benedetto Orso a.k.a. Benny Deuce. You?"

"Call me Raphael."

As they headed for Raphael's basement room, Jonah following, Benny Deuce said, "Invite *il gatto* to come along too."

Jonah meowed to that.

CHAPTER IX

"I see *il cielo* in the clouds!" cried Serafina blessing herself when a large white disk appeared against snowy woods on the hilltop.

Brilliant morning sunshine radiated Angelo's Cadillac. He stopped in the no-parking area at the main entrance of the circular two-story white brick monastery.

"I don't see no angels here—only that," Angelo said indicating a sign: "PENITENTIAL BROTHERS OF SAINT PECCATO. PILGRIMS WELCOME."

White paint had been applied over the lower part of the sign where the monastery's former name was faintly visible.

Serafina jerked a thumb at the roof where only a steel socket and wooden stump remained of a crucifix crudely sawn off.

"The Pope's double cross," Angelo said. "When he pulled the brothers' button he had the bishop transfer their chaplain. But before the chaplain left he was ordered to take the cross with him."

A man in baker's whites came from the woods reading a letter. He looked up, stared in surprise and hugged them. "Cugino *mio! Signora* Panettorio! You've come to visit?"

"A little while for our health, Claudio, if that's okay," Angelo said. He indicated the letter. "Fan mail?"

Claudio shook his head and pocketed the letter. "Somebody wants me dead. But come in and stay as long as you like. Why didn't you call?"

Angelo took the luggage out of the Cadillac's trunk but his cousin insisted on taking both suitcases.

"No time to call," Angelo said. "Let me see that letter. Nobody pushes *cugino mio* around."

Serafina gripped Claudio's arm. "You no eat enough. Food no good here?"

"*Signora*, I haven't had much appetite lately."

"Then I cook for you."

Claudio lodged them in adjoining rooms in the monastery's guest area and returned at noon. He had changed into his order's habit—gray tunic, rope belt and black leather sandals.

"Here we go around in circles," Claudio said as they strolled the main corridor of the round building.

A red, white and blue neon sign on the wall announced Peccato Pacchia and he led them through swinging doors into the monastery's tavern-cum-restaurant. Angelo jerked his thumb at the sign: "Eat, drink and be merry."

They sat in a booth in a far corner and Claudio ordered minestrone and sandwiches when the brother waiter took their order. After the waiter left, Claudio said, "I apologize for not being a more generous host but we've had to economize. I'm head baker and assistant prior but confidentially I'm not happy at the way things are going."

Serafina banged her little fist on the table, "I knew you ain't eatin' right."

"What concerns me more is whether you two are in trouble."

"The one who's in trouble is Don Topo, the punk that talks about himself like he's some other guy," Angelo said. "*Cugino mio*, who sent you that letter?"

Claudio handed it over. The plain envelope bore a Chicago postmark and was typewritten, as was the letter: "Get out or get buried."

Angelo returned the letter.

"How come to you and not to *il capo?*"

"Because the prior has been urging us to sell our bakery to the Chicago *famiglia* who have already grabbed a bakery in Illinois. And as a former English teacher I find their spelling deplorable."

"But there ain't much money in baking bread."

"There's no money in bread which is why we dropped it. We produced a nutritious high quality product that couldn't get space on the crowded supermarket shelves."

"What are you bakin' that them Chicago punks want?"

"You are now going to get the $5 tour," Claudio said.

On the way to the basement Serafina said, "How come you got tavern here not like other church places?"

"We're church orphans. We established an independent order after the Pope revoked Carlo Peccato's canonization. The Vatican said his death was a hoax to attract solvent pilgrims. So we figured let's enjoy life with our own tavern."

Claudio indicated a sign on a basement door: "BAKERY EMPLOYEES ONLY. OTHERS KEEP OUT."

"We're concerned about industrial espionage. I don't want snoopers to see my R&D."

"Not if you keep your fly zipped," Angelo said.

When they entered the bakery, a small missile whizzed over their heads. They ducked as Angelo reached for the Beretta in his waistband and Serafina groped in her purse for her .38. Claudio laughed and patted Angelo's shoulder.

"You've just encountered some of my R&D—and my fly is zipped."

The missile did a U-turn, began to wobble and crashed into plastic sheeting protecting a window. Claudio retrieved the missile and held it up.

"A variation on a theme. This is your standard two-ounce bagel but pressed flat, shaped into a V and undergoing flight trials. It's for kids who want to play with their food. We expect testimonials from the glass industry when we market this product."

"But it crashes," Angelo said.

Claudio contemplated the bagel and frowned. "I wish I had your expertise in bagel baking. You worked for Reilly's Bagels when you were in school. I'm self-taught. We attempted a boomerang design but it needs refinement."

Angelo weighed the bagel in his hand, took a precut strip of dough for a two-ounce bagel, discarded a quarter and displayed the strip.

"Now we got ourselves a 1 and a 1/2-ounce bagel. You gotta lighten up, Claudio." He shaped the dough into a wider V, flattened it more, flipped it in his palm, nodded and handed it to Claudio. "Bake this slightly harder and give it a whirl. It'll fly."

"But if it's harder we'll get kids with cracked fillings."

"Then we get more testimonials — from dentists. Whaddya call this thing?"

"I thought we'd put the bagel in historical perspective and call it the Kitty Hawk."

Angelo shook his head. "What does cats got to do with it?" He made a fist and extended his pinky and index finger, the Sicilian insult for cuckoldry. "Call it *Il Cornuto*. When customers ask we say it means V for Victory."

Serafina listened patiently and said, "Is boomerang, no? Then we call it the *Ciao* Bagel. Is goodbye-hello. Someday will save the bakery."

They sat at a small table in the bakery and had coffee with buttered bagels.

"Bagels are a fast-growing market," Claudio said. "Now we're concentrating on the frozen segment and business is picking up because we do quality work. Our big competitors stress quantity with machines making thousands of bagels per hour. But we make bagels the old-fashioned way—boiling and baking by hand. With practice my bakers and I can each make about 800 per hour. We use only the best ingredients. I may dabble in the shape but what's inside is classic whereas our competitors push blueberry, raisin and other eccentricities."

"So what's the problem?" Angelo said.

"It would be more discreet if we returned to Peccato Pacchia to confer privately. But first I'd like you to meet two of our brother bakers who also work with me on R&D." He beckoned a short, fat brother. "This is Brother Goldbach."

The brother bowed to Angelo and Serafina, smiled and patted his ample belly. "Ja, I taste everything as you see," he said.

"Brother Goldbach conducts our taste test panels."

"I look at all results and then how you say—"

"He conjectures which batch was best."

"Ja, I conjecture," said Brother Goldbach who returned to work.

Another brother sat at a work bench contemplating a bagel in each hand. One bagel had been baked crusty brown, the other smooth gold. When Claudio called, the brother placed the bagels on the bench and reluctantly left his work,

"Eureka yet, Brother Heisenberg?" Claudio said.

Brother Heisenberg, thin and fidgety, cautiously eyed Claudio's visitors.

"Maybe ja, maybe *nein*. Is always two ways of looking at a bagel or anything else. With the bagel we are uncertain which came first—the torus or the hole. So *bitte* excuse for to my work I must go."

Claudio led Angelo and Serafina to a locked door which he opened. They entered a small storeroom, Claudio locked the door behind him, put his fingers to his lips and whispered, "I developed a secret ingredient that makes our bagels taste best."

He indicated a framed photo of the grim Pope on the wall.

"The way the brothers feel about him they ignore his picture and what's behind it."

Carefully lifting the portrait off the wall, Claudio spun the dial of a safe, opened it and removed a half-gallon brown glass bottle with a large cork stopper. As he rotated the bottle against the light, Angelo and Serafina could discern granules. Claudio said, "I alone add a precise quantity of this ingredient to each batch of dough, an ingredient I prepare myself. I keep the secret formula in the safe too."

"Why do you show us this if it is so secret?" Angelo said.

"Only time two people keep secret is when one is dead," Serafina said.

Claudio returned the bottle to the safe and replaced the Pope's portrait.

"Angelo, if something happened to me I'd be grateful if you'd see to it that our bagel production continued with the same formula."

After they left the storeroom, Claudio excused himself to take a phone call and Serafina asked Angelo, "If he gets whacked, how can you open safe without combination?"

"I looked over his shoulder each time he turned the dial."

At Peccato Pacchia the trio sat in a far corner booth and had espresso and chocolate chip cookies. Claudio leaned over the table and whispered, "Angelo, you asked me what the problem is. Actually there are two both related: The prior and the Chicago *famiglia* represent one problem because the prior is in their pocket awaiting a payoff when they take over the monastery. Meanwhile our bagel trucks are being hijacked and our brother drivers roughed up. The second problem involves me personally as you saw in that letter. I infer I'm the party of the second part in a Chicago contract."

Serafina grabbed Angelo's arm. "Why fart around with *il priore?* You follow Brass Rule of Pietro *mio*: 'If somebody tries to screw you, screw the fucker back twice as hard.'"

A beefy brother about 6'6" with red hair fringing his bald pate threw open the swinging doors and strode to the bar. He seized the arm of a frightened brother bartender who dropped a glass that shattered on the bar. As the bartender yelled, the giant forced the bartender's bare arm toward the broken glass.

Angelo got up and rubbed his hands as he neared the bar. The bartender's bare arm was just touching the glass, which pricked his skin. He screamed as a drop of blood coursed down his arm. Angelo's index finger tapped the prior on the shoulder.

"*Scusi* but maybe you shouldn't fight with a peaceful man. If you make him too angry he don't know when to stop and he'll kill you. Fight with a mean man like me who never gets angry."

"You're next," the prior said bearing down harder on the bartender's arm.

Angelo knelt, stuck the ends of two wooden matches between the sole and upper of the prior's sandal and lit them. The prior observed with interest the flame advancing toward his foot but retained his grip. When the flame charred his sock, he stamped his foot on the polished oak floor until he released his grip. Then he hopped holding his foot with both hands as Angelo clapped in time.

"Why did you do that?" the prior said. "I can't stand pain."

"I can't stand the sight of blood."

Meanwhile the bartender had retreated to the far end of the bar. He poured a double scotch, dribbled some over his scratched arm, patted it with a bar napkin and downed the rest.

Shaking his fist at the bartender, the prior squared his shoulders and indicated his belt. While the other brothers wore rope belts, the prior's was linked metal plates featuring a massive inscribed chrome buckle fastened under his belly, which he stuck out and said: "I am Cannibal O'Toole, holder of the world wrestling championship title, now serving the Lord as Brother Primattore."

Angelo bowed. "And I am a mean man who asks *per favore* why you beat up on peaceful people."

"To keep in practice like so," said the prior lunging.

Angelo sidestepped, stuck out his foot and tripped the

giant who crashed to the floor. Then Angelo smacked the barrel of his Beretta alongside the prior's skull. He was snoring peacefully when six brothers loaded him onto a stretcher and staggered to the infirmary.

Angelo went for a walk in the snowy woods with Claudio and Serafina.

"*Il esperto* Benny Deuce will be lookin' for me," Angelo said. "He can't tie his own shoelaces but has never missed on a hit. I take care of him and retire Don Topo permanent and also his *marionetta*. Iron Al. Then I am *il capo* of the Scempio *famiglia*. But I don't go back to Brooklyn before I straighten out them Chicago *goombata* for you."

Serafina chewed furiously on an unlit cigarette and shook her head.

"Stay here. You can't make Brooklyn like it was."

But Angelo shrugged. Claudio led them to the parking lot and indicated one of the monastery's three small refrigerated bakery vans. It had two bullet holes on the same side—one through the front bumper and the other in the upper body near the roof.

"Good shootin'," Angelo said. "Like kneecappin'. They don't hit no vital spots because they just wanna deliver a message."

Claudio nodded.

"I was driving that day heading up our town road en route to the freeway to make deliveries in Milwaukee. The shots came from the woods. They could have put a few through the driver's window and finished me off. Why didn't they?"

"They wasn't interest in you then. If the bakery driver got hit and went off the road the van woulda been totaled. They just wanna motivate you to cooperate so they don't havta damage the van much. Since they wanna take over your business, they make bullet holes easy to patch. Why bother stealin' new vans?"

Claudio indicated the windshields of all three vans. Visible were rosaries placed over rearview mirrors and statuettes of saints on the dashboards.

"Santa Beretta would protect them," Angelo said. "She never fails."

Serafina jerked a thumb toward the monastery. "*Il priore* is a rat fink."

"He told the brothers' council that to have peace we should accept the Chicago *famiglia's* picayune offer," Claudio said.

"Let's have a sitdown," Angelo said.

They got into the cab of the van with the bullet holes. Angelo, who was behind the wheel, told Claudio beside him, "*Per favore* if you let me and Serafina stay here awhile, I take care of *il priore* for you now. Maybe them Chicago wiseguys realize it ain't safe in these woods. Might get bit by a snapdragon. Then I go back to Brooklyn and take over the Scempio *famiglia*."

"Whack *il priore* good!" Serafina said.

Ten minutes later Claudio and Serafina watched in astonishment as Angelo drove his Cadillac down the monastery's private road. Beside him was the glum prior. In a few minutes, Angelo returned alone and greeted Claudio and Serafina leaning against the van.

"He's gone," Angelo said. "He was motivated to pack real quick and I drove him down to the town road where he'll get a taxi I called."

"You a man of honor!" Serafina cried. "You shoulda whacked him!"

Angelo shrugged. "He says he's comin back with an army so I says I have bagels and espresso waitin' for him. Better he's alive and misleadin' his army than dead so a professional takes over."

Claudio hugged his cousin.

"You're giving us more than you're getting for which *grazie mille*. With Brother Primattore's departure this leaves a vacancy you could fill superbly."

"*Nipotino mio*, a promotion!" Serafina said.

"Grandma, no way."

"You meet *una signorina bella* here in Wisconsin you never wanna go back to Brooklyn. Too much street crime."

Angelo reached into the van's cab for the statuette of Saint Peccato and said, "All I wanna know, Carlo, is if you're alive or dead."

"I already pay respect at his shrine here where I see Santo Peccato in his coffin with the sealed glass top," Serafina said.

"Maybe sometimes seein' ain't believin'," Angelo said.

CHAPTER X

Far from the Brooklyn cold, Don Topo Scempio reclined on a red plastic raft on Tampa Bay, tanned and fit, his Beretta bulging in a shoulder holster complemented by a bigger bulge in his swim trunks. His left hand trailed in the blue water as his right fondled the silicone-enhanced breasts of a blonde in a topless bikini.

Adjusting his bifocal shades, he scanned a Mayo Clinic picture postcard and laughed at his wife's scrawled message: "Change of life checkup takes *molto tempo.* Why you no phone?"

He passed the card to his giggling companion. She crumpled the card, tossed it overboard as a great white shark surfaced in cascading bubbles, ground the card in massive jaws and submerged, the raft breasting the turbulence.

The blonde peeled off the don's imitation handlebar mustache exposing his real one, stuck the false mustache on her navel, wiggled out of her bikini and said, "I'll be miffed if you muff your chance at two hair pies."

He began to mount her when tapping jarred his shoulder.

"With all due respect Don Topo, Iron Al asks *per favore* for an audience," said a distant voice.

But the raft foundered, the blonde floundered, the don blew bubblegum waterwings and the great white shark burst out of the sea jaws agape.

"Help!" Don Topo cried as the face of his nephew Pasquale doorman at La Santa Spogliarellista Fraternal and Social Club, swam into view. "You the lifeguard?"

"No, Don Topo. The only pool I'm in got cues and lotsa balls. It's Patsy, son of your sister Patella. Iron Al gotta see you."

"Fun in the sun," Don Topo mumbled as his eye caught a headline in an oversize color brochure on his card table promoting retirement in St. Petersburg.

"No fun in the sun outside, Don Topo," Pasquale said. "Snowin' hard. Temp 15 above and fallin'. Wind blowin' north-northwest 20 miles an hour or 17.4 knots."

The don rubbed his wrinkled forehead and sipped cold espresso with distaste. "How many times the don tole you stop watchin' them fuckin' weather shows on TV steada westerns like us or that doubleganger radar scrambles your brains permanent. Now saddle up and get another espresso *presto* and make it hot this time. Yeah, send in *il filosofo*."

He contemplated his crotch. The pole had collapsed. . . . no tenting tonight with his girlfriend. He held out quivering hands, noted brown spots and shivered. He glanced again at the brochure and its blue sea he had sailed only a minute ago.

Iron Al carefully set the don's espresso before him and sat at the table. "Nice and hot to warm up the old bones," Iron Al said.

Don Topo hastily folded the brochure and tucked it into his inside jacket pocket but not before Iron Al saw it.

"The don got young bones," Don Topo said.

"Sure *padrone* and they feel even younger when you get yourself down to Florida."

Don Topo wagged his index finger under Iron Al's nose. "When the clown carries lighted bomb to put under king's throne, king farts and blows out the fuse. *Capisci?*"

"Sure *padrone*. Don't play with cherry bombs on the Fourth, right?"

"Why you come here now?"

"I was passin' our phone booth on the corner. That phone was ringin' off the hook. Maybe Benny Deuce, huh?"

"Why you no pick up? People on block know it's the don's phone so hands off."

"But *padrone* you always wants to be there to answer personal when you make appointment for call. You want I should go back and wait for him to call again?"

The don pursed his lips and pointed to the center of the table under which the FBI bug had been planted. Iron Al drummed his fingers there to give eavesdroppers a headache. But the don sighed and indicated the secure conference bench against the wall where they retired. Before they conferred, Pasquale entered and whispered in the don's ear. The don nodded wearily. Pasquale escorted a uniformed mail carrier, announced *il Signor* Franco Bollo and left.

Bollo, short and portly, mopped his brow despite the cold, cringed when Garibaldi awoke for a moment and growled, bowed to the don and Iron Al and kissed the don's hand.

"What can the don do for *Signor* Bollo? Some punk has dishonored your daughter? Then the don arranges a wedding or a funeral whatever you want."

Bollo shook his head.

"Maybe an unempowered person of color makes the mistake comin' into the don's neighborhood to mug you? Then the don motivates him to abandon a life of crime in our neighborhood and take his business back to his own neighborhood."

When Bollo shook his head again, Iron Al whispered in the don's ear.

"Maybe you come to deliver to the don an important letter?" the don said.

Bollo shook his head so vigorously it loosened his tongue. "With all due respect I never bother the don with that. I always give the don's mail to Patsy and I never bring mail with postage due or IRS letters or any other junk mail."

"Then what the fuck you want from the don?"

"My boy Ruggiero got trouble in school with algebra and could be left back. He ask me to help him with his homework but I no understand algebra. Ditto and likewise my wife Caterina but she no understand neither."

The don flicked an imaginary mosquito off his shoulder, "No *problemo.* The don arranges to get the teacher whacked."

The mail carrier paled and placed his hand over his heart. "But it's the School of Our Irrespressible Lady and his teacher is Sister Sessualità."

The don placed one hand over his palpitating heart and the other on his head where he felt a permanent part in his hair, a straight and narrow lesson applied by said nun's ruler when she was a novice. "Now the don understands. The don will take care of everything. Go in peace and when the don needs a favor in return you will hear from him."

Shedding tears of joy, *il Signor* Bollo blew his nose on a handkerchief, plastered a wet kiss on the don's cheek and backed out to continue his appointed rounds. The don nodded at his *consigliere,* "Now you got what is called an abject lesson the way the don solves problems. You arrange to find some algebra teacher from the public school for night work with little Ruggiero. We pay. But the don got a question: The School of Our Irrepressible Lady already teaches English, Latin and Italian, right?" The *consigliere* nodded. "Then why the fuck do they gotta make a kid also learn a dead language nobody talks today?"

Iron Al stroked his chin, shrugged and jotted the assignment on the back of an old envelope. "I take care of that new business," he said. "Now for old business, namely and to wit: Do we wait for another phone call from Benny Deuce who ain't done what the party of the first part gotta do?"

Don Topo raised a hand for silence, chewed two wads of bubblegum, blew a basketball-sized bubble and flicked a fingernail into it. The bang awoke Garibaldi who jumped to attention, barked loudly and then seeing the don pick gum off his mustache returned to sleep in disappointment.

"Jesus Christ, does the don gotta teach you everything in parallels?" Don Topo told Iron Al. "The way the don just busted this bubble is the way we bust Benny Deuce."

He extended his index finger and jerked his middle finger.

"Boom! Boom! Boom! Boom! Of which two respectably for Benny Deuce who fucked up for the first and last time and two respectably for Angelo Panettorio. We find out where that monastery is at in the boondocks because that's where the don thinks Angelo is hidin' out. For the don it will be like we say in *la diplomazia* the summit. Then when everybody knows Don Topo Scempio ain't a Mustache Pete, he goes to St. Petersburg to goof off in the sun with Maria and *la* puttana—but not on the same blanket."

"And Iron Al is the new don?" the *consigliere* said.

"*Si*. When the don goes to *il paradiso* in Florida he gives you the key to the club crapper."

"But we ain't got no lock on our crapper."

"The don uses a fig leaf of speech. But if you want, call his *cugino* Luigi the locksmith who just broke outa the slammer and tell him the don says to take care of it free. Now gas up the Lincoln and go to car wash so car looks respectable. We leave for horseshit acres *presto!*"

Iron Al fingered his throat. "With all due respect Don Topo, Angelo may be a rat fink but he was your underboss and motivated plenty of guys to swim with the fishes. You think we could use more muscle?"

Don Topo smiled cryptically. "The don is glad he got *un consigliere* who's also *un filosofo*. So get your ass over to his *cugino* Aldo the butcher and pick up a sack of big bones that don't splinter."

"You mean—?"

"Si. We take along *il Signor* Fidele who sticks to the don like baby crap on a diaper. *Il Cerbero* goes on the biggest adventure of his life."

In his corner Garibaldi awoke instantly, sprang upon the don nearly hurling him from the bench and slobbered kisses over the old man's face and neck.

Struggling to remain upright, the don cried, "Don't show so much fuckin' respect!"

CHAPTER XI

"This is the place," Raphael the janitor said as Benny Deuce drove the Thunderbird to a block razed except for an abandoned shed with a sloping tarpaper roof.

As they passed, Raphael said, "The Philistines got their clubhouse here. They nailed up scrap iron on all sides with holes so they can see who's comin' and shoot. The police is afraid to go there even though it's a crack house. They's waitin' for a court order so they can bulldoze the place for the new city parkin' lot."

Benny Deuce gave the finger to three youths in front who yelled at them.

"Where's the nearest gas station at?" Benny Deuce asked Raphael who checked the fuel gauge.

"But you got a full tank now."

"We need a little more. Before when I was in Brooklyn Don Topo says, 'Benedetto, you do this *presto'* or 'Benedetto, you do like the don tells you.' Now the don ain't here to tell me what to do. So I'm gonna do what I think because we gotta motivate them Philistines to pay more respect to your church."

They stopped at a convenience store and Raphael waited in the car with Jonah the cat on his lap. Benny Deuce bought a gallon glass jug of apple cider, emptied it in the gutter, refilled the jug with gas, capped it with a wad of windshield paper towels, paid for the gas and left the jug on the floor near Raphael's feet. Then Benny Deuce read the license plate number aloud from a parked Cadillac to confirm no 9's, unscrewed the plates, tossed them into the Thunderbird and drove off.

Raphael shifted in his seat while Jonah twitched his pink nose at the gasoline fumes.

"Mr. Deuce, I do believe it ain't lawful to put gas in a glass jug like you done. A person could have an accident because that paper plug is already soaked."

"We ain't gonna have no accident but them Philistines will."

He stopped at the clubhouse, which was on a one-way street, the driver's side adjoining the curb. Leaving the engine running and the driver's door wide open, he went to the passenger side to screen his actions. He fetched the jug, lit the stopper, held the jug behind his back and approached the three youths, who watched him warily.

"I got a present from the church for the Philistines," he said.

"Ain't nobody here by that name, honky mother-fucker," said one youth. He stood before the clubhouse door and began to draw a pistol while his two colleagues drew switchblades.

"Then maybe I leave the package in a safe place," Benny Deuce said.

He hurled the flaming jug onto the shed roof and punched the gunman who dropped a 9 mm pistol. While the other two youths took off, the gunman stumbled against the clubhouse door which burst open as a fireball exploded on the roof. Benny Deuce dived into the Thunderbird as Philistines fled through front and rear doors of the shed, which was soon an inferno.

Nearing the freeway, Benny Deuce parked the Thunderbird and installed the stolen plates but forgot to discard the LAF sign in the rear window.

When Benny Deuce was behind the wheel again, Raphael said, "Is we gonna get into trouble because you rained brimstone and fire upon them sinners?"

"We done the city a favor. By the time the cops and firemen come there won't be nothin ' left for the court to order or the bulldozer to doze . "

Since all the don's shopping was done at neighborhood stores, it was easy for Special Agent Mordecai Sachel to observe Iron Al's preparations for the trip to Wisconsin. In the cab of the plumbing van, Mordecai lowered his binoculars and told his superior via intercom, "Special Agent Sachel requests permission to enter surveillance center."

"Permission is hereby granted to Special Agent Satchel provided the matter is sufficiently important for him to leave his post."

When Mordecai entered, Haman was sitting in his green canvas director's chair. He rose and indicated a small green steel stool where Mordecai crouched, knees under chin, while Haman towered over him.

"It appears Operation Lead Pipe Cinch may be getting under way," Mordecai said.

Haman shook his head. "That operational code name which you suggested has been replaced by one I deem more suitable—Operation Big Collar."

"But—"

Haman waved his hand in dismissal. "I hereby terminate the terminology discussion. Now precisely what do you have to report?"

Mordecai consulted a small government-issue notebook with a green leatherette cover. *"Consigliere* Alessandro Savio—"

Under Mordecai's nose Haman waved an unsharpened pencil (green, No. 2, sans eraser, government issue).

"You will refrain from employing the honorific *consigliere* for perpetrator Savio or don for perpetrator Scempio. Carry on."

"This morning I have been observing perpetrator Savio obviously in haste running these errands: Having the don's

—I mean Scempio's—Lincoln Town Car washed and fueled and buying a Wisconsin road map at the service station. He also bought a large sack of bones from the butcher and at the grocery bought the following: one case of canned dog food, one case of bubblegum and one king-size tube of mustache wax."

"Is said wax for perpetrator Scempio also known perjoratively as Mustache Pete by his confederates?"

"Negative, sir. According to an informant the wax is for their German shepherd dog that answers to the name of Garibaldi, the animal we encountered at the club previously during a clandestine visit."

"Mustache wax for the perpetrator dog?"

"Affirmative, sir. You may recall one of the taped conversations between Scempio and Savio indicates the dog prefers that the wax be applied to the bristles on his muzzle once a month to project a macho image."

Haman flourished his pencil like a mini baton. When he flexed it the pencil snapped and he tossed the pieces into a government-issue green steel wastebasket an inch deep in pencil fragments. He selected another pencil from five unsharpened ones standing in a breast pocket of his coverall. Then he began to pace the narrow aisle, bumping into Mordecai's knees with each pass.

"Make a note, Satchel, to include pencils in your next requisition for office supplies."

Mordecai, notebook open on his knee, doodled with his pencil and said, "I suggest we alert the Milwaukee office to deploy a surveillance team in Wisconsin since the perpetrators' departure for that state seems imminent. Said perpetrators are apparently in pursuit of former underboss Angelo Panettorio. Object: terminating same."

Haman shook his head as he ran his pencil across shelf after shelf of audio and video cassettes, an unnerving clickety-clack causing Mordecai to clench and unclench his fists.

"You expect me to surrender this rich harvest—

hundreds of hours of admissible evidence—and turn it over to some drones in Milwaukee so they can be in at the consummation of Operation Big Collar while I get none of the credit? Negative, Special Agent Satchel. We shall follow the perpetrators to Wisconsin and arrest them there in *flagrante delicto*. I shall have the last laugh."

Haman reversed the founder's portrait from scowl to grimace whereupon Mordecai closed his notebook and stood up. He confronted his superior nose to nose in the cramped space. "Without requesting and receiving appropriate authorization from the Bureau by filing Form 3/5813?"

Haman tapped his pencil baton on Mordecai's chest. "I intend to get my piece of the pie, namely a promotion to the Bureau's elite surveillance team at Washington draining the nation's worst cesspool of crime and immorality —the capitol. If you follow orders I shall recommend your promotion to my post when I leave. If you don't—"

Haman completed his warning by flipping the founder's portrait back to scowl.

But Mordecai said, "Let the record show I comply under duress with an order that is in violation of Bureau regulation 3/1416."

"Poppycock! Now get this vehicle to a service station and check gas, fluids and tires."

"Full service or self-service, sir?"

"You do it. We'll save the Bureau 8 cents a gallon."

"May I inquire about your chair, sir?"

"What's wrong with it?"

"Nothing, sir. I was just wondering what OFFICIAL BUNS, stands for."

"It's an obvious official abbreviation for official business. While you waste the Bureau's time discussing trivialities, I focus on priorities. That is why I shall rise to the top in this chair while you are still vegetating on square one."

"Begging your pardon, sir, but may I call something to your attention outside before we depart on this covert mission?"

Haman reluctantly removed the headphones around his neck. "Granted but make it snappy."

Outside Mordecai indicated the van's license plates. Haman ran a finger across them.

"They're nice and clean. I even like plate 101-311 because the digits add up to a lucky 7."

"Sir, these are federal government plates on a covert vehicle."

"We are complying with a prime Bureau regulation—2/35711 to wit: 'All Bureau vehicles including bicycles and skateboards shall bear U.S. Government license plates. ' Satchel, your logical inconsistencies are the reason why I am commander of this operation and you are a shield bearer."

CHAPTER XII

"That waitress got a cute *culo* but she's playin' around with the wrong guy," Angelo said.

It was breakfast rush at a diner near the monastery, where he and Claudio had stopped for a snack before delivering bagels to Madison supermarkets. They were wearing Saint Peccato habits and sat in a booth. The waitress was a few booths away, her back toward them, bent over a highchair and securing a plastic bib under the bobbing blond head of a little boy. His mother beamed and the child gurgled as the waitress patted his head, shook his pudgy hand and reluctantly proceeded to the cousins.

While Claudio studied the large menu, Angelo chewed a toothpick and studied the waitress.

She was short, blue-eyed and in her early 30s. Her hand swept back copper-colored hair mussed after all the toddlers she had prepped that morning. Although she was slender, her simple white blouse was nicely filled and her black knee-length skirt hugged her hips.

As she returned Angelo's stare, her tongue darted between glossy fuchsia lips. She tapped her pen on the order pad as Claudio, peeking over the menu, crouched lower, only his hands showing.

She jerked her pen at Angelo and said, "Your menu is waiting for you on the table, Father."

"Maybe what I want ain't in there," he said chewing a

toothpick.

"Then maybe you should play with your toothpick in another pew."

She tapped her pen on Claudio's menu and he emerged blushing. "Knock knock. How about you, Father? Are you ready to order or just make a pass at the waitress like your boorish friend here?"

"Just coffee please."

"We have two big-time operators with us this morning. Nothing with it? How about some warm fresh bagels?"

"No thank you. No bagels if you don't mind."

Claudio retired behind the menu until she plucked it and confronted Angelo again, hand on her hip. "Well Father, since you're fasting for your sins I'll take your menu too and also this which you might swallow and force me to call a priest."

She snatched the toothpick and deposited it in the ashtray.

Angelo laughed and raised his hands. "Okay, I'm sorry. I was thinkin' about the Pope's health and wonderin' is he gettin' enough cantaloupes to eat in Cantaluppi. Yeah, I'll have coffee and a coupla doughnuts. Hold the bagels."

As she started to leave he said, "*Signorina*, could you just answer one question *per favore?*"

She nodded cautiously.

"Does a guy get better service from you if he's in diapers?"

"*Va all'inferno* with all due respect, Father."

Angelo applauded as she left. "That *siciliana* got more than a cute *culo*. She's *vivace*. Maybe I take her out and tame her."

"Maybe that *signorina* will slip a ring on your finger and another through your nose. That is, if she ever forgives you for the way you acted and for not disabusing her of the impression that we're priests."

But Angelo was staring through the window and across the parking lot into the snowy woods.

"You're contemplating the trip we have to make to Madison this morning?" Claudio said. "Are you as scared as I am about those Chicago *goombata*?"

"They'll be waitin' for us all right but I'm ready for them punks." The lower part of the window was fogged and he drew a horizontal line with his finger. "We go full steam ahead. They get in the way we roll over them. But then I think it's such a peaceful mornin' and we ain't runnin' dope or drivin' a hijacked truck. For Christ's sake, we're just bagel bakers. Who needs a fuckin' war?"

"But are you scared too?"

Angelo held out his steady hands.

"Maybe I drop you off at the monastery and make this run alone. It ain't worth it for you to take the risk."

"Angelo, those *goombata* always come in pairs. You can't drive and defend yourself too. I'm driving while you ride shotgun."

Chin in hand Angelo stared through the window, unaware the waitress had returned with coffee and doughnuts. He shook his head to clear it and looked up at her concerned face.

"Are you all right?" she said. "You look like you just came from a funeral."

"Just goin' to one. Sorry I acted like such an asshole. We ain't priests. We're brothers from the Saint Peccato Monastery."

"I thought so. I've heard plenty about that place."

"*Signorina*, I'm also sorry for jokin' about them babies. I was one myself once."

"I wouldn't have guessed it. I suppose that was the only time a woman was able to change you."

He saluted her with a doughnut.

She totaled the check, wrote on the back and placed the check before him with a mint. Angelo watched her go to a couple with a baby in a highchair whom she bent over to address. Angelo studied the mint and sucked it slowly. Then he took toothpicks from his pocket and tossed them into his empty coffee cup. "La *signorina* hates my guts because I'm boorish."

"That's a misconception. She's actually fond of you."

"Yeah?"

"Three reasons," Claudio said. "You're eating the first reason and I didn't even get a mint." He held up the check. "The second reason is that she wrote her name Yvonne on the back of the check."

Angelo shrugged. "So what?"

"The third reason is that under her name she wrote her phone number."

Climbing against a leaden sky, the town road slashed through dense woods as the wind whipped the antenna against the bakery van's roof and spattered rain on the windshield.

They were a few miles past the monastery, heading toward the interstate. Claudio downshifted and fingered the Saint Peccato statuette on the dashboard. Angelo, peering through binoculars, cried, "Watch it ahead!"

He grabbed his 12-gauge shotgun from the floor and pumped a round into the chamber.

As a black sedan approached, the passenger window behind the driver lowered and a gun barrel appeared. The car bore a Minnesota license plate.

"Drop your window!" Angelo cried, pushing Claudio down over the wheel.

When the sedan drew alongside, Angelo raised the shotgun and sighted over the barrel. But he lowered the weapon with trembling hands when he saw the woman driver whose rear passenger was a small boy in a cowboy hat brandishing a toy six-shooter and screaming "Bang! Bang!"

Frantically waving her hand, the woman pulled over to the shoulder while at Angelo's order Claudio parked on the shoulder directly across the road from her. She smiled at the monastery name on the van door, lowered her window, shushed the little boy and shouted:

"Fathers, I thought it would be safe to stop and ask

you directions. We're from Sleepy Eye and we're going to visit Herbie's auntie in Milwaukee but we took a wrong turn."

Although Angelo cleared his throat he was speechless, his face sweaty despite the cold wind. Instead, Claudio gave directions.

"Thank you. Fathers," the woman said as she started to pull out. "You can't be too careful about crime these days when you're lost."

But Angelo held up his hand and the woman stopped. "Yes, Father?"

"Take Herbie's gun away and buy him a hula hoop."

The mother smiled but as she drove off the boy gave Angelo the finger.

When the van got under way again, Angelo laid the shotgun on the floor and held his head in his hands, breathing deeply.

"Relax," Claudio said. "Our worries are over."

Angelo sat up and scanned the road ahead. "I coulda whacked a mom and a kid just like that." He snapped his fingers.

"Then how can you propose to return to Brooklyn for the big shootout at the OK Corral? You can't make Brooklyn as it was. What are you looking at?"

Angelo had raised the binoculars and was peering through the windshield again. "Farmers—maybe."

A mile down the road an approaching pickup towed a flatbed farm wagon loaded high with hay bales. Angelo frowned, adjusting the binoculars' focus on the pickup's Illinois license plate with a Chicago auto dealer's name on the bracket. "Down window and get over the wheel!"

"But it's only a farm truck hauling hay."

Angelo flicked off the shotgun's safety catch and leveled the barrel over Claudio's shoulders. As the pickup passed, the driver wearing an old straw hat waved but floored the accelerator when he saw the shotgun aimed squarely at him. The pickup lurched, broke the tow, fishtailed on crushed rock and overturned in the ditch.

The wagon wobbled but continued to roll ahead. When it passed the van the top hay bales flew off, a man emerged and fired an AK-47 at the van while Angelo fired three rounds at him. The man was hurled off the wagon into the ditch as the wagon overturned on him amid flying bales. But the bakery van careened with Claudio still hunched over the wheel. When Angelo grabbed the wheel Claudio slid against the driver's door. Angelo tapped the brakes and stopped on the shoulder. He stared at Claudio, leaned out of the passenger window and vomited.

The one AK-47 round had come through Claudio's open window and struck his head. Angelo crossed himself, laid the shotgun on the floor, drew his Beretta and ran to the wrecked wagon where the shooter's legs protruded from the bales.

Glancing at the overturned pickup, Angelo reached into the bales, found the shooter's bloody left hand wearing a gold wedding band and smiled when he felt no pulse. He wiped his own bloody hand on the shooter's sharply creased black trousers and noted the man's pointed black patent leather shoes and monogrammed red silk socks. He found the man's bloody face and smacked him hard with the Beretta. "That's for Claudio."

In the overturned pickup, the driver was staring through the shattered windshield at the sky as rain soaked his hair. His head was wedged against a bent window pillar. No pulse. Angelo kicked the license plate frame advertising a Chicago auto dealer. "What farmer would haul hay from the Loop to hay city?" He spit in the man's face.

In the van Angelo gently moved Claudio to the passenger seat and placed his own cap on Claudio's head to cover the wound. During the short ride back to the monastery, he told Claudio, *"Compaesano mio*, now I know what to do."

CHAPTER XIII

Benny Deuce stopped at a large sign painted on a junked barn door secured with barbed wire to a decrepit farm tractor. When he frowned Raphael read it to him: Punkinville, Founded 1850 by Silas Q. Punkin III. Best Brownie troop in Wisconsin. Welcome monastery pilgrims.

"I like Brownies when they got walnuts on them," Benny Deuce said.

"Them Brownies is into cookies," Raphael said.

They drove along Main Street and saw a tall unidentified building on the other side of the village. They passed a gas station whose sole pump displayed a sign read aloud by Raphael: "Toilet for customers only." When they passed a feed and seed store a man in a cowboy hat, his face plastered with Band-Aids, stared at them through the window. Next was a Quonset hut from whose roof a faded 48-star American flag flew.

In the window was a hand-lettered posterboard, which Raphael read aloud, "U.S. Post Office, Punkinville Chamber of Commerce, Punkinville Industrial Development Corp., Punkinville Convention and Visitors Bureau, Punkinville Herald, Punkinville Village Hall and Punkinville General Store."

With no apparent motel in sight, Benny Deuce stopped at the no-parking zone before this micro mall. Inside the proprietor had just sat in a creaking rocker near a glowing potbellied stove, a chipped coffee mug and an opened box of Girl Scout cookies at his elbow. He removed a knit woolen cap, tossed it into a box beside him that was full of hats, selected a red beret and put it on.

A little old lady in parka and galoshes with buckles open squinted at wanted posters on a bulletin board adjoining the post office counter. "When are you going to take down the one about the stagecoach bandit who writes poetry?" she said with no response. When she moved toward the door, Raphael held it open for her, its brass bell jangling, but she waved him away and waited just inside.

Eyeing the two men escorted by a skinny tomcat, the proprietor doffed his beret, donned a red and white University of Wisconsin baseball cap and said, "Mabel, go about your business. I'll let you know when your brother shows up on them postal flyers."

She snorted, tied her hood drawstrings and left, calling over her shoulder, "Up yours, chauvinist!"

The door slammed rattling loose panes.

As the visitors approached, the proprietor pursed his lips, swiveling his head up to the two men and down to the cat who circled the stove, upright tail twitching, eyes bright. The proprietor was withered with the beady eyes of a keyhole peeper.

The bare wood floor groaned as Benny Deuce stamped snow from his tennies before the hot stove. The three men watched the puddle form as the circling cat alternately watched the proprietor and the cookies.

"Where is the monastery at?" Benny Deuce said.

The proprietor adjusted his dentures for a full smile and rose so abruptly that his chair continued rocking. "You folks pilgrims?" the proprietor said pumping Benny Deuce's hand and nodding to Raphael and the cat.

"Yeah, we come to pay respect to Santo Peccato who got a bum deal from the Pope."

"So did Punkinville and our pilgrim business, my friend. But you'll need a place to stay being accommodations are crowded at the monastery to which we have the privilege of being the closest community. So I heartily recommend the Royal Punkin Motel just a baseball throw away, that is if my young granddaughter Esmeralda is pitching. See that smashed window on the side of my building here, the one patched with tape? Me and Esmeralda was playing catch in the village park last spring when she threw her rocket ball past me and clear through that window."

"How far is the village park?" Raphael asked.

"Three blocks as the crow flies. She's the pride of the third grade in Silas Q. Punkin III Elementary School. Now listen careful while I give you directions to the motel and they can direct you to the monastery from there.

"Go six blocks on Punkin Boulevard. Hang a left at Silas Q. Punkin III Elementary School. Go three blocks on Punkin High Road. Hang a left at Punkin Memorial Public Library, which holds story hour Tuesday evenings but don't tell no violent stories like 'Little Red Riding Hood.' Go three blocks on Zucchini Drive. Hang a right at Punkinville Free Parking Lot for Punkinville property taxpayers only. Go three blocks on Punkin Terrace and if you don't brake you'll run right into the lobby of the Royal Punkin Motel, luggage required, free continental breakfast served to registered guests only."

Raphael, jotting notes on the back of the road map, said, "If I calculate right, them directions take us about 17 blocks around a square and we end up at the motel that's only six blocks from here. Wasn't that the big building we saw on the other side of town?"

"I gave you the scenic route," the proprietor said doffing his UW cap and donning a boater.

"What is it with them hats?" Benny Deuce said indicating the hat box.

"Since I'm the only one working here I have to wear a lot of hats. Anything else?"

"If nobody goes to the monastery how come it's crowded?" Raphael said.

"Strange are the ways of the Lord."

Benny Deuce held up one finger. "And how come in the directions you got one Zucchini amongst all them Punkins?"

"In his salad days in Boston, Mr. Zucchini lent Mr. Punkin the cabbage for steamboat fare to go west to promote vegetarianism. But a pilgrim can get a hamburger in Punkinville if you know the right people such as yours truly. Before you pilgrims leave, enjoy some Girl Scout cookies which I'm helping my granddaughter sell."

He took the cookie box, which was empty as Jonah sauntered toward the door licking his whiskers. Before the proprietor could comment, the trio had left. Outside Jonah hopped about on the sidewalk, lifted his tail, and sprayed the no-parking sign.

"I never seen Jonah this spunky," Raphael said. "The closer we comes to that monastery the more rambunctious he gets."

When they entered the Thunderbird, the little old lady in the parka who was loitering nearby said, "What business do you strangers have in Punkinville?"

"A pilgrimage to the monastery, Granny," Benny Deuce said.

"I hear them Roman Candles carry on somethin' fierce at that monastery, drinkin' and carousin', a place no self-respectin' soul would visit. Wished you'd give me a lift there because shuffleboard at the Punkinville Senior Center ain't where it's at."

"Sorry Granny, but there may be some troubleshootin' up there so it's no place for a little old lady."

As the Thunderbird left, she threw an empty beer can which clattered off the roof.

Iron Al parked the Lincoln Town Car in the no-parking zone at Punkinville's micro mall. On the rear seat, Garibaldi barked at cringing rustics shuffling by in overalls and seed company caps.

"I never seen that mutt so wide awake like Rip Van

Twinkle just got up from a deep sleep," Iron Al said.

"He ain't got balls but he still got 'em," Don Topo said as Iron Al shrugged. "And don't call him no mutt. That don't show no respect to his KKK registration."

Meanwhile Garibaldi pressed his massive left forepaw against the window which the don noted and said, "It's No. 2."

Iron Al grimaced but snapped a leather leash on Garibaldi's chain collar and led the noble shepherd to the no-parking sign where Garibaldi gauged range, windage and trajectory and bombed.

Don Topo lowered his window and observed the steaming mound dropped bang on the base of the sign. *"Bene!"* the don cried. *"Bombardiere mio!"*

Garibaldi barked and wagged his tail as the don joined his two companions on the sidewalk and said, "Maybe the don should eat like Garibaldi because *la constipazione* only makes the don shit pebbles. For a happy life keep closed *la bocca* and open *il ano.*"

But this enthusiasm was not shared by the store proprietor visible through the hut's glass-paned door who shook his fist. When the proprietor noted the Lincoln's New York license plates, he slipped on his mackinaw, pulled a blaze orange knit cap over his ears and stepped outside as the bell jangled.

"If you could crap like that you'd have a face like an orange and not like a lemon," Don Topo told the proprietor.

But thrusting a gloved finger at the evidence, the proprietor said: "You're talking fruit but I'm talking turds and the law."

Garibaldi, shifting into attack mode for the first time in the don's service, bared his fangs, barked furiously and lunged against the leash. The *consigliere* grasped the leash with both hands and dug in his heels as the proprietor retreated.

But the don patted Garibaldi's head who quieted as the proprietor backed against the door.

"You makin' a mountain from a molehill of *la merda*," the don said. "He's just a puppy. You got plenty shovels inside so just scoop it up and dump in your garden. Is good fertilizer."

"Poppycock!" said the proprietor groping behind for the doorknob.

"Why make trouble when we can have nice sitdown and straighten everything out? But if you say a nice puppy like him can't take a crap the way *il Dio* wants, then I gotta report you to the ASPCA."

"Yeah," said the *consigliere* glad to be holding a slack leash. "You'd be aidin' and abettin' canine irregularity when you order a puppy to keep a tight *ano*."

"The boondock air musta give him a charge," the don said. "He never acts like this in Brooklyn. *Per favore* now we're lookin—"

But the proprietor who had often viewed Mafia movies held up a trembling hand and said, "With all due respect you're looking for a nice motel, right?" The don nodded and smiled. "Well, my Uncle Ahab on my mother's side runs a real cozy little place. You just get yourself back on the freeway heading east and follow it as the crow flies to Milwaukee and—"

"Milwaukee?" the *consigliere* said. "How far?"

"Only about an hour's drive. But—"

The don shook his head and Garibaldi growled lunging at the proprietor who immediately provided brief directions to the Royal Punkin Motel.

"I'm giving you the short route," he said.

Raphael racheted his tilted neck up to the top tenth floor of the Royal Punkin Motel. He and Benny Deuce stood near the Thunderbird parked in a yellow-painted no-parking zone before the main entrance. Benny Deuce scanned the parking lot. Of several hundred slots only a half-dozen were occupied. "The more I gets involved in this contract, the more I thinks things ain't kosher like they seem," Benny Deuce said.

Over his shoulder he slung a black nylon garment bag acquired after it had fallen off a truck in Brooklyn. Raphael lugged his cardboard suitcase lashed with clothesline tied in a Gordian knot which he patted reassuringly.

Jonah paused to lick a candy bar wrapper discarded on the pavement and followed them into the deserted lobby lushly carpeted in white.

"As empty as my church on Sunday mornin'," Raphael said. At the gleaming mahogany reception desk Benny Deuce pounded the nickel-plated dome bell, which bounced onto the floor. On the desk was a newspaper opened to the nation's most challenging crossword puzzle nearly completed in purple ink. Beside it were *Webster's Official Crossword Puzzle Dictionary* and *The Random House Dictionary of the English Language,* second edition, unabridged.

A dwarf appeared with a fresh pink carnation in the lapel of his black suit, a manager's ID plate pinned under a pink silk hanky in his breast pocket, his sandy Vandyke beard neatly groomed. He briskly rubbed his soft hands and switched on a 200-watt smile. "We welcome you to the Royal Punkin Motel located in the tourist paradise of Wisconsin. It is as unique as sighting the ERNE clasping ALOE in its talons and soaring above ADA during ADAR. Or in the clues, sighting the sea eagle clasping the century plant in its talons and soaring above an Oklahoma city during a Jewish month."

"Oh," said Benny Deuce.

"No two-letter words if you please. Now what can we do for you gentlemen?"

"Watch them pronouns because I don't see no plural," Benny Deuce said.

The manager pointed to the wall. Glaring down from a large oil portrait was a portly chap with muttonchops. Under the portrait was an engraved brass plate: "SHELTER FOR THE RIGHTEOUS."

"Also welcoming you is Mr. Silas Q. Punkin III, pioneer founder of Punkinville. He established the village's first business, a loggers' social club, on this very site. Do you gentlemen have a reservation?"

"What for?" Benny Deuce said. "The only thing your rooms is filled up with is air."

The manager adjusted his carnation and his smile. "And how long will you be staying with us?"

"Till we pay respect at the monastery."

"I envy you PILGRIMS a.k.a. HAJJI a.k.a. PURITANS while sedentary me just does crossword puzzles. By the bye, are you Italian?"

"No, Sicilian."

"Then you possibly may know a six-letter word for silence."

The manager's pen was poised over the puzzle. But Benny Deuce shook his head and put his finger to his lips. *"Omertà,"* Benny Deuce said.

"Thank you," said the manager completing the puzzle.

He slid a leather-covered registration book across the desk and handed a pen to Benny Deuce. "Do you prefer a double room to conclude your affairs or adjoining rooms?"

While Raphael fiddled with the knot on his suitcase Benny Deuce's voice plummeted into the basement. "Your best double with twin beds and none of your lip, Peewee, or you're gonna find yourself a head shorter when you stand on tippytoe to look in the bathroom mirror."

The manager's hand fluttered over his hair strawberry blonde and frosted. Benny Deuce registered as John Z. Smith, Brooklyn, NY, while Raphael registered as Acting Reverend Raphael, Pacifico, WI.

From his hit kit, Benny Deuce produced several $100 bills, which the manager viewed respectfully.

"How much?" Benny Deuce said.

"I suggest our Imperial Sovereign Suite which has a spacious double room, sitting room and kitchenette all enhanced by a complimentary continental breakfast. Our regular rate is $300 per day. But since we're in the slow season you may have it for $100 per day, initial payment preferred in advance." He cupped his hand to his ear. "Did I hear a meow?"

Jonah, vainly mousing in the lobby, jumped on the desk, rubbed against the manager's arm and purred.

"My what a pretty kitty but somewhat under-nourished. Yours?"

"Mine, sir," Raphael said. "Named him Jonah because he don't like to get wet. But he's hungry."

"After the bell captain takes up your luggage I'll have him bring a complimentary saucer of milk plus a can of tuna and a potty box from our kitty contingency reserve."

"You is indeed a cat lover."

"Seven letters, FANCIER, would be more precise."

Benny Deuce tossed a $100 bill on the desk and received the key. The manager retrieved the dome bell from the floor and tapped it once with his pinky.

"Front!" he cried.

Then he removed his carnation and manager's ID plate, placed the carnation in a crystal bud vase, pinned a bell captain's brass badge on his lapel and stepped around the desk. He slung Benny Deuce's heavy garment bag over one shoulder, took Raphael's suitcase and led the way to a bank of elevators, holding the door for Jonah who entered cautiously.

At the tenth floor the manager-cum-bell-captain showed them to their suite, opened the drapery with a flourish to display a panoramic view of the parking lot, patted Jonah's head, accepted a $5 tip and was half-way out the door when Benny Deuce laid a heavy hand on his shoulder. "One question. How many rooms you got?"

"Three hundred in addition to the grand ballroom, five spacious conference rooms and our delightful coffee shop."

"How many of them 300 rooms is rented?"

"Well, that's more than one question but I can provide an estimate." He tapped a pocket calculator. "At the moment, including your suite, the grand total occupancy rate is precisely 2.00 percent."

"I ain't good in the numbers. How many rooms got people in them?"

"Six."

"Ain't that kinda low?"

"Somewhat. But as I indicated this is the slow season. During the busy season, we were always booked solid. That ended a year ago and it's been slow ever since."

"How come?"

"We are the closest motel to the Penitential Brothers of Saint Peccato Monastery and aside from our friendly locals, bracing air and fall foliage, the Saint Peccato shrine is our only viable tourist attraction and a major source of revenue. With all due respect to the church and to you two pilgrims, the Pope put the kibosh on those brothers when he declared their Saint Peccato flim and flam. That torpedoed our nationwide pilgrim trade not to mention all the devout little old ladies bused in from Canada and Mexico."

"Praise the Lord!" Raphael said. "They have laid up treasures where burglars can't burgle and muggers can't muggle. Matthew 6:19-20."

"Precisely. That's why the Punkin Family Foundation built this motel so deserving pilgrims could be lodged in comfort at premium rates. I do wish someone would revitalize that monastery and rehabilitate their saint. I'd go on a pilgrimage there myself but I'm an eclectic."

"Brother, you got your church and I got mine," Raphael said.

"That was a great scam your motel had goin' but now you're fucked," Benny Deuce said.

"Metaphorically speaking, yes."

When the manager stepped out of the lobby elevator, he was greeted at the reception desk with a dome bell sonata played by Iron Al. Providing a howling accompaniment, was Garibaldi bracing massive forepaws against the desk and tugging at the leash held by Don Topo, who said proudly, "He practices to sing *il basso* at *La Scala*."

The manager immediately identified the two gentlemen

with their black fedoras and black coats bulging under the left arm as "criminal organization," five letters, and their dog baring fangs as "Hades guard," eight letters.

Hastening behind the desk, the dwarf removed his bell captain's badge, reinstalled his carnation and manager's ID, smoothed his hair and said, "We welcome you to the Royal Punkin Motel, gentlemen and canine."

"Cut the crapola and give us your best room," Don Topo said scowling at the "SHELTER FOR THE RIGHTEOUS" plate under Mr. Punkin's portrait. As the manager consulted his desktop terminal, the don asked, "Does that sign mean what it says?"

The manager glanced over his shoulder. "Positively, sir."

"*Bene* because we don't want no criminals cleanin' out our room when we're at the monastery prayin'."

"No, sir. I cordially welcome you pilgrims. We happen to have one spacious double right on the main floor with its own private entrance so you can come and go as you fancy. Further, it's only a short walk across the parking lot to some undeveloped land at the corner where you may conveniently walk your dog. The rate is $200 per day during—"

But Don Topo flashed a big roll, tossed two $100 bills on the desk and registered himself, Iron Al and Garibaldi respectively as John Doe, Jack Doe and Cerbero Doe with fictitious AKC number, all of St. Petersburg, FL.

When the dwarf bell captain escorted these guests to their room, he gratefully accepted a crumpled $10 bill tossed by the don. "Will there be anything else you may require, sir?"

"Yeah. Flush the toilet."

"The toilet?"

"Yeah, the crapper. Make sure it works."

From the bathroom, a vigorous flush was heard as the dwarf emerged rubbing his hands briskly. "The plumbing is in excellent working order, sir. I even ran the faucets."

"Then we don't need no plumber?"

"Assuredly not, sir. I AFFIRM or AVER by the Egyptian sun god RA or the Roman sun god SOL that your concern re plumbing is water over the dam or under the bridge."

"So we give you a big tip to make sure you don't forget this if you see a walk-in plumber. *Capisci?*"

He tossed a $20 bill at the dwarf who bowed and left.

"That punk talks cuckoo," the don said.

"And in capitals yet," Iron Al said.

"Did them plumbers tail us?" the don said.

"Maybe."

The don scratched his crotch meditatively. "But the pipe I got neither them nor my Hebe doctor can fix and my girlfriend is complainin' about the service."

"You think maybe it was Benny Deuce and some *puttana* that come in the Thunderbird we seen parked here?"

The don shook his head.

"Forget it. That *cretino* racked up his Thunderbird in Madison and the don ordered him to drive a Yugo because a Jap car is what he deserves. Besides, you seen that LAF sign in the Thunderbird window? Benny Deuce ain't got the sense of humor to make that."

But Garibaldi interrupted by hurling himself against the door and raising his right forepaw. The don, relaxing in bed, shouted to Iron Al in the bathroom, "Get your ass in gear and take the don's dog for a nice walk so he can do his No. 1. And watch he don't flood your shoe like he done yesterday."

The *consigliere* hurried from the bathroom, zipped up his fly, threw on his coat and muttered *sotto voce* as he was dragged out by the energized canine.

"That dog got things Iron Al don't," Don Topo said aloud. "If a Roman emperor made his horse *un senatore* then someday the don makes his dog *un consigliere.*"

Meanwhile, the motel manager was enjoying a midmorning break as he sipped brandy from a white bone china teacup, pinky extended. He sat in an easy chair at a large front lobby window. The elevator opened and Jonah stepped out alone scanning the lobby. When the manager saluted him with the teacup, Jonah jumped onto his lap purring and curling into a ball.

"You are such an intelligent kitty to come down in the elevator from the tenth floor all by your dear self. Surely, you recall the lion, a fellow member of your family, seven letters, FELIDAE. He was about to gobble Androcles but spared this gentleman, who had befriended said lion. Perhaps someday you may assist a little old motel manager who helped a deserving kitty."

Jonah meowed to that and groomed his coat as the manager added:

"A word to the wise: There's a vicious police dog on the premises but I will not permit him to harm a defenseless little kitty."

Jonah growled at that as the manager set his teacup on an end table. A plumber's van had just parked properly in the closest slot to the no-parking zone where the Thunderbird and Lincoln blocked the entrance. The manager stood, adjusted his carnation and gently placed the cat on the chair.

J. Edgar Haman strode in followed by Mordecai Sachel lugging both green plastic attaché cases and furtively looking about the lobby. The manager strolled to the reception desk and said, "We positively do not require a plumber. In fact, I would stake my life on it. What we do require is the six-letter name of the person who said, 'Let justice be done though the heavens fall.'"

"HOOVER, J. Edgar!" Haman said.

But the manager turned a manicured thumb down. "Elementary—WATSON, William."

Haman set his attaché case on the desk, aligned the case with the desk blotter, squared his shoulders, cleared his throat and said, "We require accommodations at the corporate rate."

The manager consulted his desktop terminal. "Sir, I regret to pipe this to you but we do not have a reservation for two plumbers or even one. Further, we are fully booked. Please vacate the premises and remove your commercial vehicle from our parking lot reserved for guests."

The manager folded his arms and stared up at Haman who selected a pencil from the breast pocket of his coverall, twiddled it, snapped it in two and tossed the pieces into the wastebasket. He was about to deliver a parting word when Jonah, who had slunk to the desk, raised his tail, sprayed Haman's trouser leg and galloped out of sight as the manager smiled and Haman exclaimed, "By the great Nixon, Reagan and Bush, confound it!"

He seized his attaché case, snapped his fingers at Mordecai and was nearing the front door when Mordecai called, "Going to the lavatory and shall be right out, sir!"

After Haman left, Mordecai asked the manager, "Do you have a pay phone?"

The manager indicated one in the corner and Mordecai dialed and whispered, "Special Agent Sachel reporting a gross violation of regulations by my superior, Supervising Special Agent Haman, to wit: Without requesting or receiving official authorization, abandoning assigned post in Brooklyn, executing an incursion into Milwaukee office area for surveillance of perpetrators, and ordering me to accompany him which I have done under duress. What? You will not consider this matter unless I first prepare a report in quadruplicate with my duly notarized signature? Forget it!"

He slammed the phone, grabbed his attaché case and asked the manager, "Who's in charge at the monastery?"

The manager shifted uneasily in his chair and examined his manicure. "It was Brother Primattore."

"Why the past tense?"

"Because the word around town is that in three letters he's OUT, in four letters French FINI, in five letters German KAPUT, ousted by the new prior."

"Who is?"

The manager stroked Jonah who jumped onto his lap again. "For a stranger, sir, you plumb murky depths."

Mordecai leaned over the desk as Jonah stared at him growling. "No megillahs please. This town and your motel are both dead on your respective asses unless the monastery pulls in pilgrims again."

"Therefore?"

"Therefore it's in your best interest to cooperate with an undercover federal agent."

"I can't answer questions about my guests."

"I'm no longer interested in the cockamamie wiseguys you've got here. I want to see the monastery's new prior on my own. My putz of a boss is waiting out in the van for me."

The manager steepled his fingers. "You are flushed with audacity."

"One can't make an egg cream by breaking an egg. The name please."

"I hear he's from Brooklyn and is misnamed Brother Angelo. And I have it on good authority that he's boorish."

"Keep me in sight as I execute this mission and perhaps you'll learn how to do it," Haman told Mordecai as they sat in the surveillance center of the plumber's van.

As ordered by the motel manager, they had moved the van off the parking lot and were now parked in the street opposite the main entrance of the motel. Haman sat in his director's chair while Mordecai crouched on his small stool.

"But it's broad daylight, sir. Wouldn't it be more prudent to wait until dark?"

"Balderdash! Newly registered guests Topo Scempio, Alessandro Savio and their perpetrator canine occupy quarters on the main floor front, which we have had under binocular surveillance. On the exterior of their window, I shall affix an inward oriented Limpet Mark III transparent micro bug. This device is so sensitive that through the glass it can faithfully record all sounds within the room including a mouse fart."

Haman left the van and ambled across the parking lot toward the window. He was wearing jungle camouflaged jacket and trousers, bush hat and shiny black dress shoes with leather heels that tapped the pavement.

As he approached, the motel's front door opened and the manager escorted the meowing Jonah outside. Haman crouched behind the don's Lincoln while the managerreturned to the lobby.

Still crouching, Haman waddled toward the target window when a car roared through the parking lot and screeched to a stop beside him. Haman reached inside his jacket for his government-issue .357 magnum revolver but the driver waved a business card before Haman's nose and cried:

"I'm a chiropractor passing through and have just published a paper on *Humongus erectus*, the rare spinal deformity that afflicts you! Make no bones about it, sir. You should stay in bed until you receive a professional adjustment."

When Haman stared blankly, the chiroprator tucked the card into Haman's hatband and drove off. Only a few yards from the target window now, Haman reached into his jacket pocket and carefully removed the Limpet Mark III bug the size of a shirt button. He held the bug between thumb and forefinger and proceeded toward the window until he encountered further visitors from both sides.

To the right Jonah, just starting his rounds, spied the plumber he had sprayed earlier. Assuming his own predator's crouch, Jona closed in on his quarry who was himself crouching under the window and reaching up to affix the bug.

But to Haman's left, a breathless Iron Al rounded the corner of the building trotting after the leashed Garibaldi whose black gumdrop nose scanned the pavement.

Claws outstretched, Jona sprang onto Haman's back as the bug dropped.

Garibaldi roared and jerked free of Iron AL who stumbled and fell. Then Garibaldi charged Haman bowling him over. Jumping off Haman's back, Jonah caught the rolling bug and swallowed it.

When Haman staggered to his feet, he imprudently drew his revolver, but Garibaldi clamped his jaws on Haman's wrist. Yelping in pain, Haman dropped the weapon and was confronted by Iron Al who pressed the muzzle of his Beretta against Haman's head. Noting the Aizilop van at the curb, Iron Al said, "We don't need no plumbers." Then pocketing Haman's revolver Iron Al added, "I save this for the Fourth because makin' noise is all this cannon's good for."

While Haman limped to the van, Iron Al firmly grasped the leash, ordered Garibaldi to sit and beckoned Jonah who approached warily.

"Always remember what *il arabo* says," he told the dog. "The enemy of my enemy is my friend—even *il gatto.*"

Jonah accepted a pat on the head from Iron Al and a polite woof. Then he meowed, rubbed against Garibaldi and slunk off on his rounds.

Before Haman entered the van, Mordecai hastily unloaded a camcorder with which he had taped Haman's debacle and locked the cassette in his attaché case. In the surveillance center Haman reversed the founder's portrait from grimace to scowl and said, "Did you happen to see what transpired out there?"

"Yes sir. As you directed I observed and it was most instructive."

Haman removed his camouflaged outfit, dumped it in a corner, donned his coverall and removed two fresh pencils from his pocket. Without twiddling he broke and tossed them into the wastebasket.

"Satchel," he said.

"Yes sir."

"Delete the aforementioned episode from your recollection."

"What episode, sir?"

CHAPTER XIV

"You are from *la* Sicilia?" Serafina Panettorio began her interrogation as she and Yvonne queued with Angelo at the velvet rope in an upscale Chinese restaurant. Angelo was wearing a double-breasted navy suit, white silk shirt open at the collar, heavy gold chain showing. Yvonne was uneasy in a conservatively tailored black suit with white turtleneck blouse and red scarf. She preferred her cobalt blue silk dress that complemented her eyes and was mid-thigh length, but didn't know if Angelo had meant it about bringing his grandmother. She rubbed her perspiring palms together.

"My mother's folks are from Sicily," Yvonne said.

Serafina in her Sunday best black dress, toyed with an unlit cigarette.

"Where?"

"Palermo."

"*Bene.* But how come you no look like *una siciliana?*"

Yvonne crossed her arms. "For the same reason the fisherman doesn't drop his line in the bathtub."

Angelo scratched his head but Serafina nodded.

"You *una siciliana.*"

"Grandma, can it. You say you want me to go out with a nice girl so I show you a nice girl."

"Scusi. *Signorina,* you work in a restaurant so you good cook, no?"

"Grandma—"

"I'm just a waitress. My dad's Irish and corned beef and cabbage is his favorite so maybe I take after him."

"What's his work?"

"Grandma—"

"He's a police officer in Milwaukee."

Serafina frowned.

"Well somebody gotta give out parking tickets."

The restaurant manager, a fat Chinese woman in a blonde wig, flaunted gold rings on all fingers and asked if they wanted the smoking or nonsmoking section.

"Grandma, you want smoking?"

"No. TV says *la sigaretta* is poison so to hell with it."

"But you still got a cigarette," Angelo said as they were seated.

"Not now," she said flipping it into the cart of a passing busboy.

Dinner proceeded quietly until Serafina took Yvonne's hand, studied the palm and said, "I tell your future. You are *bella*. You are *una siciliana*. Yet you never married, no?"

"*Sì.*"

Serafina traced a line in Yvonne's palm. "I see *la felicità* for you but why you no married?"

Yvonne took a long sip of tea and glanced at Angelo who averted his eyes. "The farmer's wife offers the thirsty donkey water but the donkey says, 'Heehaw, I'll wait for rain.' *Signora,* what I hope to give, men don't want. What I want from men, they won't give."

"*Bravo!*" Serafina cried. "*Nipotino mio,* you hear?" Angelo nodded uneasily as Serafina held up her hands, wiggled her left pinky saying, "One," wiggled her right pinky saying, "Ten," and added, "Signorina, show me how many *bambini* you want."

Angelo covered his face with his hands and spread two fingers to peek. Yvonne's index finger tapped Serafina's left pinky, and then flipped along all the fingers like a stick across a picket fence as Serafina's eyes widened and her mouth dropped open.

"Ten *bambini*?" Serafina said.

"No, 10 lovers. I don't know if your *nipotino* has the *cojones* to make even one *bambino*."

Serafina laughed and hugged Yvonne.

"He can make 10—all boys! Angelino, when we finish take me back to the monastery and then you take *la signorina* home like gentleman."

The waiter, a Chinese youth with gold-rimmed glasses, placed a small black-lacquered tray beside Angelo, nodded to the tray which contained the folded check, winked and left. Angelo took the check, unfolded it and found an enclosed slip of paper with a penciled message.

"What is it?" Serafina said.

"A coupon for a free egg roll next time we come. I'm goin' to the can. Be right back."

In a booth at the men's room he cocked his Beretta, replaced it in his waistband and passed through swinging doors into a large noisy kitchen.

It was a four-wok restaurant resounding with vegetable chopping. Waiters with loaded trays snaked through the staff and gave Angelo a wide berth.

With his hand inside his jacket, he scanned the room. Apparently, everybody was Chinese. Someone touched his back and he spun around but it was the waiter, who had presented the check with the note. The waiter smiled, winked through his glasses, pointed toward the rear and left with a tureen of soup.

Angelo pushed through the employees, snatching and nibbling an egg roll from a waiter's tray. Waiting near the rear exit was a white man in chef's hat and tunic but his trousers were dark. Both hands were in sight. Angelo could not quite place the man who nodded gravely.

"You sent my fortune but not the cookie," Angelo said.

The man smiled. He removed the chef's hat and tunic and laid them on a box where he retrieved his suit jacket which he slipped on. In his shoulder holster was a .357 magnum. They shook hands while the kitchen crew looked elsewhere.

"I got my grandma and girlfriend waitin' out there."

"Need a good lawyer? I'm Mordecai Sachel."

"You're a plumber who's sweatin' a different joint."

"And you're a *gonif* who needs a friend."

Angelo took two almond cookies from an opened box and offered one to Sachel who declined. Angelo ate them both and wiped his hands on a clean white apron hanging on the wall.

"Maybe I don't like your underwear. I wear Jockey but you wear a wire."

Sachel shook his head and opened his jacket. "See for yourself."

"You're takin' a big chance."

"I've quit because my boss is a shmuck. When I tried to blow the whistle on him, even sending the Bureau a videotape of his screwup, they did nothing because they put a premium on incompetence. So I've applied for my Wisconsin law license based on reciprocity because I had enough years in practice before my brief liaison with the FBI."

"Lookin' for clients here?"

"Just one. You're taking over the monastery. I'm Jewish and we're both from Brooklyn so perhaps we'll go together like bagels and lox."

"We ain't got no affirmative action program to hire a Jewish brother. We're lookin' for *un consigliere* but that guy needs an S&W more than he needs a J.D. Also OSHA might say the job environment could harm your health."

"You're in more danger than I am. There are things I know that you should."

Angelo glanced over his shoulder. "You eat yet?" When Mordecai shook his head Angelo took a boxed takeout dinner off a tray. "Enjoy with *il padrone's* compliments." When Mordecai hesitated, Angelo said, "Your only risk is that it might be roast pork."

Mordecai laughed and took the carton. "This could

make me an accessory."

"Not to a misdemeanor."

"How did you know that?"

"I may be a boorish *goombah* but I ain't illiterate. A guy don't need a law license to read *Black's Law Dictionary.* Stop by the monastery tomorrow for breakfast. What size suit do you wear?"

"Forty-two long. Why?"

"I have you talk to our human resources director and if he says okay you get our official Saint Peccato habit with rope belt and sandals."

"Who's your human resources director?"

"Me," Angelo said, strolling back to the dining room.

"Coffee?" Yvonne said at the door of her apartment.

"It wouldn't hurt," Angelo said.

She hesitated with her key poised over the lock. "It might. It's time for what your profession calls a sitdown."

He took her key, opened the door, held her arm and said, "You've seen too many Mafia movies."

As they passed through the living room, he jerked his thumb at the TV. On it was a framed photo of Yvonne with a group of young girls. Everyone was in uniform.

"My Brownie troop, the best in the state. Those little girls will surprise you with the wonderful things they can accomplish if you just give them a goal."

In the small yellow kitchen, he stood close behind her as she prepared drip coffee. He placed one hand tentatively on her hip but she moved his hand away. "Maybe I get you an espresso machine for your birthday so you make good coffee."

She turned and faced him. "You can be damn insulting at times."

He backed away. "I'm supposed to be the tough wiseguy but the way you busted my balls over dinner about your 10 boyfriends I wonder."

She kissed him on the cheek. "I'm a tough wiseguy

too," she growled mimicking him.

They sat in the kitchen at a small oak table, its top gleaming under a pulldown stained glass lamp depicting oranges, lemons and limes. He raised a white china mug to his lips but set it down when he saw the motto in pink lettering: "Thank god she made me a woman."

"Hey, don't forget you're half Sicilian."

She lifted her mug in a mock toast. "And don't you forget the other half is Irish and that I was christened Yvonne, not Hey."

Angelo noted his folded napkin on the table while hers was spread on her lap. He did the same, extended his hand and took hers. She placed her other hand over his and stroked it. They sipped their coffee silently. Then he drained his cup and stood up.

"Good coffee. *Grazie.* I better go. Us bagel bakers get up early."

At the door, he took her hand, hesitating about what to say. She put her arms around him, kissed him firmly on each cheek and then full on the mouth. "Say hello to your grandma for me."

"Hey—I mean Yvonne—when are we gonna have our sitdown?"

She hugged him again and kissed him on the neck. "We've already had it."

CHAPTER XV

Suddenly awake, Angelo slid his hand under the pillow and gripped his Beretta. In the darkness, someone had entered his locked dormitory room at the monastery.

He sat up slowly and in the green glow of the digital clock on the night table, he saw movement near the door. Resting his elbows on the comforter, he cocked the pistol and released the safety catch as the intruder froze. *"Alto,"* Angelo said. "And I ain't talkin' music." Angelo switched on the bedside lamp as a smiling man in a ragged gray habit raised his hands.

"*Come sta*, Don Angelo," the man said.

"Put 'em down."

The man complied lowering his hood disclosing a gaunt unshaven face, deep shadows under the cheekbones. Angelo put the pistol's safety catch on but left the weapon cocked within reach on the night table. He waved the man to a chair near the door, sat on the edge of the bed, yawned and glanced at the clock. It was 2:25 a.m.

"You make house calls?" Angelo said.

The man nodded. Angelo ran his fingers through his hair. His pajamas were rumpled.

"After Claudio's funeral yesterday I ain't slept so good. Carlo, how come he's planted in the monastery graveyard while you got whacked too but are still breakin' and enterin' above ground?"

Carlo Peccato pointed to the ceiling and clasped his hands in prayer.

"You seen me in my sealed coffin at my shrine," he said. "You gotta take a leap of faith."

Angelo shook his head.

"The Pope snatched your button and told you to take a flyin' leap yourself because you wasn't dead enough when you was made a saint. Now you're tryin' to give me the same bam and boozle."

But Carlo Peccato extended his arm. "Feel if I'm a ghost or not."

Angelo waved him away. "Sister Sessualità told us in second grade if we was like doubtin' Thomas we'd go *all'inferno* with no parole. But it's just that you look solid like a brick shithouse not like them see-through ghosts in the movies."

Carlo laughed and tapped a bulge on his chest. "With permission I show you proof. Don't believe what you see in them fuckin' movies. Them special effects guys with all their drinkin' and swearin' and pussy chasin' will never make it upstairs to check the joint out. It ain't all heavenly up there. Somebody gotta take out the garbage and go for coffee."

He tapped his chest again and when Angelo nodded Carlo reached inside his habit and produced a bundle of letters secured with a red silk garter. He tossed the bundle on the bed and folded his arms.

Angelo snapped the garter. *"La signorina* had a lotta bounce," he said sniffing the letters. "Smells like un *bordello."*

Carlo shrugged.

"From a lady pilgrim who had a special devotion to me. She left her garter at my shrine. What you're holding is mail from her and from other pilgrims before our repo Pope took back my halo."

Angelo scanned a few letters and nodded. "You had a good scam goin' there."

"And what you're readin' is only the letters had checks

or cash. The bullshit ones I dumped."

Angelo slipped the garter around the letters and returned them.

"So what can the don do for you, Santo Peccato?"

"Don Angelo, you better write this all down."

After fetching a pad and pencil from the night table, Angelo said, "The don is ready."

Carlo held up three fingers. "*Uno*: Lean on the Pope to give me back my button. Mary Magdalene was a hooker and got hers so why shouldn't a man of honor? *Due*: After I get my button back hire a marketing outfit to improve my image. A saint is a saint is a saint. I wanna see busloads of pilgrims again comin' up here to pay respect at my shrine and leave donations — cash, check or major credit cards. I wanna see our gift shop movin' out Saint Peccato T-shirts by the gross with the slogan, 'The Comeback Saint.'"

Angelo, scribbling rapidly, said, "In the saints book they'll call you Carlo the gabby. What's next?"

"*Tre*: Get my feast day changed from April 1 which the Pope set as a joke to a date showin' more respect—April 15. I wanna be called the patron saint of taxpayers who ain't otherwise got a prayer of payin' them Washington loan sharks."

Angelo dropped the pad and pencil on the night table. "That's all you want? Nothin' else?"

Carlo beckoned, entered the dark corridor followed by Angelo in bathrobe and slippers and led the way to a door. "Today it's just an unused storeroom they keep locked," Carlo said. He waved his hand over the door, turned the knob, entered and flicked on a light. The room was jammed with crutches, canes, walkers and wheelchairs.

"I ain't been here yet," Angelo said. "We got a rec room for old football players?"

Carlo waved his hand over the room. "We used to call this the Lourdes depository where true believers left their stuff after being healed at my shrine."

"You were peddlin' snake oil?"

"You go to a high-priced quack and he don't give you no guarantee so whaddya expect from a freebie saint? All I know, like Christ says, these sufferin' pilgrims took up their sleepin' bags and walked the walk while them doctors just talked the talk. We get a couple of lawyers' letters now and then. But since we're broke we're judgment proof. Anyway how can they subpoena a saint?"

When they left the storeroom, Angelo said, "You forgot to lock the door."

Carlo reached for his pocket and stopped in embarrassment. "I'm a fuckin' saint so why do I need a key to get through doors?"

Angelo laughed.

"You done time for B&E and you never heard of a master key?"

"Just remember what Sister Sessualità warned you about."

"She's an old fart but still teachin' a couple of grades at the School of Our Irrepressible Lady," Angelo said. "I heard she got *un cugino* in Washington is *un padrone grande* in the church. I hope he dumps *la Gorgone* in an old folks home down there so she never bothers us again."

They headed for Peccato Pacchia, the deserted monastery tavern where Angelo tended bar and drew them each a beer. As they faced each other across the bar, Angelo said, "With all due respect Carlo, the don asks a personal question: How come your don in Milwaukee puts out a contract on a good producer like you just because you go AWOL to serve holy mother the church?"

Carlo held his glass up to the light and frowned. "Without punks like him we wouldn't have no martyrs like me." He drained his glass in one long gulp and wiped his mouth on his sleeve as Angelo watched in admiration.

"Now the don just made the leap of faith," Angelo said.

"*Bene.* You remember the old Sicilian proverb? When the fox catches his paw in the trap, a gypsy lets him go. Then the fox rewards the gypsy by showin' him where the pot of gold is buried."

"Sure, everybody knows that one. It's what they call a *bubbe-mayse*."

"A what?"

"*Bubbe-mayse*. I learned Latin when I was an altar boy. But I ain't seen no foxes around here though I'm still lookin' for the pot of gold."

Carlo held out his glass. "Put a head on it this time." This too was downed in one gulp. "Now where was I?"

"I never heard of a saint gettin' loaded in a monastery bar at three in the mornin'. You was talkin' about foxes and gypsies."

Carlo set the glass down on what he thought was the bar.

"Forget the broken glass though I'm surprised to see you bombed on only two beers," Angelo said.

Carlo pointed to the ceiling. "It's the change in altitude on top of this hill. Before I came here I could drink anybody in my *famiglia* under the table."

Then he wagged his finger under Angelo's nose. "The only reason the Pope pulled the plug on me was because I didn't give him his cut of the take from the pilgrims."

Angelo wiped the bar with a towel and said, "Well, you know the rule in our business—50 percent always goes upstairs. Though I heard that the Pope said reports of your miracles and death was greatly exaggerated."

Carlo dismissed that with a shrug and eased himself onto a bar stool. "We had a good business goin' here. Them pilgrims crawled outa the woodwork all over the U.S. of A., Canada and Mexico to pay respect at my shrine and light a candle to goose their petitions up to heaven. We had $5, $25, $50 and the king-size $100 candles that burned for a fuckin' month. "Then we got a 900 number to hear their quickie petitions at $5 a minute. And for them pilgrims wantin' it in writin' we put in a fax machine. We sold $25 Saint Peccato dashboard statuettes of genuine simulated ivory made in Hong Kong at 79 cents apiece."

"I seen them in the bakery vans."

"Yeah. I gave the monastery a license to steal."

"Okay Carlo, so we just took a walk down memory lane. So what?"

Carlo gripped the bar to steady himself. "Don Angelo, I want for you to figure out a miracle scam to make me The Comeback Saint like it'll say on my T-shirts. Right now I feel like that other guy who also got his button yanked by the Pope when he didn't do nothin' wrong neither."

"Who?"

"Saint Christopher who invented traveler's checks. Also get hold of a smart lawyer to convince the IRS and the Wisconsin revenue people we is a church again and deserve our exemption back."

Angelo helped Carlo to the tavern door.

"I am seein' a lawyer this mornin'. Now get back to polishin' them golden stairs while I get back to sleep."

"Is the shyster a Hebe?"

"Yeah."

Carlo staggered down the corridor into the dark calling as he disappeared, *"Mazel tov!"*

"You not only need a lawyer—you need an army for what's closing in on you," Mordecai said.

He and Angelo were walking through the monastery woods in the morning drizzle. Mordecai dug his hands into the pockets of a Burberry trenchcoat as rain dripped off his Brooklyn Dodgers cap.

Angelo huddled in an old canvas parka. He cast a stone down the hill and smiled when he heard the stone strike.

Mordecai selected a baseball-sized stone, wound up and hurled it farther, the thump resounding in the woods.

Angelo drew his 9 mm Beretta. "We ain't in the Stone Age no more. Pull your cannon."

Mordecai drew his .357 revolver as Angelo selected a beer can from a pile of empties he kept for target practice.

"Straight up as I tell the bartender," Mordecai said. "These big rounds travel."

Angelo hurled, the boom of the heavy revolver echoing over the valley.

"You missed!" Angelo said.

Mordecai returned the revolver to a shoulder holster and shook his head. "There was nothing left to come down except fragments blown into the next county. Now I'll toss."

Angelo, sweating in the wind, fired. When the undamaged can fell at his feet, he kicked it off the hill.

"Where the fuck did you learn to shoot?"

"When I was in the fifth grade I was the BB gun champion of Midwood."

"So?"

"So perhaps as your *consigliere*-designate I can see when my don is on the mark or off it. As *capo* here you're vulnerable to assassination by the Brooklyn or Chicago families or a RICO bust by the FBI."

Angelo punched Mordecai playfully on the shoulder. "How can Rico bust me if he got whacked himself at the end of that picture?"

"You've seen too many Mafia movies. But your fiscal situation is cause for concern. Your monastery's sole income is derived from a bagel bakery that commands merely a sliver of the market. You have lost your religious exemption for taxes. Finally, the Vatican has discredited your Saint Peccato as a mountebank whose devotees have stopped visiting his shrine or sending contributions." Angelo leaned against an oak tree whose withered leaves dripped rain that pattered his parka.

"You're inferrin' I'm the boss of a two-bit outfit?"

"It's veracity."

"That bad, huh?"

"That's my categorical affirmative."

Over a beer at the monastery tavern, Angelo said, "You're the new *consigliere*. But now I gotta fill another job."

"To whom does that remark pertain?" Mordecai said.

"An interpreter."

HAROLD KNOLL

CHAPTER XVI

Outside Yvonne's apartment door Angelo heard the sound of revelry by night. He frowned and muttered, "Who's she partyin' with?"

He held a bouquet of pink roses swathed in tissue paper against the cold, started to leave but shrugged and pushed the buzzer.

When Yvonne opened the door, he looked beyond her and his eyes widened. Three shouting little girls in brown jumpers and white blouses were scurrying about the small apartment.

"Come in and join the fun," Yvonne said.

She was wearing a green uniform dress covered with a batter-stained apron. She took his black leather jacket and black beret and hung them in the closet. When he presented the bouquet, she looked over her shoulder to confirm the girls were occupied. Then she kissed him on the cheek and placed the roses in a vase on the living room coffee table. "Why didn't you phone you were coming?" she said. "But you came at the right time because we've made lots of cookies."

"Who are these kids?"

"Part of my Brownie troop from Punkinville. We're baking chocolate chip cookies for our ice cream party tonight."

"I gotta go. I'm sorry I never do nothin' right with you."

"Yvonne, they're starting to burn in the oven!" cried the tallest Brownie with glasses, braces and a uniform sash

127

adorned with achievement patches.

Marching Angelo to the sofa, Yvonne hurried into the kitchen. When the cookie crisis ended, Yvonne introduced him to her Brownies who lined up before the sofa.

"I'm Esmeralda Chance," said the tall girl. "I'm the senior Brownie in our troop because I have the most Try-It patches and I'm already in third grade. All the other girls in my troop are second graders. My associates here are Clytemnestra Tinker and Guinevere Evers. I'm into baseball."

"It figures," Angelo said bowing.

The girls raised their right hands with three middle fingers extended, the thumb holding down the pinky.

"I wish I could answer but I don't know the right finger," Angelo said.

"What they just gave you was the Brownie salute," Yvonne said.

After the girls retired to the kitchen to bake more cookies, Yvonne sat beside him on the sofa. They had cookies and fresh brewed coffee. She took his hand but he glanced nervously at the kitchen so she gave him another cookie.

"I gotta go. You got your Brownies to take care of."

"They may be young girls but they can take care of themselves. Never forget they're Girl Scouts."

"I just come here to say I'm sorry."

"And?"

Her tongue darted over her lips.

"And I like you and wanna see you again—sometime." He sighed.

"Quite a romantic speech from *il Signer* Toro. Have another cookie."

"So you're a Brownie leader."

"It's been wonderful. I tell the mothers how lucky they are and do you know what they say? 'Stay single. You're the lucky one.' Can you imagine?"

"Yeah."

Mothers arrived, nibbled cookies and helped their daughters into coats and boots. Angelo fidgeted when he was introduced to the women who smiled in appraisal. He sighed again when the mothers and Brownies left.

"All my Brownies are super but those three girls are my favorites," Yvonne said.

"I guess you gotta clean up the kitchen so I'll go."

He was led into the kitchen and winced when she fetched an apron and approached smiling. But she hung the apron in a closet. The kitchen was immaculate, the sink empty and the scrubbed cookie tins drying in a rack on the counter.

"The Girl Scout motto is 'Be prepared,'" Yvonne said. "So I've encouraged them to be ready for any situation they meet — even cleaning up after a party."

"Yeah, but they're only little girls."

"They can do more than bake cookies." She squeezed his arm playfully but firmly as she mimicked him saying, "Now I gotta go."

They laughed and sat at the kitchen table. She took both his hands, her blue eyes glistening. "It's not like the movies, is it?" she said.

"Mafia movies?"

"No, girl meets boy. They go to a movie. Then they go to bed."

"We ain't been to the movies yet."

"Do you think I'd go to bed with you?"

"I dunno. You're different."

She leaned over and kissed him on the cheek. "Well I want to but I can't yet. It's not *what* two people do but *why*."

He nodded, shifting uneasily in the chair because of his erection. "I gotta go," he said and they laughed.

At the door, she hugged him and he touched her cheek to wipe away a tear.

"My mother tells me not to give up on Mr. Right," she said.

"Because she's *una siciliana*. And what does your father the cop say?"

"We won't discuss that." She tucked his white silk

scarf inside the collar of his leather jacket. "Last night I dreamed I was at your funeral. I don't want to lose you."

"Dreams is all in the head."

He kissed her on the forehead and said as he was leaving, "It'll be okay. I'm the only don ever had a *goombah* saint for a bodyguard."

At 8 a.m. the Lincoln Town Car stopped with a jerk in the no-parking zone at the monastery's entrance and Don Topo got out of the front passenger seat. He was accompanied by Garibladi, who leaped from the rear seat and howled with excitement as the don tugged the leash.

"Zitto!" the don commanded to quiet the noble shepherd who eagerly applied his black gumdrop nose to the pavement.

The don was in clerical black and Roman collar. He adjusted his black sunglasses and false black handlebar mustache, clasped a worn black leather breviary to his chest, tucked a white cane under his arm and grumbled at Iron Al's driving.

Bending his ears back to facilitate exit, the *consigliere* struggled out of the driver's seat. His fuzzy pink Easter bunny suit provided by a costumer bulged at what the don termed the "droop seat." Iron Al sneezed through his perforated pink rubber ball nose and itched where pipe cleaner whiskers had been taped to his cheeks.

Don Topo had obtained his priest's outfit free. As Iron Al in mufti distracted the peevish pastor of St. Zucca's Catholic Church in Punkinville with a litany of sins venial and mortal, the don burgled the rectory.

He selected the portly priest's Sunday best outfit together with breviary and a life-sized fiberglass statue of Saint Rosalia, patron of Palermo. This last *la Signora* Maria Scempio needed for a shrine in their new home at St. Petersburg.

However, the two mafiosi were unaware Saint Zucca's pastor was the notorious Maximum Elmer exacting stiff tolls in his dusty three-seater confessional. His parishioners willingly drove to distant churches to offer a few Hail Marys and Our Fathers and a pledge to "straighten up, fly right, vote Republican and support pro-life."

Hence, Iron Al received a formidable penance for sins dating back to kindergarten where he had passed out sampling sacramental wine and was revived only by repeated whacks of Sister Sessualità's ruler.

The pastor rapped his gavel on the confessional divider and said, "Five hundred Our Fathers, 500 Hail Marys and $500 in cash, no checks, to help repair the church roof. No payment means no absolution and a slow grilling in hell's blast furnace that will make St. Lawrence's martyrdom look like a weenie roast."

Now Don Topo waited impatiently for response to his banging on the monastery's door knocker, a massive bronze horseshoe.

"Nobody answers because it's a bad luck horseshoe pointing down so luck runs out," Iron Al said.

"You stupidstitious," the don said banging the knocker so hard that it flew off and landed on the Easter bunny's foot.

The *consigliere* dropped his Easter basket and hopped on the sound foot while holding the injured one in his paws. The basket spilled chocolate eggs and his hidden Beretta across the sidewalk.

As Garibaldi attacked the goodies, the don vainly jerked his leash and blasphemed while the dancing Easter bunny wagged his head and retrieved his pistol and remaining eggs.

Reneging on his pledge to the pastor of the Church of Our Irrepressible Lady, the don said: "Imitation priest can say whatever he goddamn wants because *il destino* has kicked the don in the *cojones* again. How we gonna whack Don Angelo inside monastery when the priest and the Easter bunny who come to pay respect is freezin' outside monastery?"

The don's teeth chattered in the wind. But when the

shivering bunny sought a restorative by dipping into the chocolate eggs in his basket, the don slapped his paw. Then the bunny tugged his cottontail until an urgent message was acknowledged by the don.

"Makin' No. 2 here don't show respect. Wait till we get inside and find a bathroom."

However while the bunny sulked, Garibaldi slyly lifted a hind leg and drenched the shrubbery.

"*Bravo!*" said the don. "Garibaldi don't got no prostrate trouble like some old farts the don knows."

Finally it occurred to the don to try the doorknob. Locked. When Iron Al hopefully jerked a paw at their Lincoln, the don shook his head.

"Imitation priest and Easter bunny come here to whack Angelo and ain't goin' home till we take care of the party of the second part and also the party of the first part what fucked up and is drivin' a Yugo. We find another door."

They went to a side door also locked but spied a nearby doublehung window open slightly. This the don raised, peered within at an unoccupied grocery storeroom, unleashed Garibaldi, signaled to Iron Al for a leg up and received an enthusiastic shove that propelled him on all fours across the tiled floor. Garibaldi followed in one bound.

Don Topo staggered to his feet, straightened his mustache and retrieved his fallen cane, fedora and breviary. He adjusted his sunglasses and leashed the dog. Then he awaited the Easter bunny who managed to clamber unaided into the room while holding his basket with the Beretta visible under the few surviving eggs.

Iron Al started to dip a paw into an opened candy case when the don rapped his breviary between the bunny ears. "For shame Easter bunny tries to rip off church. Only priest can do that."

The don stuffed a handful of chocolate bars into his coat pocket and cautiously opened the door. He scanned the corridor, assumed a pastoral bearing and ventured forth with white cane tapping flanked by the Easter bunny and the noble shepherd.

They proceeded along the main corridor, the perimeter of the circular building, until Don Topo accosted a brother. He was more startled by the direct approach of the blind priest than by the bunny and canine companions.

"Where's the don at?" said Don Topo flourishing his white cane under the brother's nose.

Garibaldi strained at the leash while the brother backed against the wall.

"Begging your pardon, Father, but whom are you inquiring about?"

"Don Angelo, *il padrone* here, to give him a Easter present."

"Oh, now I see. I mean you're seeking Brother Angelo, our new prior. He's in his office down the hall. Permit me to see you there, Father, and I am touched to see that you read your breviary in Braille."

He took the don's arm but the don shook him off. "I ain't never read my Bible in jail because I never been busted. Whaddya take me for, some punk? Just tell me where Don Angelo is at and I find it mine own self and give him what's comin' to him."

The don raised his sunglasses, rolled his eyes and even crossed them.

"You can see!" the brother cried.

"Damn right. Now where the fuck is Angelo at?"

"It's a miracle!"

"Just a few Hail Marys to Santo Peccato done it except I gotta go easy on watchin' TV for awhile. Now which door is it?"

"Third on your right, Father. I must go and tell the brothers."

"Yeah. Also tell 'em to put up the knocker the right way for good luck."

But the brother had already hurried off as the trio moved along, the don wildly swinging his cane and tripping brothers within range.

The elevator door opened in the corridor and Serafina in baker's whites and chef's hat exited pushing a cart of pastries she had made in the basement bakery. She was en route to the brothers' tavern-cum-restaurant but stopped and bowed to the approaching blind priest. The role of the dog was obvious and although the presence of the giant Easter bunny was unusual she had come to expect this at the monastery.

"*Buon giorno, padre mio,*" she greeted the don she had never met before. "Can I offer you some of my *pasticceria* which I have here in this cart before you?"

"*Grazie, figlia mia,*" he said lifting his dark glasses and pointing with his white cane. "Maybe a half-dozen of them cannoli over there and what we got left over we put in a doggie bag for my friend here."

She started to hand over a platter of pastry when the don added: "We goin' over to give Don Angelo a little surprise."

Serafina noted the pistol butt protruding from the few remaining eggs in the bunny's basket. She instinctively reached to her waistband for her .38 Chief's Special but recalled she had left the revolver in her room for cleaning,

Instead she shoved the cart into Don Topo bowling him over as the leashed Garibaldi barked and the bunny fumbled with his pistol.

"Help!" she screamed and ran to alert Angelo.

The don jettisoned his cane, dark glasses and breviary, tried a nearby unlocked door, unleashed Garibaldi and ushered his two companions into a large dimly lit room. Sighing with relief, Iron Al doffed his bunny costume and retrieved his pistol from the basket, which Garibaldi cleared of the remaining eggs.

"Where the hell are we?" Iron Al whispered.

"Shh," Don Topo said. "We're in church."

"Well, so long as we're here maybe I sit in a pew and start workin' on them 500 Hail Marys and 500 Our Fathers since I already give the priest $500 to put in the fix for me with *il* cielo."

"No. Jam your ass against the door while I look around."

"But suppose Angelo shoots through the door?"

"Then you never be constipated because you got two assholes."

In the apparently deserted chapel a few votive candles flickered to the left of the altar. There were no windows. "How come no stoplight at the altar?" Iron Al whispered from the door.

"When the Pope took away the button from them punks they made it a Protestant church so we don't have to show no respect."

The don stuck a wad of bubblegum into his mouth and flipped the wrapper into a pew. "Alessandro, now we gonna fight like men of honor to make good on the contract. Then we die happy because we prove we ain't no Mustache Petes."

"How about your retirement home in St. Petersburg?"

"Sometimes a man gotta do what he gotta do."

"Nobody never called me a Mustache Pete," said Iron Al cringing against the door. "Maybe we just tell Angelo we come to play an impractical joke and he laughs it off."

"Maybe you better feel in your pants to see if you swapped your *cojones* for a pussy. And cock your piece because you're gonna need it."

The *consigliere* reluctantly complied as the don cocked his own Beretta and moved slowly down the aisle. Garibaldi stayed at the don's side, big ears erect, sniffing the carpet.

The don patted the noble shepherd's head. "*Bene*. The don can count on you, *compagno fedele*." Behind them the door shuddered under pounding. Garibaldi responded with ferocious barks but stayed close to his master. As they passed the shrine of Saint Peccato, the don paused and shone his pocket flashlight at the glass-topped coffin. The figure of the saint in his gray habit was clearly visible within.

"Carlo looks like he never croaked," the don said.

Nearing the front pews, the don squinted in the candlelight at an apparent life-sized statue to the right of the altar. He noted the tattered gray habit with hood up, the figure's arms outstretched, bare feet in torn sandals

"Holy Carlo," the don said brandishing the pistol. "You took a flyin' leap for yourself from *la tomba* to *il altare?* You afraid a priest whacks you so you got hands up? But a priest no whack *un santo* because *un santo* is already *morto*."

He ignored the door pounding, stood before the figure and examined it closely in the candlelight.

"I never seen a statue like this," he said jabbing the pistol into the soft middle.

Braced against the door, Iron Al called: "That's soft sculpture like I seen on pubic TV." The don peered into the dark hood, barely discerning the gaunt face.

"Don Topo Scempio from Brooklyn comes to pay respect to Santo Peccato and Don Angelo Panettorio. But first Don Topo gotta be sure you *un santo genuine* and not *un impostore* like Santy Claus."

He waved Garibaldi away who was sniffing the figure's habit. Raising his pistol, the don released the safety catch. But the figure grabbed the don's wrists and kneed him in the groin as the pistol fired into the ceiling and the don collapsed in pain. Pocketing the pistol, the figure vanished in the shadows. Then the chapel door burst open hurling Iron Al into the aisle.

Guns drawn, Angelo, Mordecai and Serafina rushed in.

While Serafina disarmed Iron Al and hauled him to his feet, Angelo motioned Mordecai to remain in the rear. Then Angelo ran toward the don who was trying to rise.

"*Avanti!*" Don Topo commanded and the growling Garibaldi leaped through the darkness toward Angelo. "*Benissimo!*" the don cried but he beat his fists on the carpet and added "*Traditore!*" when in mid-leap Garibaldi yodeled joyfully and caught a marshmallow Angelo had pitched. It was this infamous bribe that had motivated the dog to permit FBI buggery in the don's club.

Angelo stepped back before Garibaldi's slobbering salutation. Then commanding the dog to heel, Angelo walked with him and Mordecai to Don Topo who was sitting in a front pew with his head bowed.

"With all due respect Don Topo, the don gotta interrupt your prayers to pat you down."

Tears coursed down Don Topo's cheeks as he said: "*Camerata mio,* don't bother. The don ain't packin' now and it's too late for him to pray."

"We'll check that out for ourselves," Mordecai said but Angelo took his arm.

"Don Topo is a man of respect," said Angelo straightening the don's false mustache. "He climbed the mountain because it's a question of honor. Ain't that right, Don Topo?"

"*Si,*" the old man said hoarsely. "Maria say, 'Why we wait to go to St. Petersburg?' And the don says, 'Because the don ain't no Mustache Pete that runs away. The don gotta do his last rah-rah.'"

Angelo put his arm around Don Topo and helped him to his feet.

"The don shakes like a little old lady," Don Topo said.

Angelo put his finger to his lips and nodded toward Serafina guarding Iron Al at the door.

"You never know when a little old lady with *cojones* will show up. Relax. You won't get whacked. We have a sitdown and straighten everything out."

"You no understand. The don ain't afraid for you or little old ladies. It's the other guy."

"Brother Mordecai? He does only what I say."

"No, it's Holy Carlo. He was here."

"That's a scam. He's in his coffin at his shrine here. Some punk is runnin' around dressed like him to bring the pilgrims back. I was so near that con artist I could even smell his garlic."

Don Topo shook his head, his black suit dusty and

rumpled.

"Santo Peccato was up at the altar. The don touched him. The don ain't been chairman of the parish council of the Church of Our Irrepressible Lady for 20 years — never lost an election—not to know *un santo* from a punk. Santo Peccato takes the don's piece, knocks the don on his ass and goes through the wall like a ghost."

Serafina and Mordecai approached with the hapless Iron Al. She crossed herself with Iron Al's Beretta but then pointed the pistol at him again.

"Don Topo seen Santo Peccato!" she cried. "It is a sign from *il cielo!*"

"What the don can't figure is why *un santo* needs the don's piece," Don Topo said.

"Someday we more understand the ways of *il cielo*," Serafina said.

"Grandma, Carlo's a con man. He'll use the piece to knock over another bank like he used to do in Milwaukee," Angelo said.

But Don Topo, pale and trembling, looked up at the chapel's vaulted ceiling, dropped to his knees and crossed himself. "It's a fuckin' miracle!" he cried.

CHAPTER XVII

"I ain't seen this many trees since my first grade field trip to Prospect Park," Benny Deuce said.

He, Raphael and Jonah had left the Thunderbird on the town road that morning and climbed through the woods toward the monastery. Above them bluejays and crows shrilled alarm as Jonah prowled through the snow. He growled as he paused occasionally to lick cold wet paws.

A panicky chipmunk too far from his hole was bitten in the neck, shaken soundly and carried in the cat's jaws. "*Il gatto* done the hit right," Benny Deuce said.

He and Raphael leaned against a big oak while Jonah breakfasted. After a washup, the cat, tail erect now, resumed the trek.

"Mr. Deuce, I got a question," Raphael said.

"Shoot."

"How come we didn't go up the road to the monastery?"

Benny Deuce indicated the cat. "He got his priorities in order. His No. 1 job was puttin' meat on the table so he didn't mail out no RS-Teepee to that chipmunk. Likewise we tippytoe through the woods so we can pay respect to a certain party of the second part who's gonna be real surprised he didn't get no RS-teepee neither. *Capisci?*"

Jonah, head cocked, meowed but Raphael frowned. When they sighted the monastery Raphael said: "After you finish your business, I hope you'll ask them to take me in this time so I can serve the Lord even as a doorkeeper in his house. I done what you asked and showed you the way here."

Benny Deuce drew his Beretta and crouched as he walked, scanning the woods ahead.

"When the chicken flies with the eagle the hawks scram," he whispered.

"But I never seen a chicken fly that high," Raphael whispered.

As they left the woods and approached the rear of the monastery, Garibaldi, lurking behind a garden tractor, sprang howling ferociously.

"Don Topo's here!" Benny Deuce cried.

He leveled his pistol at Garibaldi but before Benny Deuce could fire Jonah leaped. The cat struck Benny Deuce's pistol which clattered on the sidewalk while Garibaldi charged Benny Deuce sending him sprawling on his back. As the cat snarled at Benny Deuce, Garibaldi stood on his chest barking until Angelo and Mordecai appeared.

Angelo picked up Benny Deuce's Beretta while Mordecai motioned with his .357 revolver for Benny Deuce to rise. When Angelo commanded Garibaldi to sit at his side the dog wagged his tail and promptly obeyed.

Despite trembling, Raphael managed to help Benny Deuce to his feet.

"What brings you two gentlemen to the Penitentiary Brothers of Saint Peccato?" Angelo said.

Benny Deuce nonplussed looked to Raphael whose hands were raised, fingers crossed.

"Would you believe a pilgrimage?" Raphael said.

CHAPTER XVIII

Supervising Special Agent J. Edgar Haman in a freshly pressed coverall sat behind the wheel of the plumber's van and snapped a pencil in two as rain pattered on the windshield. He was listening to a radio meteorologist who had just predicted sunny with no precipitation.

Haman lowered his binoculars from the sullen sky to focus on the sole aircraft at the Punkinville International and Regional Airport, a vintage Piper Cub. Its elderly owner wore a brown leather jacket, brown leather helmet with goggles, white silk scarf, riding breeches and brown boots.

He kicked the tires, spat on his hands, gave the wooden propeller several feeble jerks and was bowled over when the engine fired. The tiny airplane bounded over the grass while the pilot cringed under the passing wing. Then the plane became airborne, banked and flew into a cloud.

When Haman approached, the elderly gentleman frowned at his coverall and said, "I don't need a plumber. Get me aspirin with seltzer and a twist."

"You'll have to cool your jets, old timer."

The pilot raised himself on one elbow. "I was off to the Penitentiary Brothers of Saint Peccato Monastery to do aerial photography for their new brochure to hoodwink pilgrims into coming back."

Ignoring the plea for assistance, Haman said as he headed back to the van:

"I'll be over there myself in a few minutes but the only photography those perpetrators will get is mug shots with a number underneath. Incidentally, it's Penitential not Penitentiary."

"Same difference etymologically," the pilot said.

Haman sneered as he entered the van and heard the fax machine clattering in the rear. He ripped the message out, sat in his director's chair and read the following from the New York office: "Your insubordination and flagrant disregard of territorial jurisdiction are cause for termination of Operation Big Collar. Report forthwith and without delay to this office for promotion to Group Manager, Grade 12-Z and reassignment to the Staten Island sub-unit office. Special Agent Sachel's resignation is hereby rejected and he is discharged for willfully displaying initiative."

Haman shredded the message and flipped the founder's portrait from grimace to scowl. Hearing an aircraft engine, he hastily laid out four arrest warrants he had previously prepared for Don Topo, Iron Al, Angelo and Benny Deuce. For authorization Haman signed the Honorable Roy Bean.

Then lugging his folded chair he ran toward the grass strip where a small helicopter had just landed. He ignored the fallen aviator who cried: "Look out for my little putt-putt that will come home to Daddy!"

Haman boarded the helicopter, the folded chair protruding into the protesting pilot's lap.

"Who do we charge this trip to?" shouted the pilot.

Waving his agent's ID card Haman shouted: "The FBI of course!"

"Should I land on the town road near the target?"

Haman shook his head. "Closer. I want to drop right in on those perpetrators!"

CHAPTER XIX

"You make fun of Don Topo when you say you ain't in hijackin', dope, gamblin', loan sharkin' or even *la prostituzione*," Don Topo said.

The sitdown was in the monastery's executive committee room upstairs in the center of the circular building. Overhead was a large plastic dome skylight.

"With all due respect it's true," said Angelo at the large round conference table topped with white plastic. When Don Topo leaned forward Iron Al did likewise.

"And your racket is now bakin' Jew doughnuts?" Don Topo said.

Mordecai, sitting beside Angelo, frowned.

"*Si* like I learned from Reilly when I was a kid in the neighborhood," Angelo said. "Crime don't pay no more for wiseguys because them politicians in Washington gave themselves a license to steal. Have a bagel."

Angelo passed a plate of bagels and cheese but Don Topo shook his head. "Alfonse the dentist, *cugino mio,* stuck so much gold in the don's mouth it's like Fort Knox. When he finishes Alfonse say, 'Don Topo, eat whatever you want exceptin' them cast iron Jew bagels.'"

Mordecai drummed his fingers on the table, sighed and said: "We had Don Topo's Lincoln washed and gassed up so he's ready to go back to Brooklyn now with Iron Al."

"But not with *il traditore*," said Don Topo shaking his

finger at Garibaldi lying beside Angelo.

The noble shepherd casually examined the pads on his front paws.

Serafina entered, bowed to Don Topo and placed a covered basket before him.

"For your trip," Angelo said.

The four men stood up while Don Topo embraced Angelo as the two *consiglieri* watched.

"When you see Benedetto, tell him *per favore* all contracts canceled," Don Topo said. "He can dump the Yugo and steal himself a nice new Thunderbird."

"I tell him if I see him. *Buona fortuna* for your retirement in St. Petersburg." Then Angelo embraced Iron Al.

"Ditto to you as new don."

As Angelo escorted the pair to the door, Don Topo said, *"Per favore* Don Angelo. The don and Iron Al don't got their pieces. Lotsa criminals on the road."

Angelo indicated the covered basket Iron Al was carrying. "For your trip you got bread, cheese, salami, *vino* and two Berettas caliber .22 One is a free replacement for the don's piece Carlo took and the other is Iron Al's."

Don Topo wept and bowed. *"Grazie.* Don Topo Scempio of the best *famiglia* in New York says *arrivederci!"*

As the Lincoln slowly descended the monastery road, Don Topo told Iron Al who was driving: "Too much excitement on that mountain for a tired old man. When you hit the freeway step on it so we get back to peace and quiet down below."

"We just gotta make what the shrinks call a altitude adjustment," Iron Al said.

Meanwhile back at the executive committee room, Angelo asked, "Them two sons of bitches gone yet?"

"Si," Serafina said.

"Then *nonna mia, per favore* bring in Benny Deuce and *il nero.* And don't forget *il gatto."*

CHAPTER XX

Throbbing prompted Yvonne to join customers looking up through the diner's windows. Then she hurried into the parking lot and saw a small helicopter cruising over the trees. She stared to confirm what she had first seen through the windows:

Tethered to a cable under the helicopter was a man in a chair oscillating through the treetops.

"What's he selling?" said the diner's Greek proprietor, a stout man girded with a white apron.

"Trouble," she said running back to the diner and dialing the phone.

Some miles from the monastery, Iron Al drove the Lincoln along the town road nearing the freeway and a comfortable flatland trip to Brooklyn.

"The car's engine farts like our old espresso machine," Don Topo said.

"It ain't our engine. Look up in the sky!"

"Is that a airplane headin' right for us?" the don said.

"With all due respect that's no airplane. That's a heelyocopter."

"Did they pick up a hitchhiker?"

"Don Topo, that's no hitchhiker. His legs is covered with branches and he's comin' in so low I can see the letters on his coverall. It's the plumber from across the street."

The don peered through the windshield as the

oscillating airman passed directly overhead dropping twigs on the Lincoln. Iron Al switched on the windshield wipers as the don banged his bony fist on the dashboard.

"*I frutti e la verdura!* No matter what kinda presentation he makes we still don't need no fuckin' plumber!"

When the brother who answered the monastery phone said the prior was at a meeting and could not be disturbed, Yvonne asked for Serafina.

"Angelo has sitdown with a *goombah* and *il nero* he brought here," Serafina said.

"Warn Angelo right now there's a helicopter coming your way dragging a plumber in a chair!"

"But we don't need no plumber even one sittin' down," Serafina said. "And I don't want *i aeroplani* over the house!"

CHAPTER XXI

The wind lashed Carlo Peccato's tattered habit as he clung to the roof over the monastery's entrance.

Struggling to keep his footing, Carlo hoisted a heavy cross he had made from two-by-fours. He set this in a steel socket from which he had pried the stump of the cross the departing chaplain had sawed off and confiscated.

Carlo hammered a nail through one of the mounting holes in the socket. But when he reached for another nail they all fell from his pocket, bounced off the roof and onto the lawn. He shook the wobbly cross but was distracted by throbbing of an approaching aircraft.

Although the helicopter cruised slowly, J. Edgar Haman swung wildly in his tethered director's chair. He clenched its arms, dragged his feet through treetops and bellowed the FBI fight song whose words were drowned in the din.

Haman glanced eastward where the sun began to pierce the leaden sky and noted a small high-wing aircraft diving to attack.

"Time to pay the Piper at three o'clock high!" he cried

He risked freeing one hand from his chair, drew his .357 magnum revolver and dizzy from his ride tried to aim at the unpiloted aircraft.

At the same time, Carlo Peccato grasped the base of the cross with one hand, with the other drew Don Topo's .22

Beretta, braced it on the crossbar and despite the wind began firing steadily when chairborne Haman was nearly overhead.

Meanwhile the helicopter pilot, maneuvering toward a clearing behind the monastery, saw his windshield shattered by Haman's .357 round while Carlo's shots punched holes in the cabin overhead.

When the Piper Cub, putt-putting at full throttle, loomed ahead on a collision course, the helicopter pilot cut Haman's tether and climbed away.

The Piper Cub did a victory roll and headed back toward the Punkinville International and Regional Airport as Carlo cried, "It's a fuckin' miracle!"

A few minutes before, a sitdown was in progress in the monastery's executive committee room. Under the skylight Angelo sat at the round table facing Benny Deuce and Raphael. Mordecai stood nearby, revolver held at his side. Sitting beside Angelo was Garibaldi suspiciously eyeing Jonah sitting beside Raphael.

After brief discussion with Benny Deuce, Angelo said, "I need a good *caporegime* to help with managed competition in our bagel business. Also you will be our public relations director to help give a nice welcome when the Chicago *goombata* come back."

Benny Deuce screwed a pinky in his ear and shook the finger for clear communication. He leaned forward and licked dry lips.

"With all due respect Don Angelo, I hope you ain't sore I come to enforce Don Topo's contract on you and also to motivate *la Signora* Panettorio."

Angelo reached for a mint he kept in a bowl on the table which he passed to Benny Deuce who took a handful.

"Feel free to indulge yourself," Angelo said as he nibbled. "Them is the treat of choice for managers of *la famiglia*. Toothpicks is for *i soldati*. Now like you was sayin', the contract was only business. Even though you didn't whack me or motivate *nonna mia* to be a rat fink, you ain't in breach of contract. Ain't that right, *consigliere mio?*"

Mordecai nodded.

"To frame it in judicial perspective, Don Topo presides over a lower court while you preside over an appeals court."

Benny Deuce raised a hand.

"Per favore consigliere, a point of law. Do I gotta worry about a higher court over Don Angelo?"

Mordecai shook his head and holstered his revolver.

"The highest court is of course the families' commission: But since Don Topo is on his way to retirement in Florida it is my impression you have no exposure."

When Benny Deuce frowned, Angelo said, "He means it's a peccadilly so forget it. Anyways, Don Topo already canceled all contracts makin' them numb and verse so you is just beatin' a dead jockey. Now I welcome you to the Peccato *famiglia,* the only one named for a saint even though the Pope says he's a bum."

Angelo stood and embraced Benny Deuce as Raphael began to rise, sat down and rubbed his sweaty palms together.

"Mr. Don, with all due respect ain't you forgot about me?"

At that moment Serafina rushed in causing Mordecai to draw his revolver and assume a combat stance.

"Nipotino mio!" she cried pointing to the skylight. "Crazy plumber sits in chair and hangs from *elicottero!*"

"But we don't need no plumber!" Angelo said as the skylight shattered and chairborne Haman crashed on the conference table.

CHAPTER XXII

"Per favore signor, remove your official buns from what's left of our table," Angelo said.

Haman was sprawled on the floor amid wreckage of the conference table, skylight and his director's chair. As he staggered to his feet he tramped on Jonah's tail who screeched and clawed Haman's face. But brandishing his revolver in one hand and arrest warrants in the other, Haman said, "With authority vested in me by J. Edgar Hoover and the Great Jehovah, I arrest the perpetrators herein named in these warrants duly executed by Judge Roy Bean, the law west of the Hudson. Operation Big Collar is hereby consummated."

Before Haman could continue, Angelo nodded to the crouching Garibaldi, launching the canine rocket at Haman who was hurled into the arms of Mordecai. The *consigliere* disarmed Haman, handcuffed him, tucked the warrants into a pocket of Haman's coverall and escorted him to Angelo who stood in the debris plucking twigs from his hair.

Benny Deuce gaped at Haman and said: "It's the head plumber."

"It's the inquisitor general," Mordecai said.

"It's *il buffone,*" Serafina said.

Raphael craned his neck toward the hole in the ceiling where smiling Carlo Peccato looked down, his head against the sun. Carlo waved and disappeared as sunlight flooded the room.

"It's a sign from heaven that Saint Peccato done got his halo back," Raphael said.

But Angelo contemplated Haman, turned thumbs down and said, "It's tough shit."

Haman's eyes widened.

"Haven't you seen any Mafia movies?" he said. "You can't whack, ice or otherwise terminate an FBI agent. That's not playing the game."

Angelo nodded to Mordecai who took Haman to an adjoining room where they waited while Angelo dismissed everyone except Benny Deuce. However Jonah hid behind the wrecked table and peeked at Angelo who conferred with Benny Deuce on a sofa.

"The plumber's right," Angelo said. "I never seen a Mafia movie where a *goombah* whacked an FBI guy even when he had it comin' like this plumber."

Benny Deuce propped his hand under his chin and after a long pause said, *"Sì."*

Angelo tapped the arrest warrants he had taken from Haman. "You ever heard of Judge Roy Bean?"

"I stood in front of a lotta judges but never him. Maybe he's new like a political anointment."

Angelo studied the warrants.

"The signatures and the other blanks is all filled out in the same handwritin'."

"Maybe the judge done it all because his secretary was off today—had her period. "

"And maybe this plumber ain't kosher. Mordecai tells me this guy is a loose *cannone.*"

"So they won't miss him if he joined all them other parties of the second part I took care of."

"Every hit you been on for Don Topo nobody never found no body. That's quality control." Benny Deuce blushed.

"Zero defects is my motto."

"How many punks you put away?"

Benny Deuce began counting on his fingers. When he had gone through both hands nearly twice they began to tremble. "Eighteen."

"Which one was the toughest?"

"Number 9. Maybe now I give you two for the same price.

"You got anybody else?"

Angelo laughed.

"Twenty's a lucky number for you?"

Benny Deuce shrugged. "Not really."

"Don't worry. Number 19 will go *bene*."

Angelo returned Benny Deuce's .22 Beretta and they embraced.

"Anything else on your mind?"

"With all due respect two things. First is Raphael, the guy I told you about who was an actin' pastor when I brung him here. He wants to be chaplain for the brothers."

"How long is his sermons?"

"He says only five minutes."

"Hired. What's the second?"

"*Il gatto* behind the table. You mind if he keeps lookin' at you like that?"

Angelo glanced at Jonah who risked another peek and hid. "A cat can look at a don," Angelo said.

HAROLD KNOLL

CHAPTER XXIII

When Angelo awoke, the early morning sun streamed through the white curtains in Yvonne's bedroom. She lay quietly on her side of the bed and he thought she was asleep but she was staring at the ceiling.

He reached to the night table, took a mint from the small box he always carried now and chewed slowly, scratching his chin stubble. When he returned from the bathroom she had not moved.

"Do I call the undertaker or is there a last statement?"

"I'm thinking."

When she returned from the bathroom in her pink shorty nightie he scratched the crotch of his briefs. He touched her shoulder but she pushed his hand away.

"All you get is an A for potency," she said. "How do you wiseguys put it? You've been slipping me the salami and never once during those intimate moments have you ever said you love me. And when you come, over and over again, you never say, 'Oh my God!' Instead it's always 'Wow!'"

"Dons don't phone *il capo di tutti capi* and then hang up on him. He can trace the call of any punks that takes his name in vanity, Sister Sessualità used to say."

"I wish for a change you'd show a little of that respect for me. A bimbo is a bimbo is a bimbo even if she sleeps with a don."

"Now I get a feelin' of DJ blue. At least I stopped

chewin' toothpicks like you wanted."

"Congratulations. One baby step away from boorishness." She slipped on a green silk robe and said as she went to the kitchen, "I'm not serving breakfast in bed to *il imperatore omnipotente.* If he wants to eat he will have to get off his ass and get it."

At the kitchen table they had slightly burned toast, black coffee and scrambled eggs. They ate in silence and finally he took her hand across the table. When her blue eyes welled with tears he spoke carefully, "Your eyes look like the ocean off Coney Island when the garbage scows go out followed by a million sea gulls flappin' their big white wings." When she gasped he added, "But too far away for us to smell it."

She wept freely and dabbed at her reddened eyes with a tissue. "I'm worried about us," she said.

"What's to worry?"

From the counter she took a dish towel which she unfolded disclosing his 9 mm Beretta. "You left this in the bathroom. You keep it with you wherever you go and you tell me you're not worried?"

He laid the pistol beside his coffee cup. "It's just a habit like you don't go anywheres without your panties on."

"I'll let that vulgar remark pass. How can you call a helicopter commando attack nothing to worry about?"

"That was no commando. He's an FBI nut case who's history so forget him."

She started to speak again but he gently placed his index finger on her lips, removing it when she nodded. "No questions about your business, right?" she said.

"*Si.* Somebody drops in unexpected and then drops out. Since you don't know where he's swimmin' and with who they can't make you say nothin' in court."

After they dressed he said: "Can I have another cup of coffee before I go?"

At the coffee table in the living room he fished through the pockets of his jacket, took her left hand, lifted her fourth finger and tried to slip on a platinum engagement ring, its large stone glistening in the sunlight, Her eyes widened but the ring was tight.

"No *problema.* This is a No. 6, average size. Try No. 6 1/4."

"Better but still a little snug."

"Try No. 6 1/2."

"Perfect." She hugged and kissed him. "It was so nice of the jeweler to let you borrow three expensive rings just to fit me. And that diamond is so big."

"It'll cut glass. I tried it."

"But you shouldn't have spent so much." When he shrugged she said, "You did buy it, didn't you?" When he shrugged again she added, mimicking him, "No questions about my business."

"So it's a deal. We're engaged."

He got up to go but she held him back. "Engaged with two conditions. First, a Catholic church wedding—no justice of the peace." He nodded. "Second, I will not be a wiseguy's bimbo. Cheat on me once and it's over."

"You seen too many Mafia movies."

"Just keep your fly zipped when you're around other women."

"D'accordo."

He started to leave but she restrained him again. "We're going to have babies while I can still have them. I want you home nights so we can cuddle them and read them stories. I've heard children are going into kindergarten these days without even knowing their Mother Goose."

"Them little punks. Their next stop is reform school. Okay, but if our first kid's a girl we name her Serafina for *nonna mia.*"

"That's acceptable — for the baby's middle name. Her first name will be Brigid so that little Brownie never forgets she's 51 percent Irish. Also, when you can afford it we'll need a little house in the country where the children can play."

"We got a thousand acres at the monastery. Just tell

me under what tree you want it. Now I gotta go."

"Just one last condition: A gentleman is supposed to kiss his fiancée when they part."

He complied and said: "Now I got one question: Sister Sessualità used to tell me I had a head like *una melanzana* when it comes to arithmetic. So I counted up all your engagement conditions and two don't seem like the right total."

She hugged him at the door. "I'm so worried about you."

"No *problema*. Benny Deuce is training a brothers' welcoming committee for the Chicago *famiglia*. Since you're off work today be at the monastery at 2 this afternoon. We're holding a marketin' meetin' to get our bagel business rollin'."

"Me? But I don't know anything about marketing."

His index finger tapped her head. "Never forget it's broads like you who buy the bagels."

CHAPTER XXIV

Maintenance brothers carried tools and debris from the executive committee's conference room after replacing the shattered skylight and table.

"Bene," Angelo said leading conferees inside.

Mordecai set up an oak easel on which he mounted a posterboard covered with gray cloth while Angelo, Yvonne and Raphael sat at the new round table. Garibaldi lay at Angelo's feet and Jonah sat on Raphael's lap. Benny Deuce sat at the side of the room, a shotgun on his lap, and eyed the new skylight.

"Knock wood we don't have no more drop-ins," said Angelo rapping the table. "The insurance company paid all damages."

"They paid immediately and didn't even question your assertion that a meteorite had struck here?" Mordecai said.

"It helps to have an adjuster who's *un cugino*," Angelo said.

Raphael fidgeted while Mordecai adjusted the easel and cleared his throat.

"We are facing two battles," Mordecai said. "The upcoming one we're preparing for with Benny Deuce's help is the Chicago family's expected attack probably led by the turncoat former prior. But the other battle is already under way in the marketplace."

Mordecai picked up a wooden pointer as Raphael

untied and retied his rope belt. Then with a flourish of the pointer Mordecai said, "I am proud to introduce the persona of our campaign."

The pointer flicked the gray cloth off the posterboard as Raphael drew back, Yvonne applauded, Benny Deuce scratched his head and Angelo exclaimed, "Holy shit!"

The poster displayed the much enlarged rectangular front panel of a product carton. At the left was a color portrait of Raphael in brother's habit. He was smiling, wore a black yarmulke and had a short gray beard. But at the table the clean-shaven Raphael frowned. A golden Star of David filled the right side of the panel. The middle of the panel had this copy:

> RABBI RAPHAEL'S CLASSIC BAGELS: Baked in tranquility by the Penitential Brothers of Saint Peccato in their Wisconsin monastery overlooking the scenic Root River. Generous pilgrims welcome.

"But I ain't no officially certificated rabbi," Raphael said. "I ain't even got the rabbi beanie you show in my picture."

Mordecai twirled his pointer, reached into his pocket and produced the traditional black yarmulke which he placed on Raphael's head.

"I crown you king of bagels with the yarmulke I received on my bar mitzvah and never wore again. Rabbi Raphael, as attorney and *consigliere* of this family I can categorically state that you have no exposure. The back of the bagel carton will have this disclaimer in appropriately small type." He consulted a card and read:

> DISCLAIMER. Rabbi Raphael is the legal name of the chaplain of the Penitential Brothers of Saint Peccato. He does not represent himself as a Jewish clergyman.

"But I ain't got no beard like it's painted on the

picture," Raphael said.

"You look good in a beard," Angelo said. "Grow one."

"Rabbi Raphael," the chaplain said stroking his chin.

Yvonne passed a small mirror to Raphael who said, "Now the board of elders of my church will ask, 'Is Raphael also among the prophets?'"

"You get royalties on every box of Rabbi Raphael's Classic Bagels we sell," Mordecai said. "We'll just have you apply in court to change your name legally to Rabbi Raphael."

"We gotta get them bagels out *presto* under the new name," Angelo said. "How long will it take the judge to make the switch?"

"Is immediately fast enough?" Mordecai said. "I've got cousins too."

Angelo went to the poster and examined it.

"How come a box for bagels instead of the el cheapo plastic bags everybody else uses?"

Mordecai held up a handful of competitors' bags designed for six standard bagels. Then he reached into his attaché case and displayed a sample carton for Rabbi Raphael's Classic Bagels. The carton was hand made and in color. Yvonne smiled and raised her hand.

"If the bagels are in an upright freezer cabinet the glass is fogged and shoppers can hardly tell one plastic bag from another. But our box will stand out there and even more so in an open freezer."

Mordecai nodded and passed the sample box around as Angelo patted Yvonne's arm. Then Angelo held up a plastic bag and asked Mordecai: "What does the K mean on this other bakery's bag?"

"Kosher."

"You mean the bagels are the real McCoy?"

"No. It's a symbol certifying the bagels were prepared in strict conformity with Jewish dietary laws which at present ours are apparently not."

Angelo looked to Rabbi Raphael who shrugged as

Mordecai continued: "We would need a real rabbi to make a diligent inspection of our bakery to certify compliance. That I would strongly recommend so we may honestly display the K on our cartons of Rabbi Raphael's Classic Bagels."

"I don't want no rabbi workin' for the FBI plantin' bugs around here," Angelo said. "We gotta make an arrangement. Instead of a K we put an L on the package bein' that L comes right after K so at least we're close to kosher."

Mordecai who had been taking notes looked up from his legal pad, capped his fountain pen and said:

"This is not supposed to be an exercise in alphabetizing. What does the proposed L really stand for?"

"It's a secret ingredient I got from Claudio that makes our bagels taste special. So I ain't gonna let no rabbi get close to it, with all due respect to Rabbi Raphael."
Raphael started to nod and then shook his head.

"Is it your suggestion that we sell bagels that are not kosher?" Mordecai said.

"I ain't sayin' one way or the other," Angelo said. "At least we got Rabbi Raphael's picture on the box. You done good with the marketin', Brother Mordecai. Now *per favore* get them boxes printed up *presto.*"

"But with all due respect what's that secret ingredient?" Mordecai said.

Angelo stood up and for want of a gavel tapped the butt of his Beretta on the table.

"When the don feels the time is right he'll put that on the agenda again. But now ain't the right time. The sitdown is over."

After the meeting Benny Deuce invited Raphael for a beer at the monastery tavern. In a booth Benny Deuce made wet circles on the table with the bottom of his glass.

"You got somethin' on your mind, Brother Benny?"

Benny Deuce traced the circles with his finger. "In my head I'm goin' around like them circles. Since I come here everything's changed. In Brooklyn I was top man in my profession. Then I come out here to do a job for my don and find out he wants to do a job on me. So since you're chaplain and all—"

"Yes, and I thank you kindly because it sure beats janitor work. Now what's your problem?"

"Well Rabbi, in my line of work I don't get to confession too often and I got a lot piled up in here." Benny Deuce rapped his massive chest.

"When was your last confession?"

"My first communion. Since then I done things would make Sister Sessualità do a skip tracin' on me and when she found me—"

"But Brother Angelo says you and your work is a role model for the whole family."

"That's just the problem and specially since I always got paid good for what I done."

Raphael leaned close to Benny Deuce. "Brother Benny, you just whisper your secret in my ear. If I can hear it the Lord can hear it too. Like the Good Book says, 'He that covereth his sins shall not prosper: but whoso confesseth and forsaketh *them* shall have mercy.'"

"You ain't wearin' a wire, is you?"

Raphael shook his head. "My lips is sealed unless you tell me to unzip them."

Benny Deuce furrowed his brow and stared far beyond the monastery walls.

"What are you doin', Brother Benny?"

"Thinkin' and it's the toughest work." He tapped his head and then his mouth. "In my profession it's safer to keep the words up here than down there. Maybe I take a rain check but I give you a down payment on the confession."

He placed a coin in Raphael's hand.

"What's this for?"

"When I was a hungry little punk in Brooklyn I used to stick my finger in the return coin slot of every pay phone in the neighborhood. The small change that people forgot bought me a coupla hot dogs a day. It's a sinful habit and when I fished out a pay phone quarter the other day I figured

I'd better hand it back." Mordecai approached.

"Sorry to interrupt, Benny Deuce, but your students are waiting for you in the woods for their next lesson on the firing range."

As Benny Deuce left with Mordecai, Raphael said: "Remember Ecclesiastes 11:1: 'Cast thy bread upon the waters: for thou shalt find it after many days.'"

But Benny Deuce shuddered as he left saying: "It ain't the bread that I'm worryin' about comin' back."

CHAPTER XXV

"Per *amore del cielo,* shoot!" Angelo cried.

He slammed the rear door of a refrigerated monastery bakery van that he, Mordecai and Benny Deuce had just loaded. But Raphael, gripping the pistol in both hands, hesitated.

"It ain't *when* I should shoot but *where.* Do I shoot the hind end first or contrariwise the front end?"

Simultaneously Mordecai cried "Front!" while Benny Deuce cried "Rear!" When Raphael still wavered, Angelo mediated by pressing his index finger on the pistol muzzle and swinging the barrel toward the van's side. It displayed in four colors a much enlarged front panel of the new bagel box.

Angelo removed his finger just in time as Raphael squeezed the trigger. A water jet fed by a large reservoir atop the plastic pistol sprayed the van's side and then the rest of the vehicle as Raphael circled it. Finally Garibaldi and Jonah inspected the van and completed the job.

"You sure there's no holy water in the chapel?" Angelo said,

"The holy water jug was empty when I refilled it because there ain't no priest here no more to bless it," Raphael said.

Angelo cupped a hand near his mouth. "Remember we gotta keep it on the q.t. that you're puttin' seltzer in the jug. At least it bubbles."

Mordecai glanced at his watch. "We'll be late if we don't hurry."

"I didn't say the prayer yet," Raphael said.

Mordecai frowned but Angelo nodded. While Raphael's companions waited with folded arms, he raised his hands to the sullen sky.

"Lord, as you sent a chariot of fire to deliver your prophet unto heaven, likewise dispatch this chariot so it may deliver our bagels—mini, regular and deli size—to our customers. Verily and amen."

"I told you he's pithy," Benny Deuce whispered to Angelo.

"Show respect when you talk about our chaplain," Angelo whispered back.

As Angelo, Mordecai and Benny Deuce headed for the van, Raphael said:

"Don Angelo, I done my part and I'd be obliged if you done somethin' for me."

Mordecai sighed but Angelo said: "Big or little?"

"Little." When Angelo nodded, Raphael said, "I ask with all due respect that you give me my button please like the Mafia movies say I'm entitled to."

Angelo looked to Mordecai who said: "His evidence is of course presumptive but we are bound to accept it in the absence of rebuttal." When Angelo frowned, Mordecai said, "Rabbi Raphael is entitled."

Then Angelo hugged Raphael. "Rabbi Raphael, we'll have a big ceremony later but now the don gives you your button anyway like you asked."

Angelo checked his habit, lifted it, undid his trouser belt, opened a switchblade and sliced off the button above his fly which Raphael accepted reverently.

"This should straighten you out," Angelo said as he Mordecai and Benny Deuce boarded the van.

With both hands Raphael held the button up to the light and said: "A two-holer."

As the van descended the private road and

disappeared, a brother sentry approached with a shotgun and gave thumbs-up. He wore a gunbelt with a holstered 9 mm Beretta. On his left arm was a black cloth band with BDR in white. His thin lips smiled.

"*Grazie* for the prayer, Padre."

"You one of Brother Benny's students?"

"*Si*. Brother Edoardo Coli." He indicated his armband. "Benny Deuce's Rangers."

"Brother Edoardo, why do you wear the color of mournin' on your sleeve?"

"That's for the souls of the Chicago *goombata* dumb enough to come up here."

Mordecai drove as Benny Deuce rode shotgun at the van's passenger window and Angelo sat in the middle scanning the town road. He fingered the plastic Saint Peccato statue on the dashboard.

"I got a feelin' they'll try somethin' different. Benny Deuce, you bring my black tool bag?"

"Si *padrone*. Behind the seat."

"Then everybody watch your rearview mirrors," Angelo said.

When they reached the crest of a hill, Mordecai cried: "I can see a long way back and we have a tail!"

"They pulled outa the woods but are hangin' back about a half mile," Benny Deuce said.

"Black late model car?" Angelo said.

"Yeah," Benny Deuce said. "Can't tell the make from here Nothin' else behind us."

Angelo cocked his Beretta and replaced it in his waistband.

"The diner where Yvonne works is just ahead before we get to I94," Angelo said. "They got a big parkin' lot that shouldn't be crowded this early in the mornin'. Now *per favore* do like the don tells you."

Mordecai parked the van on the far side of the lot near the exit. Before the trio got out, Benny Deuce stowed the shotgun under a gunnysack on the floor. He cocked his

Beretta and replaced it in his waistband while Mordecai checked his revolver and returned it to his shoulder holster. Mordecai locked the van as Angelo studied the left outside rearview mirror.

"The punks are pullin' in now," Angelo said. "Just walk casual to the diner."

After the black car parked near the van, four men in black fedoras and black suits got out and strolled toward the diner. They were observed by the brothers through a diner booth window.

"Patently perpetrators," Mordecai said.

"Dirty rats," Benny Deuce said.

Angelo, sitting beside Mordecai facing Benny Deuce, tapped a spoon on the table.

"Let's have some decorum. Them punks is just tryin' to do a contract. It's only business except we'll give them the business first."

"It ain't that," Benny Deuce said. "It's their car. It's new and black and expensive but it ain't U.S. of A. It's a Jap Lexus. Them *goombata* ain't got no respect for tradition." The disrespectful quartet studiously ignored Angelo and his companions and sat at a booth on the other side of the diner.

When Yvonne arrived to take the brothers' order, Angelo whispered in her ear and her hand shook as she poured coffee. Then she touched his hand and nodded. "Remember," he said aloud, "doughnuts, not bagels."

She tried to smile but wept away a tear as she served the doughnuts. Then she walked slowly toward the four who kept their fedoras on. Angelo held his pistol on his lap and chewed a mint.

The leader wore a purple and white striped shirt and red tie. While Yvonne was distributing menus he grabbed her left hand.

"Hey, look at that ring! Biggest rhinestone I ever seen! When you and your farmer boyfriend get hitched he'll give you a brass ring he got from the merry-go-round."

She smiled and withdrew her hand.

"Gentlemen, I'll just pour your coffee while you choose from all the nice breakfasts we have for you."

A short chap with greasy red hair patted her thigh and she grinned at him. As he continued his advances, his three associates watched appreciatively.

Yvonne tilted the heavy thermos splashing hot coffee across carrot-top's arm and then lurched against him. Coffee sloshed across the table and onto the laps of all four. The leader jumped up yelling, "You dumb cunt!"

But turning on the tears, Yvonne gestured with the empty thermos toward carrot-top.
"He jogged my arm."

The leader reached over and slapped the culprit whose head jerked back while his face turned the color of his hair.

"Cherubino, you dickhead, always you think about pussy and not business. That's why you never got your button. Now apologize to the lady."
"*Scusi,*" came the mumbled reply as Yvonne smiled again.

"Boys," she said, "it's all my fault. Your breakfasts are on the house. Order whatever you want and eat hearty."

Meanwhile Angelo, who fiercely chewed a mint as he watched this encounter, used Yvonne's diversion to slip out of the diner and run to the bakery van. He removed a heavy black nylon duffel and went to the nearby Lexus LS400. The car had Illinois plates and these bumper stickers: Front—"Respect Authority"; rear—"Support Your Local Police."

Angelo donned thin white cotton gloves and in one minute unlocked the driver's door. He noted an M16 under a raincoat on the front passenger seat and a shotgun under a blanket on the rear seat. After two minutes inside he got out, relocked the door and spent another two minutes under the rear end. Then he replaced the duffel in the bakery van while the Chicago quartet was enjoying a big free breakfast.

At his booth Angelo left two $20 bills to cover everybody's breakfast, consulted his watch, drained his coffee cup and followed by Mordecai and Benny Deuce stopped at the front counter where Yvonne handed them mints.

"You done good," Angelo whispered and shrugged when she whispered: "For God's sake be careful."

She watched while they strolled to the bakery van and got in as the Chicago quartet rushed past her.

"Baby, I left 50 bucks on the table for you," said the leader tipping his hat which had a blue cock's feather in the hatband. "I come back here again."

"That would be a big surprise," she said.

The van was moving slowly out of the parking lot as the quartet got into their Lexus and followed on the town road. Both vehicles had rounded a curve and were out of sight when an explosion rattled the diner's windows and a black and orange fireball burst over the trees.

Yvonne and the diner's owner watched through the window as a leather-covered steering wheel and a black fender plummeted into the parking lot. Then a black fedora with a blue cock's feather in the hatband wobbled in the breeze and fell just outside the window.

"What happened?" the owner said.

"Four of your customers just had a bad attack of heartburn," she said.

CHAPTER XXVI

The rapping on the window irritated Irving Q. Farchadat leaning over his desk. "How many times do I have to tell you to pull down those blinds when you come in for dictation?" he said standing and zipping up his fly. "Now get your tochis out there and tell those three shnorrers to get lost."

The brunette secretary who worked under him composed herself and rubbed her back as she went toward the door. "Mamma told me never to work for a goddamn Theory X organization."

She bent to adjust her pantyhose as a toby mug sailed over her head and smashed on the wall.

Meanwhile inside the reception room of the corporate offices of Farchadat Food Emporium, Angelo, Mordecai and Benny Deuce shifted uncomfortably on a sagging velveteen sofa.

"Did you see what I seen in the window?" said Benny Deuce holding a bulging leather briefcase.

"That's what happened to them four punks in the Jap car," Angelo said. When Benny Deuce scratched his head, Angelo added, "The big bang."

"Huh?"

"Study up on your cosmology."

Their discourse was interrupted by the secretary who slammed the inner office door behind her and dropped the shattered mug into the wastebasket. She sat at her desk, shook her empty water carafe, produced a bottle of gin, emptied it into the carafe and poured herself a half tumbler.

"To the liberation of women!" she said draining the glass.

"*Salute!*" Angelo said.

She blinked at the trio in their gray habit and jerked a blue-lacquered thumbnail at the inner sanctum.

"Fathers, my boss is one mean matzo ball so you better get your butts outa here before he calls security."

Angelo leaned over her desk and addressed her ample cleavage.

"*Signorina,* we ain't workin' no scam. We just come here to let Irv in on a legit business deal. So *per favore* tell *il padrone magnifico* that the Penitentiary Brothers of Saint Peccato is here to pay respect."

"Ain't it Penitential?"

Angelo shrugged.

"Same difference etymologically. Just tell him we're here to give him the business."

She patted her shapely bottom.

"He's better at givin' it than takin' it but I'll give it a whirl."

The inner office door was lettered "KEEP OUT!" in gold foil. With a trembling hand she turned the knob and entered shutting the door behind her.

The trio heard a booming voice within punctuated by shattering. When the secretary returned she slammed the door behind her, again dropped a broken toby mug into the wastebasket and smoothed her hair.

"Mr. Farchadat regrets he is unable to consider your kind proposal at this time and requests you to please vacate the premises at your earliest convenience if not sooner."

She slipped into a black cloth coat and wistfully stroked the worn sleeve.

"Where are you goin'?" Angelo said.

"To buy two more toby mugs for the asshole because

he just assassinated Attila the Hun and Ivan the Terrible."

"Mr. Farchadat is obviously an aficionado," Mordecai said.

She snuggled her chin into the frayed collar of her coat.

"I've called the son of a bitch a lot of things but I wouldn't go so far as to call him that."

Angelo patted her shoulder.

"Il *padrone grande* don't treat you right. What is your name, *signorina*?"

"Purità and I catch your drift because I'm *una siciliana*." She blotted a tear with her sleeve. "It ain't easy lovin' a guy who just uses you for a bimbo and a garbage can for his neuroses. Confidentially, his wife is tryin' to take him to the cleaners before she'll give him a divorce."

She rested her fragrant dark head on Angelo's shoulder and wept.

Benny Deuce patted her arm. "Don Angelo, we gotta help this *compaesana*."

Mordecai held her hand. "In my professional opinion your situation could be ameliorated if we informed said tortfeasor that his conduct is actionable. In short, he is playing a mug's game." She stopped crying and frowned at Mordecai.

Angelo patted her head. *"Signorina* Purità, you heard it right from the mouth of *consigliere mio*. So just get your cute *culo* out to wherever while we make an arrangement for you."

She smiled, kissed each brother on the cheek and with a joyful *"Ciao!"* departed as Benny Deuce waved.

Then from the wastebasket he retrieved the broken pottery and admired the bright colors. "What a pair of jugs," he said.

"Forget pulchritude," Angelo said striding toward the inner door and crying *"Avanti!"*

Irv Farchadat, chairman, president and chief executive officer of Farchadat Food Emporium, coughed after washing down a capsule with seltzer from a crystal goblet.

Then he stood, clasped his hands over his head, did a bump and grind and sat.

He shook his head at a large ebony tray on his desk displaying serried ranks of prescription medications, the entire vitamin alphabet and a jumbo bottle of enteric aspirin. An air cleaner purred on one end of his desk while a vaporizer hissed on the other.

Next he swiveled, his black leather judge's chair to face a long shelf of toby mugs lacking two in the middle. He was reaching for the mug of a little girl with blonde sausage curls, seated aghast, mouth open, blue eyes staring, when the inner office door flew open. Three strangers in gray habit marched in and ducked as the mug flew over their heads and smashed against the wall.

Angelo picked up the pieces and frowned at the child's innocent face. "Tsk tsk," he said.

"I can't tolerate a *tsitser*," Farchadat said.

"Who is she?"

"If it's any of your business—Little Miss Muffet."

"Why did you whack that little angel?"

"Can the megillah. Normally shnorrers get tossed out on their tochis, but since you're priests I'll make an exception and take one church raffle ticket if under $1."

He produced a bulging crocodile wallet secured crosswise by two stout rubber bands which he carefully removed. Then he extracted a $1 bill, replaced the rubber bands, pocketed the wallet, patted it, folded the bill into a one-inch square and flipped it to Angelo saying: "I expect change."

Angelo flipped the bill back. *"Grazie mille* but we ain't here to take your generous donation. We come to help you make more dough."

Farchadat indicated a black leather sofa. His desk was mounted on a six-inch platform from which he looked down on the seated visitors. He smoothed his long gray hair fringing a shiny pate and stroked his bushy mustache and short pepper-and-salt beard.

"Let me guess. You're selling protection from the Vatican's Wiseguy Security Service."

When Angelo shook his head and laughed Farchadat said: "Or maybe you're here to sell me a lifetime subscription to the *Goombata Journal*." Again Angelo shook his head. "Then it must be an accident insurance policy issued by the Cosa Nostra Assurance Society."

Before Farchadat could continue there was a timid knock on the door and a little man entered wearing a lavender track suit with matching tennies. "Your secretary said you wanted me, Irv."

"I did not, you *shmendrick!* Now jog your tochis out of here!"

The jogger fled as Hitler's mug smashed on the closing door.

Farchadat popped another capsule, gulped seltzer, stood, did another bump and grind and sat. Noting his visitors' puzzlement he said: "I like seltzer with a twist. That *nebech* you just saw is my security chief, my brother-in-law and another item on my tsuris list. So if you've come to sell me problems I'm overstocked and can sell them to you by the gross below wholesale yet."

Angelo dismissed this with a smile and a wave of his hand.

"I'm Brother Angelo and this is Brother Mordecai and Brother Benedetto. We just come for a friendly sitdown to talk business. Why fight when we can make an arrangement to solve your problems? But first what's with the jogger?"

Farchadat got up, moved the medicine tray aside and sat on his elevated desk.

"My wife figured all her brother had to do as security guy was to chase shoplifters. But some are husky momzerim who object to an insensitive little honky that tries to pry cans of Spam out of their pockets. Now before we talk arrangements let's hear what the hell it is you're really selling."

Angelo pointed to Mordecai who pointed to Benny

Deuce who reached into the briefcase on his lap. He produced a box of bagels, which he passed along to Angelo who tossed it to Farchadat who fumbled and dropped the box on his desk.

"You need coachin' in pitchin' and catchin'," Angelo said.

"But I'm a damn good slugger."

Farchadat sat behind his desk to examine the box. His index finger touched Raphael's portrait and the Mogen David. Then Farchadat tried to read the rabbinical disclaimer in small type, swiveled with his back to the visitors, squinted through a magnifying glass, replaced the lens in his pocket and swiveled facing them.

"In one word: *bubkes!* I've heard about your Mafia monastery, your grifter saint and the pilgrims you've fleeced. A monk peddling bagels saw me a while back and I told him no dice unless he came up with both the slotting allowance and maintenance fee for the privilege of occupying my display space. Also I told him to chop his wholesale price."

"He was my *cugino* Claudio and I'm here to negotiate for him."

"How come he isn't here?"

"Somebody made the mistake of whackin' him."

"May he rest in peace but I'm not budging one inch on the deal. Enough with the smoke and mirrors. You've got a *shvartz* rabbi who isn't really a rabbi and bagels with the Mogen David but the box has a cockamamie L instead of a K."

Angelo got up smiling, flicked open his switchblade and approached Farchadat who grabbed a toby mug for a preemptive strike.

But Angelo spread a linen napkin on the desk. Then he slit open one end of the bagel carton, removed a bagel, slit it and placed the halves face up on the napkin. Benny Deuce produced a small jar of strawberry jam which Angelo spread with the knife while Farchadat lowered the mug, patted its head and returned it to the toby lineup. With a tissue Angelo wiped the blade, pocketed it, bowed and said, "*Per favore* enjoy. We toasted them bagels for you."

Farchadat chewed slowly as he studied the bagel box. "So what's with the L? Does it mean Litvak or lox?"

"You're enjoying our secret ingredient that'll keep your customers comin' back for more. So how's the bagel?"

Farchadat finished the bagel and headed for the door. "I've eaten worse."

"Per *favore* before we go—one question," Angelo said. "Why did you whack Little Miss Muffet?"

"Because in kindergarten the little bitch added another tsuris to my list—arachnophobia. Now follow me."

He led them across an alley to the Farchadat Food Emporium supermarket. "My flagship store, No. 1 of 10 we have in Wisconsin."

Angelo nodded to Benny Deuce who went to their parked van.

In the store's frozen food section Farchadat indicated the open horizontal cabinets where row on row of bagels were displayed in plastic bags.

"Here in the coffins as we call them we have six brands of regular two-ounce bagels including our house brand. In the uprights which are the closed cabinets we have three brands of the large three-ounce deli bagels plus two brands of the one-ounce mini bagels. That already makes 11 purchase choices for the shopper who just wants a bagel for breakfast. And you drop in with an unknown brand I'm supposed to squeeze in. You show me a space and I'll put your bagels there—guaranteed. "

Farchadat folded his arms and smiled.

Angelo beckoned Mordecai who opened a trash bag. "You're a reasonable man and I like the way you negotiate," Angelo said. Farchadat backed away from the horizontal display as Benny Deuce approached wheeling a hand truck bearing cases of Rabbi Raphael's Classic Bagels. "Now *per favore* tell me which of the six kinds of regular bagels is the dog brand?"

"Our house brand. It tastes like shit and moves like molasses in the winter but I get it cheap."

Angelo flicked an index finger at the house brand. Mordecai dumped the entire section into the trash bag as Benny Deuce waited and Farchadat gaped.

"Stop!" Farchadat cried.

But Angelo gently placed his hand on Farchadat's shoulder. "Patience *amico mio* . A guarantee is a guarantee is a guarantee. We don't do no strong-arm stuff. We do marketing for a win-win situation for you and us. Brother Mordecai, you got any more room in the bag?" Mordecai nodded. "Then Irv, we took care of the No. 6 brand. Which is the No. 5?"

Farchadat tossed a bag of bagels to Angelo and said: "Can you believe broccoli-flavored bagels? And their other flavors are succotash and cauliflower."

Angelo indicated the monastery's cases Benny Deuce waited to unpack.

"Our bagels are the real thing I used to bake when I was a kid in Brooklyn. That's why we call 'em Rabbi Raphael's Classy Bagels."

Farchadat peered at a case. "You mean Classic, don't you?"

Angelo shrugged. "Same difference etymologically."

After Mordecai had dumped the No. 5 brand, Angelo nodded to Benny Deuce who filled the display's gap with the monastery's bagels.

"I'm still waiting to hear about the win-win deal," Farchadat said. "Those companies paid me slotting and maintenance bucks for exposure here."

"That's a minor detail you can work out, Irv. We give you today's whole supply free. Our wholesale price to you we make 5 percent less than your No. 1 brand. Starting tomorrow we put Rabbi Raphael in person in your store to sign autographs and bullshit with the customers." Farchadat raised both hands.

"Hold it. I need demonstrators giving out free samples

more than I need a goyisher rabbi who's a *shvartzer* yet."

"*Camerata mio*, you get both. Sure you get demos. We got the Penitentiary Sisters of Saint Peccato to give away free bagels with cream cheese all week."

"That's Penitential," Farchadat said.

"Etymologically the same difference. Also our public relations director wants to pay you respect. Brother Benedetto, let go of the truck and shake hands with *il padrone*."

Farchadat reluctantly extended his hand which Benny Deuce grabbed in one hamlike paw and released when Farchadat winced.

"We assign Brother Benedetto as our goodwill ambassador to stand outside your front door, hand out cents-off coupons and look in customers' bags when they leave to make sure they bought the right bagels. And look at his smile." Benny Deuce grinned as Angelo said, "A mouth fulla crowns all gold."

"That's extortion, isn't it?" Farchadat said.

"Indeed a court would probably regard that as prima facie evidence for extortion," Mordecai said.

"But I like your MO," Farchadat said using both hands to pump Benny Deuce's paw.

Angelo shook Farchadat's hand and whispered, "For the clincher we go back to your office for a sitdown. We make you a deal nobody else can because we take care not only of your business problems but your personal ones too."

"You're a mensh," Farchadat said.

As they started to leave, Farchadat's brother-in-law jogged by. "Any security matters I can handle, Irv?"

Angelo took the loaded trash bag from Mordecai and thrust it into the little man's hands. "Yeah," Angelo said. "I saw a poor people's food bank in the neighborhood. You jog yourself over there and deliver them bagels compliments of the Farchadat Food Emporium." When the security chief hesitated, Farchadat cried, "Golem, do like the gentleman says!"

While Mordecai and Benny Deuce waited in the van, Angelo had his sitdown with Farchadat. As Angelo was leaving, a smiling Farchadat again selected the toby mug he had last picked up.

"Hey, *amico mio!*" he called.

Angelo turned as Farchadat tossed the mug underhand. Angelo caught the mug and pocketed it as Farchadat said: "Your fielding isn't bad." "And your pitchin' is gettin' better."

As the van was homeward bound on I94 Angelo said: "We got not only his No. 1 store but the other nine in Wisconsin if we take care of one business problem for Irv plus one personal problem. The business problem is holdups in the store and purse snatchin' in the parkin' lot from little old ladies we gotta protect."

"What's the personal problem?" Mordecai said.

"We gotta motivate his wife to settle the divorce reasonable so he can marry his secretary Purità."

"But the young lady didn't even indicate they were engaged," Mordecai said.

"That'll be a nice surprise for both of them."

"I have no recollection that we have an order of nuns at the monastery as you indicated to Mr. Farchadat. When was this established?"

"As of right now."

Angelo displayed the toby mug he had received. "What position did this guy play for Cleveland?"

Mordecai examined the mug. "Why that's Mahatma Gandhi."

"*Si.* Irv told me this guy used to be with the Indians."

CHAPTER XXVII

Mrs. Candy Farchadat frowned but plunged into her lawyer's starched white boxer shorts while he yawned and tugged at her black string bikini panties.

After a few bounces on a heart-shaped water bed in a leading Madison hotel they lay back spent but unfulfilled.

"When I addressed your bar, Uriah, was I awesome or just exciting?" she said stroking a solitary wisp of hair on his 34 chest.

"E pluribus unum."

"Oh Uriah, you're such an impressive attorney even when I don't understand you. Do you think an implant would enhance my boobies?"

He adjusted his gold-rimmed glasses. *"De minimis non curat lex."*

She kissed his furrowed forehead. "You're so flattering. You're the smartest divorce lawyer in Wisconsin. Would you like seconds?"

He sighed and shook his head. "A recess is indicated."

"Do you really think we can zap Mr. K'nocker?"

"I am employing my infallible DP strategy."

"Uriah, I love it when you flog your smarts."

"Flaunt is the intended term my dear and the abbreviation signifies the first principle of litigation—deep pockets and the pursuit thereof."

She cuddled against him.

"After you put the kibosh on my penal servitude to this *bulvon* and we're both rich you'll keep your promise?"

"Recapitulate."

She stroked his due process. "All the other times we went to bed you promised you'd divorce your wife, marry me and we'd honeymoon in Las Vegas."

"The rule of res gestae would make such a declaration admissible as an excited utterance."

"You sure seemed excited every time you made that promise."

"And we enjoy attorney-client privilege," he said stroking her personal chattel.

She lay back and contemplated her bangs in the mirrored ceiling.

Meanwhile during the brightly lit hearing the adjoining room door had been silently unlocked and opened just enough for a camcorder lens and microphone. Then the door opened wide to admit Angelo, Mordecai and Benny Deuce in gray habits. Angelo continued to tape while the pair sat in bed clutching the sheet around them.

Switching off, Angelo passed the camcorder to Mordecai and applauded while Benny Deuce locked the door and drew his Beretta.

"Bravo!" Angelo cried. "The good news is we don't need no retakes."

"Objection!" Candy's attorney said. "Breach of attorney-client privilege."

Angelo consulted Mordecai who said: "Objection overruled. Learned counsel is out of his breeches."

Candy dropped her side of the sheet and shook both fists at her attorney as the penitential trio stared.

"You fink! Don't you know three dago hitmen when you see them?"

"Objection!" Mordecai said. "I'm Jewish."

But Candy continued to cross-examine her attorney. You're working for Irv too, aren't you? I'll kick your demurrer into next week, you goddamn shyster!"

"Mrs. Farchadat, objection please. I assert categorically I am not a party to this balls-up."

"*Silenzio!*" Angelo said. "Ain't nobody gonna ask what the bad news is? Then I tell you anyway. You don't get no Hollywood contract."

Candy drew the sheet around her again and said: "End the megillah already. What do you torpedoes want?"

Angelo nodded to Benny Deuce who put away his pistol.

"We represent *il Signor* Farchadat who wishes no harm to you *signora* or to your lawyer. Me and my brothers come here from our monastery to have a little sitdown so you can get your freedom, fly away like *il cuccu* and be happy."

As the three brothers applauded, she tossed off the sheet, got out of bed and in slow motion wiggled into a red silk robe. Then she flicked her finger at some chairs. "You want a sitdown so park your butts over there." Turning to her attorney she said, "Johnny-Come-Prematurely, I'll handle these negotiations so shut up."

The attorney complied, dressed and sat on the edge of the bed, his briefcase beside him. Candy strode to Angelo and tapped him on the chest. "How much is my goddamn freedom going to cost me?"

But her perspiring attorney interrupted and handed his briefcase to Angelo saying: "You people prefer liquidity of course. Herein I have $5,000 in small unmarked bills I carry for such contingencies I tender this honorarium in exchange for the tape in your camcorder. It's a simple quid pro quo between professionals. Agreed?"

But Angelo tossed the briefcase back. "That offer does not show respect."

"Asshole!" Candy yelled at her attorney. "Haven't you ever seen a Mafia movie?"

"*Consigliere mio*, ain't that extortion which is illegal?" Angelo asked Mordecai who nodded. "For what we got in the camcorder we don't want $5,000, $10,000 or even $100,000."

"Then with all due respect what the fuck do you want for that tape?" Candy said.

Angelo bowed and smiled. *"Signora* Farchadat, we are Penitentiary Brothers of Saint Peccato and we pay you respect by first asking you *per favore* put on your dress because we took solemn vows to stay away from pussy. In fact we even gotta report a wet dream when we go to confession."

She slipped into a black sheath dress hemmed eight inches above the knee. Then giving her attorney the finger she sat in a chair beside Angelo.

"Before we start, shouldn't it be Penitential?" she said.

"Same difference etymologically. Now if you and your lawyer okay the offer I make then I promise as a man of honor to burn this tape and not make or send copies to his wife, to the divorce judge, to the State Supreme Court that regulates lawyers' licenses, to his law partners and to the media."

Candy moved closer to Angelo, put her hand on his shoulder and said: "Keep talkin'."

Angelo cleared his throat as he watched her reaction. "No *problema.* You have no children so no custody fight. You just accept *il Signor* Farchadat's generous offer of $25,000 in cash and the nice new red Ford Escort he bought you last year. You take your clothes and other personal stuff. You take your four cats and their four litter boxes and you move out *immediatamente. Finito."*

She slapped Angelo on the shoulder and was winding up to do more when Benny Deuce intervened.

"Bullshit!" she cried struggling in Benny Deuce's hold. Irv is a fuckin' millionaire!"

But her attorney approached, stopping outside the range of her flailing arms. "My considered opinion is that the good brother has achieved an apparently equitable balance of interests which it may be prudent to entertain. Therefore to put it in the vernacular, you win one and you lose one."

When Angelo nodded, Benny Deuce released Candy

who grabbed her purse and stared coldly at the four men.

"You win," she told Angelo. Then confronting her attorney she said, "And since you charge for our time in bed, here's your fuckin' fee!" She swung her purse which smacked his jaw sending him sprawling across the rumpled bed. "If you dare to send me a fuckin' bill I'll cut your balls off and mail 'em to your wife!" While her attorney staggered to his feet helped by Angelo and Benny Deuce, Candy wept and said, "The clock's tickin' for this gal who's a three-time loser with husbands."

Angelo hugged her. "*Signora*, next time will be lucky for you. I was an orphan but now I'm *il padrone* of a big family."

He handed her a handkerchief and she blew her nose loudly. Then she kissed him on the cheek and said before leaving: "Why didn't I meet you five years ago? I could have been the meatballs in your pasta."

Her attorney gingerly touched his aching jaw. "No billable hours from her tonight and she even committed misfeasance in bed."

But Angelo patted his arm. "Cheer up. *Consigliere mio* will back me when I say you just done a nice matzo by servin' *la signora* pro boner."

HAROLD KNOLL

CHAPTER XXVIII

"They look boorish," Angelo whispered to Benny In white smocks, Angelo and Benny Deuce arranged packaged ground beef at the rear of the Farchadat supermarket.

Approaching were two young black men wearing black athletic jackets, black jeans, black baseball caps bills reversed and black hightop basketball shoes. The pair's swagger deteriorated into an anxious shuffle along deserted aisles.

It was 11:05 p.m. just after closing. The last customers had left, the door locking behind them. Directly outside at the wheel of a battered sedan, engine running, a young black man stared into the supermarket.

"Here comes the two *melanzane* lookin' for role models," Angelo whispered. "I take the tall husky one who looks disadvantaged."

"And I take the little skinny one who looks underprivileged."

Limping slightly, the store manager carried a sturdy canvas sack with the evening's receipts toward his office near the meat department. He winked as he passed Angelo and Benny Deuce.

"*Stupidaggine,*" Angelo whispered to Benny Deuce. "They don't even wear masks."

The two robbers flourished .357 magnum stainless steel revolvers with six-inch barrels and accosted the manager as he reached the office door. Above it were two conspicuous TV security cameras. When the pair saw themselves in the security mirror beside the door they touched their faces in alarm. "Where is them ski hats at?" said the tall one.

"You was supposed to brung them," said his short colleague as the manager waited calmly, money sack on the floor and hands up.

"Then grab the bread what we come for," the tall one said .

"Bakery department over there," said the puzzled colleague waving his revolver in the indicated direction.

"Your *padrone* means for you to pick up the bag," Angelo said as he and Benny Deuce raised their hands.

But the leader pointed his revolver at Angelo. "Keep out of this, honky motherfucker." Then to his colleague he said, "Do like the honky done told you."

When the short man bent to comply he fumbled with the sack and dropped his revolver. It fired into a wall knocking down a framed public service poster which struck the leader on the head and sent him staggering against his partner. When they recovered they raised their hands as Angelo and Benny Deuce displayed their Berettas.

The manager disarmed the robbers, passed their revolvers to Angelo and Benny Deuce, retrieved the money sack and entered his office where he placed the sack in the safe. Angelo and Benny Deuce ushered the robbers into the office and shut the door.

"I'll wait in the store while you do what you have to," the manager told Angelo. "Also I'd feel better if you'd let me borrow a piece in case their driver came in looking for them."

Angelo handed over a revolver which the manager checked spinning the cylinder. "Are you sure you know how to use it?" Angelo said.

The manager tapped his hip. "When I came home from Vietnam I brought back a wooden leg and a sound knowledge of small arms."

He stood guard outside the office door while Benny

Deuce relieved the robbers of their wallets and passed these to Angelo. "Now *per favore* you two gentlemen kneel and bow," Angelo said.

The trembling pair obeyed but the leader protested.

"Hey man! You ain't gonna do to us what they do in Mafia movies is you?"

Angelo pressed the muzzle of his pistol against the back of the leader's neck while Benny Deuce followed suit with the colleague. When the Berettas were cocked this prompted both robbers to scream for mercy.

Then Angelo stroked the leader's neck with the pistol barrel. "You're only seconds away from *il inferno* unless you listen good to a proposition I make to you."

"I'm listenin'. Like you folks says, 'It's nothin' personal because it's just business.'"

"*Si*. We just wanna motivate you to do a little favor for *il Signor* Farchadat who owns the store."

"Sure man. We like to do favors for rich white folks." The leader nudged his colleague. "Don't we?"

"Cool," the colleague said.

"*Bene*. You tell all your underprivileged and disadvantaged friends that when they want to knock over a supermarket they stay away from any Farchadat store. *Capisci?*"

"You mean we don't have to give up a profitable life of crime?"

"Live and let live is my philosophy. But if a Farchadat store does get knocked over or a little old lady is hassled in a Farchadat parkin' lot, then we come lookin' for you and your little *compagno*." Angelo removed the drivers' licenses from the wallets but returned the wallets. "We know who you are and where you live. You accept my proposition?"

Both men agreed emphatically.

"My public relations director will take you back to your car and will explain to your driver what I told you. If the driver don't accept the proposition you know what will happen to all of you."

"That motherfucker will accept!"

Angelo nodded to Benny Deuce who began to escort the two robbers through the store as the manager watched.

"Wait!" Angelo said.

Both robbers stopped and raised their hands.

"You walkin' on the sign you shot down. Maybe you turn it over and see what it says."

The leader complied and held up the sign.

"*Bene.* Now take it along for a souvenir."

The public service message adorned with a simpleton's face said, "Have a Nice Day."

CHAPTER XXIX

The rickety speakers' stand swayed in the wind in the Farchadat Food Emporium parking lot. When a high school band marched past, Irv Farchadat covertly twitched a pinkie in time with the bouncing bosom of a strutting drum majorette.

Behind him a 50-foot banner was stretched above the store's entrance displaying Raphael's smiling portrait with this message: "CONSUME NEW RABBI RAPHAEL'S CLASSIC BAGELS."

Beside him stood his secretary Purità impatiently drumming the fingers of her left hand on the two-by-four rail. Brilliant morning sunshine failed to highlight her new ring whose tiny stone barely twinkled in its silver setting. She covered the ring with her right hand and said: "Irv, who's going to be your secretary after we get married?"

He patted Purità's arm without taking his eyes off the drum majorette who wiggled in her white satin hot pants.

"Remember our agreement, my little hamantash. You'll be queen of Farchadat Manor while I'm king of the Farchadat Food Emporium."

"My *mentore* Don Angelo would feel you didn't show him and me respect if you balled that teenybopper you're drooling over. And my el cheapo ring don't show respect neither."

Farchadat stroked his bald head, smoothing bygone

locks

"I resigned from pussy poaching when I gave you that ring which is in good taste and which I positively will not exchange. Right now I prefer to concentrate my executive attention on our new promotion for Rabbi Raphael's Classic Bagels."

Dismissing this with a shrug, Purità continued, "Tomorrow we interview my aunt Innocentà who just quit as secretary to her bishop in Chicago."

"What did she quit for?"

"He went to jail for child molestation."

"She was all shook up?"

"No he was because she's the strict Catholic that blew the whistle on him. She says a priest's dick is only for peeing while a married man's dick is only for giving his wife babies when he ain't peeing."

Farchadat scratched his crotch. "How old is this lady?"

"Aunt Innocentà is 60—old enough to help you concentrate on the bagel and not on the hole."

"An old maid?"

"How did you guess?" Purità paused to throw a kiss to Angelo who stood nearby with the monastery delegation. "The Penitential Brothers of Saint Peccato saved your salami and I'm glad you won't forget to save their bagels."

Farchadat placed his hand on her left hand and straightened the ring. "My little knish, even if your aunt can type I'll still hire her."

"Irv, as long as you're in a good mood I've got a problem. This cold wind is blowin' through my old cloth coat like toilet paper. You Jews all have relatives in the fur business."

Farchadat fingered her coat and smiled. "I hear you loud and clear. Get yourself down to my cousin Myron who's got a boutique on the far west side. Pick out anything you want, tell him I sent you and that he's to bill me remembering that I never pay retail."

Purità kissed him on the cheek. "Oh Irv, my first mink coat."

"Who's talking mink? He's in the sweater business."

As Farchadat bent to rub his bruised ankle, a little old lady pedaled an ancient balloon-tired bike through the crowd scattering irate spectators. She wore a white jumpsuit, cervical collar, hightop basketball shoes and black cyclist's helmet topped with a white streamer. Bolted upright over the rear wheel was a bulletin board on which a hand-lettered poster proclaimed: "STAMP OUT GENTEELISM!"

She leaned the bike against the speakers' stand, removed black leather cyclist's gloves and slapped them on Angelo's back. "What's up, sonny?"

When Angelo jerked his thumb at the 50-foot banner, she shielded her eyes against the morning sun and swiveled to scan the message. "What's with the syntax?"

"Liquor and cigarettes but not bagels yet, *signora.*"

She reached into her backpack, brandished an 18-inch oak ruler with a brass edge and as he flinched, whacked him across the shoulders.

"A teacher!" he cried.

"Why belabor the obvious? I'm a retired UW-Madison English professor." She jabbed the ruler toward the banner. "NEW is a vague modifier here. What's new—the rabbi or the bagels?"

"Both, *signora.*"

"And what's with CONSUME? Isn't EAT acceptable?"

"That was the idea of *consigliere mio.*" Angelo indicated Mordecai who disappeared in the crowd when she brandished her ruler at him. "He said CONSUME is more respectable than EAT."

"Pettifogger! Are they shooting a movie here or is all this tsimmes for real?"

"We're introducing Rabbi Raphael's Classic Bagels baked by the Penitentiary Brothers of Saint Peccato."

"You deserve another *klop* for that Freudian slip but forget it. How come a *shvartz* rabbi who's the eponym for

Jewish bagels baked by dagos in a church yet? These are the fruits of cultural diversity?"

"Testing *uno, due, tre,*" Farchadat said over the loudspeakers.

"Why this pidgin Italian from you people? If I ever hear an entire grammatically correct Italian sentence I'll plotz."

"But I like Italian pigeons," Angelo said. Then to change the subject so he could listen to Farchadat's imminent speech, Angelo added, "Did you hurt your neck, *signora?*"

"Father, I thought you'd never ask. I just wear this sucker to keep my chin up and maintain a positive attitude. Now where's the free lunch?"

Angelo bowed and indicated the entrance.

She trundled her bike into the store despite employees' protests and collided with the jogging security director. He reeled into a display of spaghetti sauce jars splashing the floor with glass and goo.

Meanwhile Farchadat addressed the crowd: "Rabbi Raphael's Classic Bagels are a revolutionary breakthrough in baking. Demand the bagel box with Rabbi Raphael's picture. It's your unconditional no-strings-attached guarantee that you're getting what you deserve."

Mordecai applauded and told Angelo, "He should have been a lawyer."

Encouraged by Angelo, Raphael hesitantly mounted the speakers' stand. Farchadat introduced him to vigorous applause from some black spectators. Raphael adjusted his yarmulke and said:

"Brothers and sisters, it ain't so long ago that when white folks invited a black man to climb up onto a platform he was likely to get a rope." He mopped his brow with a blue bandanna. "So until Mr. Farchadat gave me this microphone I wasn't sure what kind of reception I'd get."

Another round of applause from black and white spectators reassured him.

"Brothers and sisters, hurry inside for your free bagels with cream cheese and coffee. When you sink your pearly whites into my bagels you break down the walls between races and religions. We all goin' to the same place upstairs." He jabbed an upright finger. "So munch in good health. Shalom!"

A bearded Hasid in the crowd waved his black hat and cried. "You ain't a *shvartz* shnorrer! You're a *tzaddik*!"

He joined the stampede into the store led by Farchadat, Purità and Raphael. Following were Yvonne and Serafina in the gray habit of the Penitential Sisters of Saint Peccato.

Angelo scanned the parking lot, smiled and handed fliers to Benny Deuce. "Me and Mordecai will go inside to help. You give these out here when the customers show up. Tell 'em to use the coupon to buy one and get one free."

After Angelo and Mordecai entered the store, a middle-aged man with a butch haircut and a pot belly was stopped at the door by Benny Deuce, who grabbed the customer's shoulder and stuffed a flier into his hand.

"But Father, I already usher Sundays, go to bingo Tuesdays and stone the abortion clinic Thursdays."

"Relax. See that coupon? Get your ass inside, buy a box of them bagels and get another box free. Just in case I'll be inspectin' your grocery bag when you come out."

"Hey! You're not in our parish, the Church of Our Insufferable Mother. What kinda swindle is this?"

Benny Deuce shoved the customer against the wall. "Penitentiary Brothers of Saint Peccato, that's who we are, smart ass, and fuck the etymology."

The customer shrank further against the wall. "That's the Mafia outfit, ain't it? I'll buy whatever you say but I just got one question: What's a bagel?"

Meanwhile in the store, customers jammed the aisles around the frozen food section. Farchadat had returned to his office while his fiancée Purità joined Serafina and Yvonne in serving at a long buffet table.

"*Nipotino mio* Angelo says you're *una siciliana*," Serafina told Purità.

"Don Angelo is a wonderful guy," Purità said. "He made an arrangement with my boss Irv so that now we're engaged when I used to be just a bimbo here."

Serafina handed her a bagel with cream cheese.

"You make a good wife for a Jewish man. He knows how to make money and you know how to cook. I make you No. 3 Penitential Sister of Saint Peccato."

"But I don't want to be a nun."

"First eat, then talk."

The Hasid alternately sampled a bagel with cream cheese in one hand and a bagel with lox in the other. Between bites the Hasid said:

"Rabbi, we got a regional meeting of Hasidim coming up next week in Madison and I personally invite you to be with us. We pray, dance, sing, eat and drink."

"Sounds like a gospel meetin'. I'll go if you buy enough of my bagels to have there for a nosh."

"Rabbi, like the Talmud says, 'A bagel gladdens the heart and ain't bad with peanut butter neither.'"

The little old lady cyclist rapped Raphael's shoulder and indicated the Hasid heading for the checkout with an armful of bagel boxes. "How come that Holy Roller gets lox with his free bagel while the rest of us just get cream cheese?"

Raphael interrupted dispensation of bagels and autographs. "For the same reason in the wilderness when manna fell from heaven: Moses got sour cream on his blueberry blintzes while the children of Israel only got potato blintzes with salt."

She stamped her hightop shoe on his foot. "I know my Torah and that's not in it."

"You're talkin' Torah but I'm talkin' Midrash," Raphael said stepping back.

The little old lady shook her head. "I can't believe a *shvartzer* with so much learning."

"You never heard of the lost tribe of Falasha in Africa where it's one big suntan parlor?"

But she stared so intently at his crotch that he covered it with both hands and backed away more.

"Unzip, show me the salami and I'll believe."

"Another doubtin' Thomas," he said turning his back on her and resuming his chores.

Nearby Angelo greeted the middle-aged man with the butch haircut who seemed dazed.

"Father, where can I get two boxes of bagels?" he said clutching the coupon flier.

"Try a free one," Angelo said handing him a bagel with cream cheese.

The man bit down hard and produced a broken tooth.

"I'm sorry about that, *signor*," Angelo said. "We bake 'em real crispy. Just tell Farchadat's and their insurance will pay the dentist."

But the man seized two boxes of bagels, backed away and said over his shoulder: "It had to come out sometime. I just want to get by the bouncer at the door."

After the man left, Mordecai said, "Benny Deuce has done well in flier distribution."

Angelo indicated the trembling customers who were queuing to buy Rabbi Raphael's Classic Bagels while glancing anxiously toward the store entrance. "He done better than that," Angelo said. "Benny Deuce has mastered the first principle of marketing."

"Which is?"

"Get close to your customers."

When a black man in navy homburg and British warm reached into the open freezer for a competitor's bagels, Raphael took his hand away and shook it. "Brother, why is you passin' up my bagels for a honky brand? Don't you see my picture on my affirmative action bagels?"

Raphael's hand was abruptly removed by the customer, who selected his preferred brand and said, "I am not your brother."

As the customer shouldered his way toward the front, Raphael called: "Be sure to say *ciao* to our public relations director."

Five minutes later the customer returned, tossed the competitive bagels back into the freezer, grabbed two boxes of Rabbi Raphael's Classic Bagels and said, "Uncle Tom!"

Farchadat stopped by, clapped Angelo on the shoulder and indicated the void in the freezer. "Fantastic!" Farchadat said. "You've sold out your bagels and the day isn't done yet. Your worries are over."

"We still got some Chicago competitors to take care of. Another van is comin' soon from our bakery to restock. Irv, we've taken care of your business and personal problems. Now with all due respect we ask you to keep your part of the deal and give our bagels special treatment in all 10 of your Wisconsin stores."

"Done! What's your marketing secret?"

Angelo nodded to Benny Deuce who had come in for more fliers. Benny Deuce scratched his head and adjusted the Beretta in his waistband, which bulged inside his habit.

"I guess it ain't what you say that counts," he said

"Then what is it?" Farchadat said.

Benny Deuce tapped his waistband. "It's how you say it."

CHAPTER XXX

A wheezing Hyundai climbed the hill reaching the monastery's entrance as the engine died.

Brother Edoardo Coli cocked his shotgun and motioned to the driver who came out with hands up. He was a bearded little man wearing a white yarmulke.

"Don't shoot!" he said. "I'm a friend of Angelo Panettorio."

"Name?"

"Reilly."

When Brother Edoardo frowned, the bagel baker added, "Before that it was Flynn but I changed it to Reilly so I'd be able to answer what my name was before I changed it."

"And before Flynn?"

"What else—Cohen."

When Reilly was ushered inside, Angelo took him to the monastery's tavern where Angelo had beer and Reilly a glass of tea with lemon and two lumps of sugar which he dipped in the tea and sucked.

"Don Topo told me where you were before he left for St. Petersburg," Reilly said. "All my Jewish customers have also moved to Florida so I retired and stopped by just to say hello to my dear friend. Then I go on to California to live with my son and his family who are kindly making room for me in the basement. For room and board all I have to do is babysit my grandchildren, mow the lawn and walk the dog."

Angelo ordered another glass of tea for Reilly with bagels, lox and cream cheese.

"Great bagels," Reilly said between bites. "They have a certain *je ne sais quoi* I never tasted before."

"*Grazie.* I was taught by a master. Now forget about goin' to California."

"I'm not?"

Angelo hugged his old friend. "Reilly, I make an arrangement for you. I need a bakery manager because I got too much to do already as *il padrone* here. I pay you good and throw in meals and a nice room not in the basement. We call you Brother Reilly and give you a Saint Peccato potato sack like I'm wearin'."

"But I'm Jewish."

"So is our *consigliere.* He got his button and you'll get yours."

"But in the Mafia movies it's a closed shop for southern Italians only."

"*Landsman mio*, at the monastery things ain't always what they seem. A deal?"

"*L'chayim!*" they said clicking glasses.

"So what do you want me to do first?" Reilly said.

"When I worked in your bakery you was always handy fixin' machinery."

Reilly held out his hands wrinkled but steady. "I like to tinker and this is my digital equipment. Near the end of WWII I graduated from NYU in mechanical engineering, got drafted and the army in its wisdom put me in baking school. I've been in the dough ever since."

"*Benissimo!* First you do a rush job producing our *Ciao* Bagel. But you also gotta tinker with a special machine me and our maintenance brothers put together to serve them bagels. The machine still don't work right."

"A vending machine for bagels?"

Angelo laughed. "Yeah. Fast food." He summoned Benny Deuce. "Get Reilly squared away. Give him everything he asks for *presto* especially for the *Ciao* Bagel project. And make sure he gets a whole bunch of tea bags, lemons and sugar lumps."

"I'm honored you're starting me with such a big program, a regular crash project."

"Yeah. Crash is a good word for it."

Reilly finished eating and said, "But I just have one question. I hope you bake bagels here the way I taught you —no cockamamie flavors and always boiling before baking for a crispy crust. Can you imagine some bakeries skip boiling to make the crust like a wet dishrag?"

"I know a customer at Farchadat's supermarket in Madison who can guarantee our bagels are al dente. We make 'em your way. Like the lady poet says, 'A bagel is a bagel is a bagel.'"

Reilly laughed.

"She referred to roses but it's applicable." Then he stroked his beard and felt the edge of Angelo's coarse sleeve. "To think I'll be wearing a monk's habit and running a bakery in a monastery. Angelo, so many changes are happening to me."

Benny Deuce blanched as he escorted Reilly out and heard Angelo say: "Just ask Brother Benedetto: When you come to this place you're never the same again."

Alone in the Saint Peccato Chapel, Benny Deuce knelt in a front pew and consulted his little black book by flickering candlelight from the altar. The title page said: "BENEDETTO ORSO'S BEST HITS." He nodded as he thumbed through the entries scrawled in pencil, one page for each subject. Finally he came to the last name, No. 19. It was J. Edgar Haman, the first federal agent to make the list. Benny's hands began to shake.

When he heard the pew creak, he turned Beretta in hand to confront Carlo Peccato kneeling beside him. Benny Deuce replaced the pistol in his waistband. But when he tried to stuff the little black book into his habit the book kept falling out.

Carlo Peccato picked the book off the floor as Benny

Deuce covered his face with his hands.

"*Per favore?*" Carlo asked. Benny Deuce slumped in the pew and nodded. "Santa Rosalia!" Carlo said as he turned the pages.

Benny Deuce clasped his knees. "It's true, Santo Peccato. I done all them things."

"*Figlio mio*, for shame! You done 19 and the last one's a fed?"

"At least forgive that one because 9 is my unlucky number."

"Benedetto, you expect me to forgive such dishonorable stuff? I been in court often enough to know what we got here in your notebook constitutes a material breach of contract. And the Mustache Pete who runs your *famiglia* back in Brooklyn never called you in for a sitdown?"

"Don Topo paid me to get rid of them guys and I done it. The end justifies the meanness. I also done that last contract for Don Angelo the same way."

"How you done it is the question."

"Couldn't you hear my confession, Santo Peccato?"

"Why me?"

"Because you're a no-good *goombah* like me and I'm too ashamed to go to a priest. If I get whacked myself when the Chicago *famiglia* comes here, then I go straight to *il inferno*. I can hear *mamma mia* in Palermo hangin' out the window with the wash and screamin', 'Benedetto's swimmin' with the fishes, not flyin' with the angels!'"

Carlo Peccato got up, clasped his hands behind his back, paced up and down the chapel aisle, glanced at Benny Deuce after each lap and muttered. Finally, he returned to the pew.

"I direct dialed *il cielo* and got your answer loud and clear: You gotta repent for your rottenness. You gotta wash your sins in divine detergent. In the final analysis you gotta get an ethereal enema."

Benny Deuce stood and waved his hands imploringly. "With all due respect Santo Peccato, I dunno what the fuck you're sayin'."

"I'm sayin you gotta get real talk therapy so I give you a referral. I'm sayin' go see our Chaplain Melanzana."

But Benny Deuce raised his hand. "I brung Rabbi Raphael here myself when he was just a church janitor. Since we got an affirmative action *famiglia,* Don Angelo opened the books and gave Rabbi Raphael the button. So it don't show respect to call a made rabbi an eggplant."

"*Scusi,*" Carlo Peccato said blowing out the altar candles and plunging the chapel into darkness. "Even a saint can make a venial sin."

Rabbi Raphael trudged through the monastery woods followed closely by Benny Deuce.

"And like you just told me you was well paid for what you done to all them innocent folks?" Raphael said glancing back.

"*Si,* but they wasn't so innocent, Rabbi. Some of them was welshers who skipped out. One punk kidnapped the statue of Our Irrepressible Lady with 20 grand in $100 bills the parish taped on for carryin' in her feast day parade. And one son of a bitch never visited his *mamma* in the Little Sisters of Ninfomania Nursing Home—not even on Mother's Day. But you gotta understand, Rabbi. It's like the Mafia movies. In the family, business is business and if you don't do a contract you get the business yourself."

They sat on a fallen tree.

"You didn't do it to no kids?" Raphael said.

Benny Deuce drew himself up proudly. "Not even with the irrespectable way them teenagers behave today."

"No ladies?"

"Never. Don Topo said for me to just motivate *la Signora* Serafina to talk. But instead she motivated me to get the hell out of her house and stay out." He rubbed his lower back. "The chiropractor says my sack-of-iliac still needs more treatment for what that little old lady done to me."

"Better I don't hear too much of the details because that might make me accessible after the fact like I seen on the TV cop movies," Raphael said. He cupped a hand to his ear and listened to the tranquil sounds of the forest. "The birds of the air and the critters on the ground all live in peace like one big Disney cartoon. So it won't be easy for the Lord to forgive you for what you done since a human bean is supposed to have more smarts than animals."

Benny Deuce rubbed the sleeve of his habit over his sweaty face.

"I forgot to mention a legal complication I asked Brother Mordecai about. He's a Jew lawyer and they got the most moxie. I asked if hypodermically speakin' a guy does wrong if he takes a lot of dough in a contract to do somethin' one way and he does it but kinda in another way because he thunk his way was better. Brother Mordecai looked real serious and said that constitutes a moot case."

"It sure constitutes moot to me. And you dumped them victims where?"

"Congeniality, Wisconsin. Could you just ask the big *padrone* in the sky would he make an arrangement for me?"

Raphael held out his hands, bowed, closed his eyes and prayed silently, lips moving. When he looked up smiling, Benny Deuce smiled too.

"The Lord declares you is forgiven even if it is a moot case, Brother Benny."

Benny Deuce clapped Raphael on the back. Raphael would have been hurled to the ground had he not gripped the fallen tree with both hands.

"Che bello!" Benny Deuce cried.

"But the Lord got two questions. No. 1: He never heard of Congeniality, Wisconsin and can't find it on his official state road map. No. 2: If Congeniality exists, why in heaven's name did you pick such a godforsaken spot to dump them victims when you coulda picked the usual places in Brooklyn like Canarsie or Bath Beach?"

Benny Deuce looked up to an inquisitive crow on an overhead branch, cogitated slowly with wrinkled brow and smiled when his shoulder received the bird's calling card.

Then he saluted the crow, flicked off the blob and said:

"It's as plain as this crapola. Answer No. 1: Yes there is a Congeniality, Wisconsin. It's way up north as far as you can go on State Highway 13 in Bayfield County without gettin' your feet wet in Lake Superior. I wound up there one time because I was lost. On my first hit I was skip tracin' a horseplayer who left Brooklyn owin' Don Topo a lotta vigorish. I'm drivin' in Wisconsin on I94 tailin' the guy north-northwest when I takes a wrong turn off the freeway at Eau Claire and goes due north to Congeniality."

"How come you goes a couple hundred miles outa your way and don't notice nothin'?"

"I'm a member of the Audubon Society and I was kinda preoccupied because it was my Big Day in May."

Raphael lifted his yarmulke to scratch his head. "You was rejoicin' because you was gonna commit the sin of which you confessed?"

"No Rabbi. My Big Day is countin' as many different birds as I can in one day. I was up to 99 already since I seen a lotta odd birds on the freeway and was hopin' to get past that number when I spotted a Canada jay. I ain't never seen that one before bein' accustomed to his cousin the U.S. of A. blue jay. So I'm passin' through this little town when their cop stops me and writes two tickets.

"'What for?' I says since I ain't doin' nothin' illegal. And the cop says, 'One ticket for jay watchin' and one ticket for drivin' with New York plates, both of which is illegal in Congeniality.' When I ask for travel directions back to the freeway he says, 'We don't give no travel directions to strangers.' Then a crowd of shitkickers starts throwin' tomatoes and stuff at my Thunderbird egged on by the cop."

"You was angry?"

"Hell no. I was happy because I found the perfect place and when I caught up with that horseplayer that's where I dumped him. That punk and all the other parties of the second part was never heard from again no matter how long their wives and girlfriends left the porch light on."

"But you ain't said why Congeniality ain't on the state map."

"Them locals don't believe in advertising."

Raphael cupped a hand to his ear again. "The Lord got a P.S. He says you still feel guilty about a sin you done over and over, a sin hurtin' you so bad it was like puttin' a contract on yourself."

Benny Deuce smacked his palm on his forehead as Raphael cried: "Confess!"

"It's fettuccine Alfredo! I love it better than sex. I see a plateful of pasta loaded with eggs and cream and butter and cheese and I gotta have it even though I know it's like pourin' cement into my heart."

Raphael cast his eyes heavenward and cried: "Lord, you done heard it right from the horse's mouth. Brother Benny's talkin' big CO—a cholesterol orgy. Is this miserable sinner's confession now kosher with you?"

He closed his eyes, cupped an ear toward the ceiling once more and finally smiled. "Brother Benny, thus saieth the Lord: 'You was lost but now you is saved. I stamp your confession with my golden seal what has a big K on it. Go in peace.' The Lord got another P.S. which is: 'When them Chicago Philistines descend on this holy place with their chariots and war horses, you got my permission to smite them dudes hip and thigh.' Thus endeth the Lord's sound bite."

"*Grazie*, Rabbi."

As they returned to the monastery, Raphael fingered his yarmulke. "Us rabbis carries a heap of secrets in here. There ain't nothin' that could happen at this monastery that would surprise me now."

CHAPTER XXXI

The new black Porsche 968 lurched back and forth with grinding gears as the driver jerked the six-speed shifter. Irv Farchadat strode through the clinic parking lot at Madison and rapped on the driver's window. The driver reluctantly lowered it a few inches and said, "Irv, I've got to deliver twins so make it snappy."

"Shut if off, Sy. Never forget who put you through medical school after I promised Dad on his deathbed to look after my kid brother who was always the favorite."

Dr. Sy Farchadat fumbled with the ignition key and switched off. Then after a frantic search he found the door lock switch. Irv Farchadat eased into the passenger seat.

"What's with the shifting mishmosh? A Caddy isn't good enough for my brother the doctor?"

"Not for an OB who needs a fast car to get to the hospital and deliver twins."

Irv Farchadat peered at the instrument panel. "You need a 180 mph speedometer on the autobahn, not the Beltline."

Sy started to bang his fist on the dashboard but drew back and banged his head instead. "It's not the car that worries me. It's what waiting for me at the hospital."

"What's to worry? You've delivered twins before."

"There's a lawyer in the family who's unreasonable and aggressive."

"The husband?"

"No, the patient. She's a first-time mother who demands an easy delivery and healthy blond fraternal newborns with no forcep marks or she'll ream my ass. Lately I've been spending more time in court than in my office. OB is malpractice city. Who needs stress? I'll become a dermatologist with nights and weekends off because those patients never bleed, never get well and never die. Now I've got to get to the hospital."

Sy reached for the ignition but Irv snatched the keys . "I got a friend who needs your services Saturday night."

"You know I won't do abortions for your bimbos. Use a condom next time."

"Sy, this is your chance to do a big *mitzvah*. My friend is a monk who heads up a monastery in the country. They're nice quiet guys who just want to say their rosaries and do whatever monks do, but they expect to be hit Saturday night by Chicago gangsters. My friend was tipped off by a cousin in Chicago who has a brother-in-law in that mob. So all my friend asks is backup medical attention provided on the spot and on the q.t."

Sy grabbed for the car keys but his brother held them out of reach.

"What kind of mishegaas is this?" Sy said. "You've seen too many Mafia movies. Gunshot wounds have to be reported. That monastery needs an emergency care practitioner not an OB man so why ask me?"

"Because you've had more malpractice suits filed against you than any other quack I know."

"So? It goes with the OB territory."

"It also proves you can handle stress. Maybe you'll just have to slap on a few Band-Aids and I'll be there with my girlfriend to help you."

Sy wrested the keys from Irv and started the engine. "Get out! I won't do it!"

Irv opened the passenger door and smiled. "Sy, you seem to forget your malpractice insurance premium comes due soon and you asked me for a loan."

The obstetrician jiggled the shifter. "Give me a call when you need me. I'll have just the job for you as my physician's assistant."

The little old lady in the white jumpsuit, black cyclist's helmet with white streamer, cervical collar and hightop basketball shoes pushed her old balloon-tired bike into the Punkinville micro mall. The proprietor dozed in a rocker beside the unlit potbellied stove.

When the door's brass bell jangled he reluctantly opened one eye, noted the cyclist wheeling her bike toward him and opened both eyes wide.

"Sonny, where's the monastery?" she said bumping the front wheel on his foot.

"The who?"

"Get the bat guano out of your ears. How many monsteries do you have in the vicinity anyway?"

He studied her bike and jumpsuit both peppered with road dirt.

"You can't bring that bike in here."

"Stuff the non sequiturs. I repeat, Mr. Shmegegge, where is the Penitential Brothers of Saint Peccato Monastery?"

The proprietor rubbed his eyes and slapped himself so hard on the cheek he nearly fell on the floor.

"For a second there I thought I was dreaming you was my mother-in-law from Hustler making good her threat to move in with me and my family. But she doesn't travel by bike being partial to a broom. Where are you from anyway?"

"Madison. I just got off I94."

"It's illegal to ride a bike on the freeway."

"Only if they catch you, hayseed."

The lanky proprietor rose slowly out of his rocker and stared down at her. "You mean to tell me your bicycle outdistanced the state troopers?"

"Affirmative. It's easy if you hitch a ride behind an 18-wheeler with a macho driver. Now let's can the Q&A which I can't abide from a yokel off his rocker."

"Lady, you better stay away from that monastery. The talk around town is that Armageddon is going to break out there Saturday night when the Chicago Mafia raid the place. But our constable is a law and order man who'll have the perpetrators under lock and key quicker than you can say—"

"Shut up. Go see a dentist to treat your diarrhea of the mouth. I've already heard about the raid and you still haven't told me how to get to the monastery."

When the proprietor saw the message on the bulletin board bolted on the bike's rear wheel he said, "Why does your placard anathematize genteelism?"

She rolled the bike over his feet and headed for the door.

"Mind my extremities!" he cried while she replied: "Fowler, save us!"

She nearly collided with a little old lady wearing a parka and unbuckled galoshes despite the dry early spring day The proprietor wagged a bony finger at the old lady in the parka.

"Go on about your business, Mabel, and peruse the seed packets some other time."

But Mabel was already chatting with the cyclist as they reached the sidewalk.

"You're on a pilgrimage to the shrine of Saint Peccato?" Mabel asked.

"Pilgrimage bullshit. That saint's only a grifter if you catch my drift. It's just that I love those dago bagels with the *shvartz* rabbi's picture on the box. It's a triumph of multiculturism."

"But can't you just get them bagels at a store?"

"You're not in the loop. I heard this morning at the launderette in Madison from a yenta whose cousin in Chicago said the Mafia there is coming up to the monastery Saturday night to give the brothers a *klop* and take over bagel production."

"What difference does it make who manufactures

them goldurn bagels?"

But the cyclist tapped her belly.

"The difference is here. The brothers' secret ingredient makes their bagels taste better than fettuccine Alfredo with no guilt. If the Chicago gonifs take over, the brothers will flush their secret formula down the toilet. Then we'll all get heartburn from Rabbi Raphael's Classic Bagels because they'll taste like the competition—shit."

Mabel hoisted a foot onto the no-parking sign and briskly fastened her gaolsh buckles.

"I've been a closet feminist long enough in this male chauvinist town. It's time us gals became proactive. You're welcome to crash at my pad and we'll drive up to the monastery to help the brothers. We've got to protect them bagels. But just one teeny question."

"As long as it's relevant," said the cyclist buckling the chin strap of her helmet.

"What in tarnation is a bagel?"

The pickup's siren gurgled and died as the vehicle skidded to a stop on bald tires in the no-parking zone at the Royal Punkin Motel entrance.

Doubled up behind the wheel was a wizened gentleman in a soiled white cowboy hat. His face and hands were plastered with Band-Aids. He vainly kicked black plastic cowboy boots against the jammed driver's door and contemplated the open window.

But he shook his head, gritted his teeth and gingerly wriggled past the passenger seat where an upright roll of four-point barbed wire awaited delivery elsewhere. As the roll plucked at his frayed red, white and blue striped shirt, he said: "I get the doggoned point."

One kick sufficed to propel the passenger door onto the sidewalk. He replaced the door lettered Punkinville Feed and Seed Store, securing it with another kick. When this caused the siren atop the cab to resume gurgling, he rounded it into submission with his fist.

Then he began to pin a chrome-plated six-pointed star

on his shirt. But he winced, faced the pickup for privacy, unbuttoned his shirt, applied a Band-Aid to his chest, rebuttoned and completed pinning. The star said: "Punkinville Constable. *Res ipsa loquitur*." Seeking a Latin scrap for the pioneer village's motto, Silas Q. Punkin III had petitioned a departing circuit judge on horseback. The judge surveyed the solitary mud street and false front general store-cum-saloon, scribbled on an old envelope, tossed it to Punkin and collected $1 in coins.

"It's all Greek to me," Punkin said.

"The thing speaks for itself," said the judge galloping off and splattering him.

"But what does it mean?" Punkin cried.

Now the constable hesitated at the entrance but finally wiped his boots on the welcome mat. He ambled into the lobby, boots squeaking, a simulated mother-of-pearl handled .45 single-action revolver wobbling in a plastic holster on his hip. He tiptoed to the desk in a vain attempt to stop squeaking and greeted the dwarf manager perched on a tall stool who was doing a crossword puzzle with a fountain pen.

Without looking up the manager asked: "What's GNU, African antelope, three letters?"

When the constable's dim bulb failed to flicker, the manager glanced over each shoulder and beckoned him. The constable moved so close to the desk that his cowboy hat brim crested the wave in the manager's permed hair. The manager capped his pen and tucked it behind the mauve handkerchief in the breast pocket of his black suit jacket. He sniffed stale beer on the constable's breath, wrinkled his nose and leaned back.

"Another lost cat?" the constable whispered going to the side of the desk as the manager shook his head.

"For once we expect more of you than rescuing stranded pussy or driving your pickup in the big Punkinville parade."

The constable rubbed his hands and beamed.

"You mean the village board is finally puttin' in our

first stop-and-go light outside my store so I can set inside and aim a radar gun through the window at traffic perpetrators?"

"Your loquacity brings to mind the Greek god of the winds, six letters. On the contrary, I was referring to a forthcoming event. It is our great opportunity to restore the Royal Punkin Motel to its former glory and to buoy this community's declining economy."

The constable snapped his fingers.

"Then the village board has okayed puttin' in that hazardous waste landfill after all, the one that'll have a heavenly glow at night for all the pilgrims to see?"

The manager sighed and put the crossword puzzle away.

"Although you're going down and I'm going across we're not interlocking. A gentleman guest that checked out today is a commercial traveler in ladies' intimate apparel. He confided that when he had passed through Chicago this week a bartender said a friend in the Mafia reported the monastery would be attacked Saturday night.

"To help clear the way for return of the pilgrims and restoration of the village's tourist revenue, we must hazard life and limb to help the Penitential Brothers of Saint Peccato. Otherwise, Punkinville will become as extinct as a New Zealand bird, three letters, MOA. Therefore I propose you deputize me so together we may fight under the banner of the Greek god of war, four letters, ARES."

By this time the constable had backed away to the front door, which he was vainly tugging when the manager said: "The door will remain locked until you hear me out and I release the nonpaying guest switch."

"Never trust the hearsay testimony of a traveling salesman that gets into ladies' drawers," the constable said.

"No sirree. I march to a different drummer."

The manager beckoned the constable who reluctantly shuffled back to the desk where the manager said: "Unless I have your immediate pledge of cooperation and am deputized instanter, I shall notify my uncle who is chairman of the Punkinville Village Board which you seem to forget employs the constable."

"But why risk your neck climbin' up that monastery hill to fight perpetrators when you can stay here snug as a flea in a dog's ear and do your crossword puzzles?"

"Like the volcanic U.S. peak, four letters, HOOD, because it's there."

The constable tugged down the brim of his cowboy hat and cleared his throat.

"Raise your right hand. Under the powers of eminent domain vested in me, I hereby deputate you to assist me in hot pursuit across municipal boundaries seeking perpetrators from Chicago also known as the Windy City. Such hot pursuit bein' legal even though it's the sheriff what otherwise got authority outside the village limits, not me."

The manager extended his hand and when the constable tried to shake it, the manager said, "The deputy's badge."

"I keep one at the store for when I deputate my cousin to sweep up after the sheriff's mounted posse that rides in the big Punkinville parade. I'll bring it by soon."

As the constable turned to have another go at the front door, the manager said, "Two final items: First, why does your cousin crave the Augean task of sweeping up after 100 horses?"

"He says it may be horseshit to you but to him it's his bread and butter. And your second item?"

"When will you arm me appropriately for the monastery mission?"

The constable dug into a hip pocket and laid a .22 derringer on the desk saying, "My backup shooter is just right for you."

But the manager drew himself up to his full height of 3 feet 10 inches. His index finger flicked the tiny weapon off the desk and into the constable's hands.

"I shall require a banger long, hard and potent—

specifically your 12 gauge double-barreled shotgun."

Early Saturday evening, Yvonne coaxed her old Toyota up the dark private road to the monastery barely reaching the entrance when a cloud of coolant burst from the hood.

Thunder rumbled in the sullen sky and rain began to fall as the car doors flew open. Yvonne and three Brownies, all in uniform, hurried into the monastery where Angelo and Serafina greeted them.

"You should not be here tonight with the kids," Angelo said.

"That's what your sentry Brother Edoardo also told me. But the car was overheating while I was driving the girls home to Punkinville from a meeting with our Girl Scout Council officials. We argued so much about the amount of money the council returns to us from our Girl Scout cookie sale that I forgot to look at the heat gauge when we were driving home. This is the only building until we get to Punkinville."

Angelo and Serafina took the group to the monastery's tavern where she served hot chocolate. Then Reilly came up from the bakery with a large platter of cookies still warm from the oven. He leaned over to Angelo and whispered:

"The *Ciao* Bagel machine is ready whenever you need it tonight."

"*Benissimo!*" Angelo said. Then Reilly announced:

"Since I've been bakery manager here I've wondered what else besides bagels we could bake for more income. So I developed these experimental cookies which have my special dough, candied fruit, pecans and white frosting. What do you girls think?"

Before the cookies disappeared, Angelo pocketed the last two. He was addressed by the tallest Brownie with the most achievement patches on her uniform sash.

"Don Angelo, we met in Yvonne's apartment when we girls were baking cookies. I'm Esmeralda Chance and you've also met my young associates Clytemnestra Tinker and Guinevere Evers. The Girl Scout Council claims we're learning free enterprise by selling their cookies, but what's to stop us from cutting a better deal selling Brother Reilly's?"

In support her two colleagues tapped their spoons on their cups.

"Good idea," Angelo said. "But we better get a second opinion from our *consigliere*."

Benny Deuce, guarding the door, fetched Mordecai.

"I've got much on my docket right now," said Mordecai whose revolver was holstered on a gun belt buckled over his habit.

But Angelo patted his shoulder. "*Per favore consigliere mio*, we need your wisdom for just one minute."

After Yvonne explained briefly, Mordecai nibbled a cookie Angelo presented.

"Without researching the matter I assume you would probably not be permitted to sell competitive cookies as Brownies even though the proceeds went to your proposed worthy venture. But it is my impression you could sell cookies under the sponsorship and brand name of another group and wearing said group's uniform."

Angelo saluted Mordecai.

"After we take care of them *goombata* tonight *per favore* make us a charter for the Junior Penitential Sisters of Saint Peccato Cookies baked here."

"I'll drink to that," Esmeralda said raising her second cup of hot chocolate.

Mordecai left to check the monastery's defenses while Benny Deuce left to inspect Yvonne' s car.

"I have AAA," she told Angelo when she accompanied him to his office. "Couldn't I just call them to look at my car?"

Benny Deuce, a Beretta secured in his rope belt, knocked and entered.

"Her engine's blown. Probably a bum head gasket."

Angelo indicated the phone and when she lifted the receiver she said: "It's dead."

"Lightning," Angelo said. "We got walky-talkies for up

here but they don't reach far."

"But I have to call the girls' mothers who'll be worried."

"No way till it's over. You go back to the tavern where Serafina's takin' good care of them little girls."

Yvonne left escorted by Benny Deuce but returned five minutes later with him, Serafina and the Brownie trio. Angelo, listening on his walky-talky to sentries' reports, looked up in surprise and switched it off, "Did you little girls run out of cookies?"

Yvonne nodded to Esmeralda who stepped forward, bowed and said, "With all due respect Don Angelo, we thank you for taking us in and watching out for us till you can get us home . "

Angelo stood and returned the bow. "*Prego*. And what can I do for you, *signorina*?"

"Can we have a sitdown?"

"Si, but we can't have it standing up."

Angelo waved the group to chairs while Esmeralda sat beside his desk. She pointed to one of the achievement patches on the sash across her pinafore.

"I'm the only one in my troop who has earned a scientific patch for studying frogs in the Punkinville pond. So I ask your permission for us Brownies to help in your infirmary in case anybody needs medical assistance tonight."

Angelo looked to Serafina and Yvonne who both nodded while the two other Brownies said: "We want to earn a scientific patch too."

"Okay," he said. "Also the infirmary is a safe place for you. Yvonne will be there to watch over you and Serafina will be on guard outside the door."

He extended his hand to Esmeralda who surprised him by kissing it. As the group was leaving, Angelo said: "Two questions *per favore Signorina* Esmeralda: First, how come you know just what to say and do here?"

Esmeralda casually buffed her fingernails on her sash. "Don Angelo, maybe it's because our motto is 'Be prepared' or maybe it's simply because I've seen a lot of Mafia movies.

Your second question *per favore?*"

"What do you want to be when you grow up?"

She reached into her small purse and produced a scuffed baseball.

"Right now I'm ready to pitch for your monastery's baseball team so we can cream any order in the church— even the Jesuits. When I grow up I'll be on the mound for the majors."

Angelo sighed and reached for his walky-talky. "Practice, practice," he said.

CHAPTER XXXII

His face sweaty, Raphael knelt backward on the kneeler in a rear pew and scraped a putty knife under the seat.

"Ain't you assbackwards?" said Angelo who had quietly entered the chapel with a 12 gauge pump shotgun.

"I didn't mean no disrespect to the Lord, Brother Angelo. But it's his temple and I'm his minister what gotta cleanse it especially with all the visitors comin' tonight."

He indicated a coffee can labeled PARK YOUR GUM HERE he had placed near the entrance.

Angelo looked around the chapel. Pews were polished, hymnals neatly arranged in racks behind the pew, carpets vacuumed.

"You done a good job in the little time you been here and your five-minute sermons don't put nobody to sleep. But I'll tell maintenance that chapel cleaning is their department, not the chaplain's. Tonight you better stay in your room where it's safe."

Raphael laid down his putty knife and holding his lower back rose groaning. He led Angelo to the sacristy, unlocked a cupboard and removed an ancient single-shot .22 rifle, split stock bound with masking tape but steel bright. He took cartridges from his pocket.

"If them Philistines from Chicago come tonight I'll be right beside you. When I was a boy in Mississippi, my daddy gave me this rifle on my twelfth birthday. Whenever a squirrel or rabbit got in my sights, we had meat that night. I was ready to defend my church with it all by myself till Brother Benny come and brung me here."

Angelo sighed. "That's some tool but maybe we find somethin' else for you to do tonight."

He hugged Raphael who said as Angelo left, "My Bible will show me what to do."

Rain pattered against the dark stained glass windows, which rattled in the thunderstorm. They flashed in the lightning and displayed Saint Francis of Assisi chatting with a wolf as three smiling piglets watched.

Alone in the chapel, Raphael moved to a front pew, knelt rifle beside him, gray head bowed, gnarled hands holding his worn King James Bible. He turned to the 91st Psalm for reassurance and to I Samuel 17:40 for guidance.

Raphael became aware of movement against his left thigh and looked at Garibaldi who lay down beside him.

As Raphael patted the shepherd's head, a meow announced the arrival of Jonah who curled up purring at Raphael's feet.

Closing the Bible, Raphael meditated and looked over his shoulder on hearing scratching. He dropped his Bible when he saw Carlo Peccato in a tattered habit in the pew directly behind, his hair crudely cropped.

Carlo scratched a pencil stub across a sheet of paper laid against a hymnal on his lap. Lips moving, he printed, stopping to ponder spelling, deleting a doubtful word for a simpler one. At the bottom of the sheet he sketched a map.

He folded the sheet, placed it in a soiled envelope, sealed and addressed it to Angelo. Below he wrote, "To be opened when I'm gone." He signed this Carlo Francis Peccato with a cross and date. Then he smiled at Raphael. "They picked a winner when they made you chaplain."

"But I was just the janitor of a little Bible church. I read real slow, write slower, preach a little and sit down. I ain't a real preacher who can go on for an hour after the end of his sermon."

Carlo sat beside Raphael and hugged him. "It takes more than a red hat to make a cardinal."

"Brother Carlo, I seen cardinals with a cowlick but never a hat."

Carlo laughed but then blessed himself.

"Rabbi, I ask you for *un perdono* to forgive me for what I said to Benny Deuce. You ain't no eggplant."

Raphael scratched his head. "Never thought I was nor broccoli neither but you is forgiven, Brother Carlo."

Tapping the envelope on his knee, Carlo said, "You heard *i briganti* are gonna hit us tonight?"

"The Philistines?"

"I dunno their names. Could be Phil or Stan. Same difference."

"The Good Book has told me how to fight them."

"*Bene.* I'll be there too with a 9 mill. We'll kick their butts but they will pierce my body. It's Armageddon."

"Amen. John 19:34 and Revelation 16:16. But I'll smite them hip and thigh. We shall overcome. The righteous always prevail. It's the law of the Medes and the Persians. I won't let the Philistines hurt you because I know who you are."

"Who am I, *figlio mio?*"

"Folks say you're a phony-baloney ghost but they never seen you in a white sheet like the KKK. I say you're Saint Carlo Peccato, son of David and a prophet of the Lord. Hallelujah!"

Carlo nodded.

"*Bene.* After tonight I won't be with you no more but I'll still be with you."

"Brother Carlo, I just can't puzzle that out."

While Garibaldi and Jonah remained silent in the pew, Carlo led Raphael to the shrine of Saint Peccato where they looked at the coffin with the sealed glass lid. Raphael peered at the figure within and then at Carlo.

"Why is you holdin' that empty beer can in there?"

"I used to collect cans to sell to the recyclers for dough to help the poor and buy me a six-pack once in awhile. Now I gotta go outside and see what's doin'. When the pilgrims hear what we done tonight they'll come back again to pay respect and leave donations. And maybe if we ever get *un siciliano* Pope he'll give me my button back."

Raphael displayed Angelo's pants button. "I got mine from Brother Angelo and you can have it."

Carlo studied the button and shrugged. "I can wait. Now *per favore* take this envelope and keep it safe on you because inside is my last will and testosterone. When I go to that big monastery in the sky you give the envelope to Brother Angelo and tell him I said to open it."

Raphael took the envelope in both hands, weighed it and carefully placed it inside his habit. "You'll let me hand over the envelope? That's a big honor. Before you go, Brother Carlo, can I ask you one question?"

"Shoot," said Carlo opening the door.

"Is you twins?"

But Carlo just called over his shoulder as he left: "Rabbi Raphael, tonight we need all the angels we can get."

A small school bus with 12 no-good pilgrims bounced over potholes as a thunderstorm swept the crushed rock town road. On the side of the bus lightning illuminated SICILIAN VESPERS PAROCHIAL SCHOOL, CHICAGO. Above was the school's coat of arms with the motto REMEMBER 1282, commemorating a pious demonstration in medieval Palermo. The coat of arms depicted gold chickpeas on a red field.

The wiry driver clamped a white-knuckle grip on the steering wheel as he glimpsed the road between futile jerks of the windshield wipers. When visibility worsened, he grabbed a rosary hanging from the rearview mirror.

Looking over the driver's shoulder was Cannibal O'Toole, sometime Prior Primattore. "Stop!" O'Toole cried. "Somebody's ahead!"

"I ain't stoppin' for no ambush!" the driver said but O'Toole jammed his size 15 shoe on the brake pedal.

The bus skidded to a stop as the driver wrestled the wheel with one hand while the other clung so hard to the rosary that it broke scattering beads on the floor.

"Why it's two little old ladies riding a bicycle in this weather," said O'Toole peering through the windshield "And that must be their car in the ditch."

The ladies had just begun to wobble away on the bicycle from a dented VW Beetle with a rear bike carrier.

When O'Toole reached for the lever to open the front door his hand was shoved away by the driver.
"Little old ladies can be trouble," the driver said.

This was confirmed by 10 heavily armed gentlemen passengers who cried: "Likewise!"

But O'Toole applied his infamous vise grip to the hand of the driver who yelped in pain. Then O'Toole opened the door, leaned out into the rain and lightning and shielded his eyes with his hand to read a poster on the bulletin board bolted upright to the bike's rear wheel. The poster said: "STAMP OUT ENTHUSE!"

O'Toole shut the door and addressed the driver who was sucking his bruised fingers: "You're right."

When the driver rammed the shift into low gear, the bus fishtailed showering the cyclists with gravel and mud. The little old lady in the cervical collar and jumpsuit swerved the bike toward the bus while Mabel, straddling the bike's rear package rack, slammed an aluminum bat against the side of the bus.

The driver veered away and the bus lumbered along the edge of the ditch, sideswiped an oak, blew a tire, shattered windshield and windows, hurled the invaders to the floor and stopped.

First to climb back into his seat was the driver who blinked against the downpour and held his aching head in his hands.

"Sister Depravazione warned me that if I brought her

bus back with one teeny scratch she would use her iron yardstick for a niblick and whack my balls. All because my cousin the don asked me to borrow him the bus to repay a favor."

Whereupon lightning flashed and showed Mabel standing on the hood and swinging the bat. As it flew through the open windshield, the driver and O'Toole ducked but the mafioso behind them didn't. Bong! went the bat and down went the mafioso leaving 11.

"Who is this casualty?" said Cannibal O'Toole.

"Izzy Speranza," the driver said. "He's from a multicultural family."

Ignoring the groaning Speranza, O'Toole buckled his championship wrestling belt around his camouflaged coverall. He attached a big cowhide holster holding his .44 magnum revolver with a six-inch barrel.

"Don't abandon me in this hellhole!" Speranza cried and lapsed into unconsciousness.

But O'Toole cried: *"Avanti!"*

He slid on rosary beads and charged to the front but the door had been jammed shut in the crash.

"Advance to the rear through the emergency exit!" he cried. "The monastery road is just ahead."

Reluctantly following, his colleagues shouted *"Deficiente!"* and *"Imbecille!"* to which O'Toole replied *"Grazie."* When they got outside, they saw the little old lady cyclists, who had drawn first blood, already riding their bike onto the monastery road.

The storm lashed O'Toole and his 10 commandos laden with firearms as they stumbled along the muddy town road. The mafiosi directed at his broad back such expletives as *"Pazzo!"* and *"Buffone!"* receiving a further *"Grazie"* from O'Toole.

Meanwhile on the steep monastery road the cyclists dismounted. The little old lady in the jumpsuit led with the handlebars while Mabel pushed from the rear.

As they meandered in the dark up the winding road, a

guttural voice cried: *"Alto!"*

A warning shot flew over their heads and smacked a tree trunk.

Brother Edoardo in a camouflaged poncho stepped onto the road from the thick woods and turned a flashlight on the two ladies and their muddy bike. He motioned with the barrel of his M16.

"Vieni qua!"

"What in tarnation is that gentleman saying?" asked Mabel from the rear.

"A Sicilian welcome," her companion said. "That sucker knows a bagel lover when he sees one."

But Brother Edoardo swung his rifle their way and said: "Why you come to this place?"

The little old lady in the jumpsuit passed the bike to Mabel, marched up to Brother Edoardo and said:

"We didn't come here to talk to the monkey. We came to see the organ grinder."

The rain beat down on the trio as Brother Edoardo's expression evolved from belligerence to puzzlement and finally to joviality.

"Hah, you make joke," he said patting the little old lady on the shoulder and calling up the road:

"Two little old ladies comin' up to see the organ grinder."

To which an unseen sentry in the dark called: "Okay."

Standing on tiptoe the little old lady patted Brother Edoardo's shoulder.

"And you'd better get your head out of your ass because the Chicago gunsels are down below."

Brother Edoardo switched on his walky-talky.

"All sentries: The gunsels are down below!" He switched off and called after the little old ladies who had resumed their climb: "What's a gunsel?"

The little old lady in the jumpsuit wiped rain and mud off her face and called back, "Ask Bogy!"

"Keep them in sight!" commanded the deputized

manager of the Royal Punkin Motel a few minutes earlier.

Perched on a sack of feed he had shlepped onto the passenger seat of the pickup, he tipped his white cowboy hat back to peer through the streaming windshield. Also wearing a white cowboy hat was the constable gripping the steering wheel as the pickup banged into potholes on the stormy town road.

"You shouldn't have dumped that roll of barb wire," the constable said.

"This cab wasn't big enough for the three of us. It was either you or the barbed wire. But now a hunter's cry, four letters, HARK! They've stopped!"

On the town road the school bus they had tailed just crashed. But when the constable braked, the pickup whirled in the mud and hurtled into the ditch out of sight in the storm.

Although the pickup remained upright, it had tilted left spilling the deputized manager onto the constable's lap. Tête-à-tête they scrutinized each other.

"You've sustained minor facial abrasions and contusions," the manager said.

"And your face got scratched and bruised but I keep a big box of Band-Aids under the seat."

After they had treated each other, the manager loaded the double-barreled shotgun while the constable spun the cyclinder of his six-shooter.

"I got lots of calls tonight from families of them three Brownies who disappeared with their leader," the constable said. "I called the monastery being it's the only place between the Brownie meeting and Punkinville but their phone got knocked out in the storm."

Since the driver's door was jammed against the ditch, the manager reared back and stomped his new tasseled cowboy boots against the passenger door, which flew off. As the rain drenched the cab's interior, the manager said: "Rallying cry, two words, eight letters, FOLLOW ME!"

Crouching in the rain with weapons ready, they

tiptoed to the bus and cautiously entered through the open rear. Snoring peacefully, the felled mafioso was slumped across his seat, a lump on his forehead.

"Cuff this gunsel to the seat!" the manager commanded.

But the constable fumbled in his pockets producing instead a golf ball, tees, a dogeared paperback *of The Old Farmer's Almanac,* tokens for the Greater Punkinville Motorcoach System and self-stick labels promoting the Punkinville Feed and Seed Store.

The manager tapped his boot on the bus floor awash with rain.

"Trash collector, six letters, MAGPIE."

The constable shrugged, plastered a label on the mafioso's forehead and read the unconscious perpetrator his rights. When the manager and constable slid back on loose rosary beads through the rear exit, the constable said: "What in the name of corn rootworm is a gunsel?"

"Haven't you ever viewed a film about pursuit of the black bird, two words, 13 letters, MALTESE FALCON?"

The constable tilted up his cowboy hat and let the driving rain refresh his face.

"Nope but I seen a peregrine falcon in downtown Milwaukee. He was over a bank building where there's a birdie motel. Howsoever I can't rightly say your question is apropos."

After they passed the bus they came upon the Beetle in the ditch, the rear engine cover sprung by the impact.

"I'm surprised to see such a reliable little vehicle immobilized," the manager said.

"Me too," said the constable. "They even got a spare engine in the trunk."

As they started up the monastery road in the dark, they heard gunfire and saw lightning illuminate 11 men ascending ahead. When the constable did an about-face, the manager pushed him off the road and into the dense woods.

"We'll climb the hill and outflank the gunsels," the manager said.

But the constable shook himself free as they stumbled over fallen tree limbs. "This ain't no time for bird-watching," he said.

The gunfire came from Brother Edoardo who emptied his M16 at the fleeting Chicago invaders. Then he retreated a short distance up the monastery road calling in the alarm on his walky-talky. But his shots had gone high through the trees overhanging the road, showering the invaders with twigs and arousing chattering squirrels.

As the invaders dived onto the crushed rock road, O'Toole cried, "We'll hit them with a battle royal!"

But his colleagues said, *"Fanfarone!"*

Two prone mafiosi, faces in the crushed rock, turned toward each other.

"Maybe we pass the time better tellin' stories," one said. "You heard the one about the busy *puttana* went to confession on her coffee break? The priest gave her a penance of a thousand Hail Marys so she offered to swap it in trade."

"Goffredo, you ain't relevant," his companion said.

Meanwhile two defenders were executing battle plans of their own.

Yellow eyes glittering, Jonah crouched on a tree branch directly over the invaders prone on the road to escape Brother Edoardo's fire. Lightning flashed on his sleek coat when he leaped.

The bus driver screamed and thrashed on the road, his arms flailing at an unknown furry assailant that clawed his face. When the driver staggered to his feet, he dropped his revolver, which discharged sending a bullet through the leg of a nearby colleague who howled.

Now the other invaders were on their feet firing wildly in the dark as Jonah ran into the woods. When the disoriented bus driver bent to retrieve his weapon, Garibaldi barking furiously burst out of the woods. The noble shepherd sank his fangs into the driver's buttocks and as an added indignity ripped a large piece out of the seat of his pants.

As the driver collapsed in agony, Garibaldi raced through the invaders nipping right and left and dashed back to the woods. There he waited as Jonah went to repay a favor.

Since wild shots were coming down the road from Brother Edoardo and his sentries, O'Toole mustered his dispirited band. He left the two casualties on the monastery road with a pledge of prompt medical attention, ignored their replies and led the group, diminished to nine, into the woods to avoid the sentries' fire.

There the invaders became separated in the dark as they stumbled uphill scratched by thorn bushes and splashed wading across a brook. One tall and muddy gentleman, pining for Chicago's concrete vistas, said: "We're lost in a dark wood."

He did an about-face and collided with the constable who had politely turned his back on the battle to water a tree. The mafioso placed the muzzle of his Beretta against the constable's head and inquired, "Shorty, which way is outa here?"

The constable first zipped up his fly, raised his hands and slowly turned, lightning glinting on his chrome-plated badge. But the mafioso was not impressed.

"I asked you a question, Shorty!"

"To whom are you applying that pejorative?" said a voice behind the mafioso.

He turned to see the motel manager raising a double-barreled shotgun. When the mafioso leveled his pistol, Jonah leaped from an overhead branch and bit the mafioso's neck. The mafioso screamed, lowered his pistol and shuddered as his head was struck by the shotgun swung by the manager.

After the mafioso momentarily contemplated the buzzing in his head, he handed his pistol to the manager and fell poleaxed at the manager's feet.

"Thank you, kitty!" the manager cried as Jonah scampered off to join Garibaldi. "You didn't forget!"

Then the manager knelt beside the fallen mafioso and said: "Where are the Brownies?"

The mafioso opened one eye, blinked and before lapsing into unconsciousness said, "Not guilty, Your Honor. I'm a cannoli man myself."

"Tag him," the manager commanded.

But the constable was unable to affix the self-stick Punkinville Feed and Seed Store label to the mafioso's muddy forehead. Instead the constable parted the snoring gentleman's lips and inserted the fluttering label thereby diminishing the invaders to eight.

"Did you hear what he said?" the constable asked as he proceeded uphill with the manager.

"It confirms my impression that Sicilians are preoccupied with cuisine."

In another part of the woods, two mafiosi, separated in the dark from their six colleagues, debated during a stumbling ascent.

"Nowhere else in *Italia* is the cooking like we do in *Sicilia*," said a portly gentleman from Palermo who wheezed with each step.

However, his companion, a groaning Neapolitan, said: "I too am from *il Mezzogiorno,* but I swear by San Gennaro there is no difference except you overcook your pasta."

They began to cuff each other until they heard crashing through the underbrush uphill. Lightning revealed a bicycle descending upon them bearing two little old ladies, the driver pedaling vigorously despite her cervical collar. But more disconcerting was the little old lady in the parka straddling the rear package rack.

Having lost her aluminum bat in the bus assault, Mabel brandished a new wooden one obtained from the Penitential Brothers of Saint Peccato baseball team when the ladies had reached the monastery. As the two-wheeled juggernaut bore down on the mafiosi, lightning illuminated the brand on the bat which Mabel swung barely missing the pair.

"It's a Louisville Slugger!" the two malefactors cried dropping their revolvers and slaloming through the trees.

When they passed the constable and manager, the fleeing invaders were heard to say, "Pasta *di Napoli* fooey!"

"Pasta *di Sicilia* fooey!"

The manager nodded as the mafiosi disappeared downhill into the night, diminishing the invaders to six.

"Like a Trojan priest, seven letters, LAOGOON, they are still entangled in spaghetti," he said.

CHAPTER XXXIII

The double doors of the monastery entrance flew open as head baker Reilly and a helper pushed a massive wheeled object bulging ominously under a black tarpaulin.

"Park it right out in front and get it goin' *presto!*" cried Angelo in a rain-slicked parka who was guarding the entrance with Benny Deuce. "We got half of them but they're still comin' up through the woods!"

The two bakers flung off the tarpaulin revealing a machine shaped like a giant bagel with a front port. Steel shields were mounted on each side to protect the crew.

When Reilly plugged in a long extension cord and threw a switch, gauges glowed, bells rang and a whistle blew. The machine rumbled and as it warmed did a rock-'n'-roll.

"Deploy anchors!" Reilly commanded.

His helper released spring-loaded braces that gripped the pavement.

"Okay?" Angelo said.

"We'll take a shillelagh to those momzerim, begorra," Reilly said.

"And who's this guy?" Angelo said jerking a thumb at the helper.

"He's a new brother, Patrick Pending, who's a mechanical genius."

"They call me Pat for short," the helper said.

"Are you a mechanical engineer like Reilly?" Angelo

said.

"Nah. I was pinball champ of Bensonhurst."

"It figures," Angelo said resuming his inspection of the monastery's defenses.

Scattered firing continued in the woods. Meanwhile brother stretcher bearers carried lightly wounded casualties, invaders and brothers, to the infirmary where Dr. Sy Farchadat presided. One of the stretcher bearers was Brother Heisenberg.

"How's it goin' in the woods?" Angelo asked the dour baker who replied, "Uncertain."

Angelo and Benny Deuce looked up at the rickety cross installed on the monastery roof by Carlo Peccato to replace one confiscated by the previous chaplain.

"When that falls it's gonna make a big impression," Benny Deuce said.

But Angelo had already left.

At that moment lightning revealed the surviving six invaders staggering out of the woods 50 yards from the monastery entrance led by Cannibal O'Toole flourishing his revolver. As wild shots were exchanged by both sides, Reilly shouted to his assistant, "You may fire when you are ready, Pending!"

Atop the machine, a spotlight flared dazzling the invaders who froze as the machine alternately clanked and clanged. Then commencing with a smoky report midway between a fart and a belch, the machine spewed at quarter-second intervals a rock-hard frozen disk six inches in diameter: The infamous *Ciao* Bagel Mark II!

Blinking in the spotlight's glare, the horrified invaders peeked through their fingers as flying disks deviated from an initial flat trajectory. Approaching the target, the disks bobbed and weaved making evasion difficult.

Three mafiosi fell. But the other missiles sped past the target, did a tight U-turn and returned clobbering two more mafiosi in the back. With these five colleagues disabled, Cannibal O'Toole remained the only effective.

Meanwhile crouched behind the machine's shield Reilly and Pending raised landing nets, snared the returning missiles and dumped them into a hopper at the rear of the machine. From there the missiles were transported into a magazine for reuse.

Dodging a volley of missiles, Cannibal O'Toole paused to lay his revolver barrel over his forearm. One thunderous shot pulverized the spotlight and plunged the scene into darkness.

O'Toole zigzagged through bullets and as lightning illuminated the monastery's rough-hewn cross he scowled and gave it the finger.

"Sure and 'tis sacrilege!" Reilly said. He tried to block the burly invader but was shoved aside as O'Toole plunged through the monastery's massive entrance doors wrenching them off their hinges.

Pursued by Angelo and Benny Deuce, the former prior raced along familiar corridors, turned to fire a booming shot that shattered a window and was confronted by Serafina guarding the infirmary door.

"*Alto!*" she cried assuming a combat stance and squinting over the two-inch barrel of her small .38 revolver.

"With all due respect to little old ladies, you are indeed trouble. So get the fuck out of the way or I'll kick your butt!"

He lunged at her. Trembling because she had never fired her late spouse's revolver, Serafina aimed at the biggest target and fired. O'Toole grunted as his free hand grabbed his belly. Then he laughed when he saw the dent in his massive championship buckle forged of heavy alloy steel. He again charged the frail grandmother, disarmed her, and with the muzzle of his revolver pressed against her head forced her inside the infirmary and locked the door.

In the corridor, Angelo and Benny Deuce looked at each other in despair.

"What we got inside there," Angelo said, "is a nut case with a .44 magnum he's pointin' at my helpless little old *nonna*, my helpless girlfriend, her helpless little Brownies and a lotta other helpless people too numerical to mention." Benny Deuce scratched his chin.

"How can he point his piece at all them people at the same time?"

"You're talkin' point but I'm talkin' counterpoint. What's goin' on in there is a whole new ball game."

A few minutes before, the infirmary had been busy but surprisingly tranquil. Lightly wounded patients, brothers and invaders, lay on cots tended by Dr. Sy Farchadat and his volunteers.

Especially cheerful were the invaders who received bagels and cream cheese with their choice of espresso, beer or wine instead of the expected two behind the ear. The only grumbler was Irv Farchadat commissioned bedpan orderly by his physician brother.

Yvonne and her Brownies tidied the infirmary while Purità kept a pot boiling in the infirmary's kitchenette in response to the obstetrician's frequent order: "More hot water!" But he smiled when he said it.

All labored or rested under the eye of an armed brother sentry whom Benny Deuce had appointed inside guard while Serafina guarded outside.

Purità, observing Dr. Farchadat's ministrations, plucked Irv Farchadat's sleeve as he headed for the bathroom carrying a leaning tower of bedpans.

"Hold it!" she said.

"I am holding it and if I drop it we'll all be in deep doo-doo."

"Lighten up, Irv. I just say *grazie* for bringin' a great doctor for when we get married."

Irv carefully placed the bedpans on a table.

"Great doctor? He's a kvetcher who hates medicine. We don't need him. We had the grand opening a long time ago and we're a perfect fit."

"Then Dr. Sy is the first kvetcher I ever saw who whistles while he works. I need him because I want lots of *bambini*."

"Okay, but in the *bambini* department I'm the guy who handles Part A while Sy just delivers in Part B."

"Bedpan!" Yvonne cried from the other end of the infirmary.

Irv grabbed a bedpan and said over his shoulder: "We'll discuss this some other time."

But Purità shook her head. "No talk. Action! You be sure to always set it up on the night of the full moon so all our *bambini* are boys. "

Above the bathroom's constant flushing, came Irv's voice-over:

"Why did I get myself into a hole just to sell more bagels?"

The infirmary door flew open as Cannibal O'Toole burst in with the captive Serafina and cried, "Everybody freeze!"

O'Toole surveyed the room:

Yvonne and her three Brownies stopped housekeeping. Irv Farchadat braked and dropped an empty bedpan he was rushing to deliver. Dr. Sy Farchadat, who had poured some brandy to calm a nervous brother, downed it himself. Purità placed a water jug on a counter and scowled at O'Toole. Serafina clenched her small fists in frustration as O'Toole still pressed his revolver to her head. And as Serafina groaned, the brother guard meekly handed his pistol butt-first to O'Toole who hurled it through a window.

While O'Toole conducted his survey of the infirmary, senior Brownie Esmeralda Chance fingered the achievement badges on her uniform sash and conducted her own.

Esmeralda winked at Yvonne who shook her head but Esmeralda nodded. Then the senior Brownie glanced meaningfully at the table on the side of the room where she had left her baseball. Brownie Clytemnestra Tinker who had been sweeping there smiled and nodded to Brownie Guinevere Evers nearby who had been arranging packaged bandages on a shelf.

Meanwhile Cannibal O'Toole addressed a visionary popcorn-munching audience beyond the ring and denounced the Penitential Brothers of Saint Peccato, "They're gutless guineas I'll ram into the turnbuckles . "

So preoccupied was O'Toole that he was taken aback when Yvonne screamed and collapsed in a simulated faint.

With this diversion, Clytemnestra Tinker backed against the table, reached behind her, grabbed the baseball and tossed it to Guinevere Evers who threw a wild pitch toward Esmeralda Chance.

The ball flew over Esmeralda's head and bounced off the wall as she scrambled to field it. While Dr. Farchadat's volunteers cheered and his brother Irv clanged two empty bedpans together, Esmeralda caught the ball, spat on it, wound up and hurled her best pitch, the infamous spitter.

At the same time Serafina jabbed her elbow into O'Toole's groin, stamped on his foot and broke free. The disconcerted O'Toole vainly tried to keep his eye on the ball which swerved right, left, up and finally down onto his gun hand. As the heavy revolver fell Serafina ran to the wall and flicked off the light switches.

In the dark O'Toole groped vainly on the floor for his revolver, contented himself with the little .38 seized from Serafina which he held in his uninjured hand and fumbled at the door latch but could not release. Recalling how he had plunged headlong into the ring to spirited applause, he stepped back and hurled his 290 pounds through the door emerging into the corridor in a shower of shattered wood. There he delivered slur No. 1: "Mazzini was a fink!"

Standing directly outside were Angelo holding his shotgun and Benny Deuce his Beretta. But it was like being in the path of a runaway train and both were bowled over firing as they missed and fell. Despite pain in O'Toole's hand and groin, he raced along the corridor toward the monastery entrance pursued by Angelo and Benny Deuce who held their fire to avoid hitting bystanders.

Meanwhile in the infirmary where order was being

HAROLD KNOLL

restored, Yvonne hugged her three Brownies.

"We never want Brownies to do what you did so bravely yet run such risks," she said. "Tonight you earned much more than Try-It patches."

But Esmeralda conferred with colleagues Clytemnestra and Guinevere and the trio replied:

"Brownies can do a hell of a lot more than just sell cookies."

After scolding the guard who had meekly surrendered, Serafina cast her eyes heavenward and said, "Santo Peccato, where are you when we need you?"

As O'Toole lurched along the corridor two four-footed avengers attacked again. Lying in wait behind a life-size plaster statue of Saint George wrestling an alligator (a gift from a Florida pilgrim) were Jonah and Garibaldi. With their customary one-two, Jonah sprang and clawed O'Toole's face as Garibaldi hurled himself at O'Toole's buttocks and bit same.

But drawing upon a great reserve of strength, O'Toole flung the cat against the wall where he lay whimpering. Then O'Toole wrestled the shephered and kicked him in the chest so hard that the noble canine flew across the floor and came to rest groaning beside his companion.

Angelo raised his shotgun but again hesitated to fire the shotgun's lethal 00 pellets in the corridor. Benny Deuce, breathless from running, fired three pistol shots at O'Toole who had resumed his flight toward the entrance. Two shots missed but the third grazed O'Toole's shoulder prompting slur No. 2: "Screw the Kingdom of the Two Sicilies!"

"He really is pissed," Angelo told Benny Deuce.

They waved to Garibaldi and Jonah, stunned but recovering, and continued the pursuit of O'Toole who had just plunged outside through the monastery entrance. He trampled on the doors he had previously torn down and brandished Serafina's small .38 in his massive fist.

Out into the night went O'Toole where rain, thunder and lightning swept over the Penitential Brothers of Saint

Peccato and their defenders gathered before the monastery for Armageddon.

O'Toole splashed through puddles and mud, holding his fire as he glanced over his shoulder seeking Angelo.

On this last leg of his journey, O'Toole encountered first the two little old ladies wobbling on their bicycle with tail gunner Mabel holding the Louisville Slugger. He swerved to check the poster on the bulletin board bolted to the rear wheel and shook his fist indignantly as he read: "STAMP OUT OXYMORONS!"

When Mabel swung at him he ducked and said: "Smart asses!"

So mightily had Mabel swung that both little old ladies fell off the bicycle, which slammed into a boulder and blew a tire. When Irv Farchadat offered to help them out of a puddle they declined and the driver said: "It's only the pedestrian ending that hurts."

As O'Toole hurtled through the crowd, he encountered the Punkinville constable straddling the sidewalk. The constable tried to steady his .45 revolver in both hands while behind him the deputized motel manager struggled to raise his double-barreled shotgun.

"Halt in the name of the law!" the constable cried as the manager shook his head and said, "Hackneyed, five letters, BANAL!"

But O'Toole charged head down and sidestepped them. The constable fired wildly, fell back from the heavy revolver's recoil and bumped the manager whose shotgun discharged both barrels into tree branches overhead. This brought down a squawking crow that landed in the lap of the fallen constable who had prudently substituted birdshot for the requested buckshot.

"Is this the black bird you was ravin' about?" he asked the manager who had fallen beside him.

While pursuers Angelo and Benny Deuce were hampered by the crowd, Rabbi Raphael ran out of the monastery with his squirrel rifle in one hand and in the other a small bulging gunny sack tied with twine.

As he ran past the two little old ladies inspecting their damaged bicycle, he thrust the rifle into the driver's hands saying, "Please hold this big little gun for me!"

"Mabel," said the driver, "it's time for a new poster."

With his shoulder bleeding from Benny Deuce's bullet, face bloody from Jonah's claws, buttocks sore from Garibaldi's fangs and gun hand numb from Esmeralda's spitball, Cannibal O'Toole pressed on, his head swiveling to seek his nemesis Angelo.

O'Toole nearly collided with Raphael who stepped back a dozen paces for room to deploy his sack. Misinterpreting this move, O'Toole raised the .38 and said, "Am I such a punk that for the main event they send only one scared nigger against a world champion?"

But Raphael swung his sack over his head and said, "I come as a shepherd without sword and shield but with the blessing of the great Jehovah!"

He flung the sack which *klopped* O'Toole's forehead and burst spilling five frozen deli bagels. The big man staggered and dropped Serafina's revolver but did not fall. Flailing his arms, he stumbled through the crowd toward Angelo waiting near the monastery entrance.

As lightning flashed over the roof, O'Toole glanced up at Carlo's jury-rigged cross and was startled to see him clinging to it as he prayed in the storm. The wounded giant extended his middle finger and shouted slur No. 3, the mother of all blasphemies: "The Pope wears army shoes!"

In response, the heavens thundered and a furious Carlo Peccato grabbed a rope he had tied to the steel base of the cross. As he rappelled down from the roof, the mightiest lightning bolt of the storm struck the cross, which burst into flame. A shower of fiery fragments cascaded over Carlo who began to glow.

As the crowd scattered, the flames enveloped O'Toole who shook his fists and emitted his infamous wrestling yell that had terrified opponents and referees. His hair and clothes were alight, but impervious to pain and unarmed he charged Angelo who stood with shotgun leveled.

Because people dashed through the line of fire, Angelo again hesitated to shoot. But Carlo drew Don Topo's Beretta and hurled himself at the fiery giant. They grappled, two shots were fired and Carlo clutched his chest and collapsed.

Cannibal O'Toole stood alone, hands raised in triumph. Then consumed in flame he staggered forward and fell at Angelo's feet.

While the monastery's maintenance brothers carried fire extinguishers up ladders to the roof, Dr. Sy Farchadat knelt beside O'Toole.

"He's fought his last bout. Shot through the heart and severely burned."

Dr. Farchadat hurried through the crowd around Carlo who was on a stretcher, tattered habit bloody, eyes staring. As the brothers wept, Dr. Farchadat found no pulse and shone a flashlight at Carlo's eyes. Cutting open the habit, the doctor examined Carlo's chest, sighed and wearily stood up.

"He's gone. Also shot through the heart. But you say he fought hand-to-hand with that *farshtinkener bulvon* who was on fire?"

Angelo nodded. He knelt beside the stretcher and held Carlo's limp hand.

"Carlo took a bullet to save me," Angelo said. "But though he's glowin' he ain't burned."

Raphael knelt on the other side of the stretcher, laid his empty sack over Carlo's chest and said:

"Upon this saint's body the fire had no power, nor was a hair of Carlo's head singed, neither was his coat changed nor had the smell of fire passed on him." He looked to the black sky and added, "I freely quote Daniel 3:27." Then he clapped his hands. "Hallelujah! It's a miracle!"

To the crowd's astonishment Carlo's eyelids fluttered. After he vainly tried to raise his head he beckoned Angelo and for a minute whispered in his ear. Then, Carlo lay still as the glow faded and his eyelids were closed by Angelo.

When Raphael whispered to Angelo they stepped aside and Raphael handed him Carlo's envelope. Angelo put a finger to his lips and embraced Raphael. Then Angelo called up to the maintenance brothers on the roof, "What's the damage?"

"Nothing!" cried a brother. "The crux of it is that the cross is gone but everything else is untouched by fire even Santo Peccato's rope!"

"It's another goddamn miracle!" the crowd cried.

Angelo locked his office door, sat at his desk and opened Carlo Peccato's envelope. The note said:

"The Milwaukee *famiglia* put a contract on me not only because I took off to serve the Lord but mainly because I also took $200,000 of the don's dough with me. I buried it in the woods 100 paces north-northwest of the boulder behind the monastery like the map shows. *Per favore* use the dough to help the Lord's poor."

At dawn, the next morning with spade and compass Angelo set off accompanied by Garibaldi who growled dutifully at trespassing chipmunks. When Angelo reached the hundredth pace he wedged the spade into the soft earth, struck something hard and uncovered a small metal box whose seams had been sealed with duct tape.

Back at his office he wiped dirt off the box, removed the tape and found 20 packets of $100 bills, 100 to a packet. He fingered a plastic statuette of Saint Peccato and said, "Carlo, like I told you before about the rule in our business — 50 percent always goes upstairs."

He placed 10 packets in the box, the remaining 10 in his safe and burned the note in an ashtray.

"Grazie mille," he said saluting the statuette.

Then tucking the box under his arm he headed for the monastery tavern.

CHAPTER XXXIV

The next morning three private ambulances and a hearse descended the monastery road against a cloudless blue sky.

At the monastery entrance Angelo threw them a mock salute. Yvonne held his arm and *Consigliere* Mordecai stood beside her. Angelo said, "The don called the Chicago don last night after the phone company hooked up service. He says tryin' to take over our bagel business was too stressful so he's gonna stick to dope."

"What surprises me is his abrupt capitulation, even rushing ambulances for his wounded and a hearse for O'Toole," Mordecai said.

Angelo smiled and chucked Mordecai under the chin.

"Ain't you never seen a Mafia movie? In our business it helps to motivate the other guy by bustin' his balls."

As they spoke maintenance brothers removed foliage that had fallen during the storm. Other brothers were on the roof raising a cross newly made in their carpentry shop.

Angelo looked up and nodded.

"Soon we're back in business."

Serafina, who joined them at the entrance, said, "Except you gotta ask the Pope to give Carlo back his saint's card."

Angelo indicated Mordecai who opened his briefcase and produced a sheaf of papers.

"Affidavits from dozens of witnesses last night. To wit: Carlo Francesco Peccato was not burned even though he stood in a flaming shower of debris when lightning shattered the cross. He was not even burned when he grappled with a perpetrator who was afire. Further, neither was the roof damaged nor the rope he used to climb down."

Joining the group as they entered the monastery was Rabbi Raphael who said, "And he glowed with heaven's light."

"Bene," Angelo said. "Now Brother Mordecai, in your cover letter to the Pope you say this *per favore:* That Carlo Peccato was 100 percent dead when he was canonized but he rose from the dead last night to defend his monastery which is miracle No. 1. When he got whacked the second time he still stuck around long enough to give all the brothers his blessin' before croakin' for good which is miracle No. 2."

"Miracle No. 3 will be if the Pope buys that *bubkes,"* Mordecai said.

"*Si,* it will take a great leap of faith for the Pope so with the letter and affidavits we send him a pair of tennies."

Serafina took Angelo aside as the others waited in the corridor.

"Nipotino mio, la nonna asks a favor *per favore,"* she whispered.

"Who do you want whacked?"

"No whack. You tell me once you will be *il padrone modesto* when you are don. But now you are don you talk of yourself like you are a public meeting." Angelo hugged her.

"The don will take it under advisement," he said as she frowned.

Bleary-eyed Dr. Sy Farchadat who had stayed the night to tend the wounded was leaving the monastery tavern sipping coffee. His white clinical jacket was soiled.

"Thanks for your affidavit, Doctor," Mordecai said. Sy rubbed a hand on his grimy forehead and shook his head to clear it.

"This has been some night but to tell the truth I enjoyed the stress. Also no crying babies. Never have I heard of a man who was shot through the heart and revived briefly to make a deathbed statement. Who knows? I might switch to emergency medicine. Now all I have to think about is how to pay back my brother Irv if he lends me the money for the upcoming premium on my malpractice insurance."

Angelo hugged the doctor.

"You done us a big favor which the don never forgets. Since the don's *famiglia* is up on a hill you got friends in high places. If some crook files a malpractice suit against you, then you just let your friend Don Angelo know. The don sends his public relations director Brother Benedetto over to straighten the troublemaker out and also the troublemaker's lawyer. We call that tort reform. So drop that malpractice insurance, stop worryin' and take time to smell the petunias."

Sy shook Angelo's hand and went to the parking lot, but before he entered his Porsche, Raphael came up and whispered, "Doctor, I'd sure like to ask you a doctorin' question but I don't have no money to pay."

"Certainly Rabbi."

Raphael fiddled with his yarmulke.

"It's kinda personal, Doctor."

"Get in."

When they were alone in the car Raphael said, "Could you fix me up so I'd pass for a real Jew bein' I ain't really a Jew nor a rabbi neither?"

Instinctively Sy's hand went to his own crotch. "That's mishegaas. Why undergo all that pain? Last night you already displayed the courage, compassion and wisdom of the ideal Jew."

"Please Doctor. I'm gonna take lessons and someday when I'm ready—"

"Another miracle on the hill. All right Rabbi, I'll do it even though I'm not a *mohel.* No charge. Who knows? You might even be ordained and run your own temple."

But Raphael pointed through the windshield to the monastery. "The Lord has lifted up the meek to serve his people in this temple."

Sy took Raphael's hand.

"We'll make an appointment soon."

"For me to go to you for the operation?"

"That can wait. A nonobservant Jew wants to come back to see you soon for a long talk. *Shalom aleichem.*"

Raphael got out of the car. *"Aleichem shalom,"* he said.

At the big table in the executive committee room Serafina tapped Angelo on the shoulder.

"Nipotino mio, with all the miracles here I still worry Carlo Peccato ain't gettin' his saint's card back because this Pope ain't *italiano.*"

Angelo hugged her.

"If *il mulo* won't go when you show him the carrot then maybe you gotta motivate him with a two-by-four."

"You made an arrangement?"

"Si *nonna mia.* Every brother here who got *cugini* in Sicily or Rome called them this morning and told them to motivate the Vatican. And our Washington friends have already motivated the papal nuncio to get on the horn to the Vatican to reopen Carlo's case."

"Bene," Serafina said. "So the papal nuncio believes Carlo is a saint?"

"Who cares? What he does believe is that he would have a big headache under his biretta if he got two behind the ear from our Beretta."

When there was a knock on the door, Benny Deuce went into the corridor shutting the door behind him. Inside the executive committee room the conferees heard two loud sounds through the door—a resounding thump and an "Ouch!" from Benny Deuce.

He entered the room closing the door behind him and rubbing a welt on his forehead. In a quavering voice he announced, "Panjandrum plenipotentiary from his specialty the papal nuncio in Washington has come for an audience with Don Angelo!"

"Show him in," Angelo said.

"With all due respect it's a her."

Angelo frowned and nodded as Benny Deuce opened the door to admit a frail little old nun in a dusty black habit who brandished her 24-inch oaken ruler with a gleaming brass edge.

"And I'll give you another *klop* if you can't remember your multiplication table, Benedetto Orso!" she cried. "Since when does 9 times 9 equal 99?"

As Benny Deuce began to mumble about bad luck numbers, she made him bend over and whacked his buttocks so hard that her ruler broke in two while he staggered into a wall.

"Excuses, always excuses from you, Benedetto. I've lost more rulers on you than on any other slow learner."

"With all due respect your holiness, they told me in reform school slow learner was pejorative and that you shoulda called me cognitively disadvantaged."

But she was blinking now through pop bottle eyeglass lenses.

"Where's Angelo Panettorio, my former pupil who's done well in baking? The papal nuncio, *cugino mio*, has sent me here to have a sitdown with Angelo about your phoney baloney Santo Peccato."

Angelo got up and hugged the nun who wept when he said, "*Benvenuto,* Suora Sessualitá. You're not teachin' no more?"

"No, they retired me early at 85, so *cugino* mio, the papal nuncio, got me a job as troubleshooter. Now where can we talk to straighten out *il imbroglio?*"

"My private office, Sister. Meanwhile everybody wait here. Benny Deuce, bring Sister some espresso and a package of bagels and lox to go."

Fifteen minutes later Angelo returned without the nun.

"She's on her way back to Washington. We made an

arrangement: Sister is gonna motivate the papal nuncio to send the right message to the Vatican about Carlo Peccato. And the don guaranteed the Penitentiary Brothers would send Sister a nice monthly donation for her pension since old folks don't feel secure on social security only."

"It sounds like a win-win settlement, the respective parties receiving what they wanted," Mordecai said.

"Not exactly. We ain't buyin' her a new ruler."

On the table Reilly placed a large platter of golden brown bagels warm from the oven but he declined when Angelo indicated an empty chair.

"There's something I want to do now with your permission, Don Angelo."

When Angelo nodded, Reilly held up the weathered gold-painted life preserver that had hung outside his Brooklyn bagel bakery. Angelo took the sign with its attached mounting chain, smiled and said, "When the don was a baker's helper for you he swiped the life preserver from a boat at Sheepshead Bay and the chain from Sol Farpotshket's junkyard. So what's with the sign, *amico mio*?"

"Before I came here I sold only fresh bagels. Frozen is acceptable but I have a warm heart and I'd like us also to sell fresh not only in stores but to drive-in customers who could buy here."

"Claudio told me the frozen bagel market is $60 million but that the fresh bagel market ain't peanuts neither," Angelo said. "It's $30 million."

"Positively," Reilly said. "And though the fresh bagel market is smaller, it's growing much faster at 31 percent a year while the frozen market is growing at 10 percent."

Angelo nodded.

"Reilly, get hold of a maintenance brother, go down to the town road and put up your sign. You also got my okay to put in a drive-up window here."

On the town road near the monastery's road, Reilly and the maintenance brother installed a post and arm from which the life preserver oscillated on its rusty chain still proclaiming: "FRESH BAGELS UPSTAIRS."

Meanwhile in the executive committee room the group was joined by Irv Farchadat and his fiancée Purità who wore the habit of the Penitential Sisters of Saint Peccato.

Irv fingered the coarse material and said, "When we go on our honeymoon in Sicily I'll do what I always wanted—bang a nun."

But she displayed a platinum engagement ring with a glittering rock.

"Irv, when we got engaged my bimbo days were over. So watch your mouth. And don't forget that when we go on our honeymoon I'd better be wearing the mink coat you promised—not a sweater."

Serafina took Purità's left hand and admired the ring.

"Is nicer than one *il Signor* Farchadat gave you before," Serafina said.

Purità adjusted the ring and smiled. "I had a sitdown with the big spender and told him to take the bargain basement special back and get me a ring that shows respect or I'd tell Don Angelo."

"I was only kidding," Irv said. "I'm happy because hooking up with the monastery has turned things around for me. In fact Rabbi Raphael's Classic Bagels are selling so well that I'm gonna open Wisconsin store No. 11 in Bloomer."

"You did a market analysis?" Mordecai said.

"Market shmarket. How can I go wrong in a place named Bloomer that's the Speed Rope Jumping Capital of the World?" He flexed his biceps. "And I feel great. The first thing I'll do when I get back to the office is dump the pharmacy I have on my desk. The second thing is have a potter make a Saint Peccato toby mug to be featured in my collection."

When Irv reached for the toothpick container on the table, Angelo placed a mint in his hand and summoned a brother- waiter.

"All toothpicks are outa here and our tavern," Angelo said. "A guy could get a splinter."

"Also they're boorish," Yvonne said.

Angelo beckoned his four-footed colleagues who sat at attention, Garibaldi barking and Jonah grooming his sleek coat. Angelo fastened a silver Saint Peccato medal on the collar of each and patted the animals to applause.

A mouse strolled before Jonah but the cat yawned and continued grooming. When Angelo frowned, Raphael said, "Jonah's gotten too fat to do a cat scan for mouses. He's found kitty paradise here."

Angelo turned next to the Punkinville constable and deputized manager who were leaving. As he hugged them for their help, Benny Deuce ushered in a little old lady who insisted on carrying her cardboard suitcase secured with frayed pantyhose. Although it was a warm spring day, the collar of her red mackinaw was turned up and buttoned while a heavy red knitted cap was pulled down over her ears.

Angelo stood and bowed as she said, "Are you the big enchilada here?"

"Si. What service can I give you, *signora*?"

She cupped a wrinkled hand to the side of her head. "Louder, Junior. I don't hear so good."

Angelo nodded to Benny Deuce who bowed, snatched her cap and presented it to her with a flourish. Her mussed hair was fiery red.

"I am Brother Angelo, prior of this monastery, *signora*. How can I help you?"

The little old lady clapped her hands to her ears in astonishment.

"It's a miracle! I hear you clear as a bell, Father. The pilgrimage up here cured me! And those quacks down below claimed I needed an ear trumpet!"

"*Bene*. You have the honor to be our pilgrim No. 1. Brother Benedetto will pay our respect by takin' you to our humble restaurant for our free homemade bagels and espresso. Then you gotta visit Santo Peccato's shrine where you got your choice of candles to light. You got the $1 introductory birthday cake size all the way up to the $50 dripless jumbo unconditionally guaranteed to beam your intentions upstairs for 30 days. And before you leave stop at our gift shop for Saint Peccato T-shirts plus assorted gewgaws and gimcracks."

"Thank you, Father. I am president of the Pigeon Falls chapter of the Penitential Servants of Saint Peccato. Those ladies sent me here to check things out after we heard on the radio you're welcoming pilgrims again. Now who can refer me to a nice quiet motel with a bar and pool where a little old lady can meditate during her pilgrimage?"

Angelo beckoned the motel manager saying, "Take good care of *la signora* because she likes pigeons. "

The manager of the Royal Punkin Motel adjusted his smile, cleared his throat and seized her suitcase.

"Madam, in six letters I anticipate your exclamation on finding a cozy nest: EUREKA! We have one vacancy at the Royal Punkin Motel in nearby Punkinville, gateway to a pilgrim's paradise. I shall personally escort you there in an official vehicle provided by the constable of Punkinville who is in attendance."

"And give Brother Angelo's regards to Pigeon Falls because he likes all *piccioni*, Italian or whatever," Angelo said.

Before the manager and little old lady exited, he told Angelo:

"Kindly convey my thanks to Brother Reilly. He has offered to help us establish the Punkinville Drum and Bagel Corps."

"You mean bugle," Angelo said.

"No, bagel. Brother Reilly promised to buy all the drums and we agreed to paint on the big bass drum, 'EAT RABBI RAPHAEL'S CLASSIC BAGELS.'"

After the manager and pilgrim had left, the constable rubbed his hands and told the group at the table, "Maybe the village board will put that stop-and-go light outside my store now that it's open season on pilgrims."

Escorted by Benny Deuce, the constable left twirling his six-shooter.

"We got the pilgrim business again," Angelo said. "Next we have Brother Mordecai apply to get our tax exemptions back as a religious organization."

When Benny Deuce returned his face was ashen and sweaty. He opened the door partway, stuck his head in and tried to shout above the clamor behind him, "Delegation to see Don Angelo!"

"More pilgrims?" Angelo said.

While Benny Deuce was considering a reply he was shoved forward by an angry mob. Drawing his Beretta he confronted a dozen male rustics shaking their calloused fists. But he replaced the weapon in the waistband under his habit after Angelo frowned.

Benny Deuce stared at the large button displayed on the delegation's seed company caps. He stepped back and wiped his face with his sleeve. The button said, "CONGENIALITY LAYABOUT COMMITTEE." The mob wore mudcaked clodhoppers, torn jeans, and T-shirts repeating the button's message.

"If you ain't pilgrims then you musta saw the sign Reilly just hung out and you're here for his nice fresh bagels," Angelo told them as Benny Deuce cringed.

The delegation's gangling spokesman pounded the table and spouted expletives while his associates offered a barnyard medley mimicking chickens, pigs, cows and goats. "Now that you've introduced yourselves, what can Brother Angelo do for you?"

"Not you—him!" cried the leader indicating Benny Deuce. "Your Mafia hitman dumped his victims up north in our village of Congeniality, Wisconsin."

"Never heard of it. Even if there was such a place you wouldn't have no environmental impact because Brother Benedetto takes pride in his work. In our profession we call that the Jimmy Hoffa arrangement."

However the leader switched to his other hand and pounded the table again. "Horse turds!"

Angelo beckoned the shamefaced Benny Deuce who

shambled through a gauntlet of jabbing elbows, hung his head and mumbled, "No. 19 is what done it."

Angelo scratched his chin as Raphael came forward, vainly tried to put his arm around Benny Deuce's massive shoulders and said, "Brother Benny done already confessed his sin to me. These folks know your dark secret, Brother Benny, so I asks your permission to do like the Good Book says: 'What I tell you in darkness, *that* speak ye in the light.' For what you done was a corpuscle act of mercy."

Benny Deuce sobbed and nodded, loudly blowing his nose in a napkin tendered by a weeping Serafina.

"I am here to serve my Brother Benny like Aaron served his brother Moses," Raphael said. "Brother Benny has a kind heart which the Lord delights to look upon. When Brother Benny was the party of the first part who was contracted to smite certain parties of the second part, he made an arrangement for them parties: Option A—Join his witness protection program and go into exile at Congeniality where they could hang their harps upon the willows by Lake Superior and unlike the children of Israel live in idleness and comfort supported by Brother Benny. Option B—Take a bullet."

Angelo stood, gulped a glass of seltzer, took a deep breath and burped.

"Brother Benedetto, from two dons you took contract retainers under false promises," he said.

The table shuddered again under pounding by the rustic leader.

"Now hush up this Mafia falderal," he told Angelo. "We come down here to complain about them 19 outsiders who is no-good layabouts which is why we disestablished this civic committee headed by me, name of Clem. Them layabouts goes to our post office to collect their witness protection checks and doodles mustaches on the wanted posters. They don't work. They play cards all day and drink hard liquor instead of watching TV like respectable citizens. When they're sober enough they go fishing even on Sunday when the rest of us has to sit in church. And now the latest layabout to arrive in our fair village is a loony who claims he's the natural son of J. Edgar Hoover, sits outside the village hall in his director's chair and has put the whole village under surveillance."

Angelo sat, exchanged whispers with his *consigliere* and said, "Before the don gives his verdict, he tells Brother Benedetto as one professional to another that he admires this slick arrangement and wants to know how it got done." Benny Deuce blushed and nudged by Raphael said, "People figure because I look like a gorilla I'm a killer but them people don't know gorillas is kindhearted vegetarians like me. At least I always seen gorillas eat peanuts I used to throw in their cage at the Prospect Park Zoo when Sister Sessualità took the class on a field trip."

Angelo nodded and said, "I done that too. Them gorillas can get the nut outa the shell PDQ which proves they got fine motor skills. So like you, Brother Benedetto, they ain't as *stupido* as they look because they never dump the nut and eat the shell."

Benny Deuce beamed.

"*Grazie*, Don Angelo. I thunk I wouldn't be in breach of contract if I just escorted them guys up to Congeniality and made them a nice arrangement. So I used my hitter fees to start my own witness protection program. That way I never hadda whack nobody though I hadda motivate some guys a little."

"How did you get new IDs for them parties of the second part?" Angelo said.

"I made an arrangement with *cugino mio* who runs a credit bureau. He gave them guys new names and new social security cards, drivers' licenses, birth certificates, diplomas and credit references. The only complaint I got from the hittees was their new names."

"What's in a name?" Angelo said.

"Cugino *mio* just wanted to show respect to Italian composers. So why do I hear bitchin' from Pancho Pergolesi,

Moses Monteverdi and Rocky Rossini? Since *cugino mio* has run outa composers he's gonna show respect next to Italian painters."

Angelo winked at the Congeniality leader. "How would Clem Botticelli grab you?"

But the leader gave Angelo a gnarled finger. Mordecai, chin in palm, studied the angry delegation and asked Benny Deuce, "Why did you select Congeniality?"

"For security because nobody never goes there unless they get lost. The locals even took down the CONGENIALITY sign the highway crew put up and replaced it with DO NOT ENTER,

Angelo stood and said, "Okay, the don makes an arrangement. He will send a bus to Congeniality *presto*. Brother Benedetto will be on board as our community relations director. He will then motivate all them witness protection deadbeats to get on the bus so we can transfer 'em somewhere else."

Angelo smiled but was dismayed when the delegation offered variations on a barnyard theme while the leader pounded both fists on the table and cried, "We want you to get us into your witness protection program too!"

Five minutes later Brother Edoardo Coli entered with two of his brother guards. All were heavily armed.

"We held a motivational sitdown with them Congeniality punks," Brother Edoardo said. "They promised when they got home to go to the nearest Farchadat Food Emporium and buy our bagels. Then we slapped the 'I Visited the Shrine of Saint Peccato bumper sticker on their pickups and let 'em take off."

Angelo nodded to the guards in dismissal and hugged Benny Deuce who said, "Now I got peace of mind because I can look forward to contract No. 20."

"To err is human, to forget divine especially on the witness stand," Angelo said as the company cheered.

Serafina left and returned with the two little old lady cyclists wearing the monastery's habit and wheeling their repaired bicycle.

"I just gave them their Penitential Sisters of Saint Peccato button," Serafina said. "They're workin' in our bakery."

Angelo noted the bike's rear poster displaying a new message: "STAMP OUT YOUR PIDGIN ITALIAN!"

"Why keep pickin' on them birds?" Angelo said. "The don likes Italian pigeons."

"As an English professor emeritus I find in my association with you characters that I have yet to hear one syntactically correct sentence in Italian," said the little old lady in the jumpsuit. "I suspect your fragmented dialogue is dredged from an Italian-English dictionary and that you cannot even order a pizza without it."

Angelo scribbled notes on a napkin and said, "*Signora* Professoressa, the don don't understand all this tsimmes about Italian pigeons. But to show respect to a little old lady the don says '*Via il gatto ballano i sorci.*' That means when the cat's away the mice will play."

The little old lady took a deep breath and steadied herself against the bike. "A miracle!" she cried. "I almost plotzed when I heard it!"

But Jonah growled and sulked in a corner.

Mordecai stood and said, "An important matter remains unresolved: Was Carlo Francesco Peccato a.k.a. Saint Peccato alive at his canonization thereby deceiving the Pope because sainthood is to be conferred only after death? And is the aforesaid deceased indeed deceased now?"

Angelo cleared his throat. "You remember last night when Carlo got whacked? When I put my ear to his mouth he whispered his secrets for a minute and then *finito.*

"He says when his Milwaukee *famiglia* put out a contract on him for goin' AWOL they sent an amateur who Carlo whacked. Then Carlo faked his own funeral at the monastery with help from his buddy Claudio. When Carlo done all them good deeds, him and Claudio set up the shrine to bring in pilgrim business. Claudio's *cugino* who's a sculptor made a soft sculpture of Carlo which Claudio stuck in the coffin and sealed the glass lid."

"But how was the canonization implemented and by whom?" Mordecai said.

"By the previous Pope who was *un siciliano* you could have a sitdown with, not like the present guy who needs more motivation."

Mordecai shook his head. "Are you implying the former Pope took a bribe?"

Angelo patted Mordecai on the shoulder and smiled. "I ain't sayin' he did and I ain't sayin' he didn't. Carlo told me last night how it was arranged but that I wasn't to say nothin' out of respect to the Holy See which is an ocean I never heard of."

Mordecai put pen and pad into his briefcase and snapped the latch shut.

"As both your *consigliere* and provider of ancillary legal services regarding your petition for restoration of Mr. Peccato's saintly status, I am frankly disconcerted. There are too many unanswered questions regarding the supposedly supernatural activities of this gentleman which you declare he discussed with you in detail for only one minute as he lay dying."

Angelo chewed a mint and folded his hands.

"*Consigliere mio*, that was just what I told Carlo after he made a great finale recitin' the Apostles' Creed. But he said, 'Don Angelo, you got your secrets and us saints got ours.'"

"Including surviving, albeit briefly, lightning, an inferno and a bullet in the heart?" Mordecai said.

Raphael stood and threw up his arms. "Ask Shadrach, Meshach and Abednego how them servants of the most high God done escaped from the burning fiery furnace!"

"You heard it from the chaplain," Angelo said. He focused through the frame of his splayed fingers. "The don sees our ad now like he was psychotic: 'Visit the Shrine of the Comeback Saint.' We'll run it in all the diocesan newspapers."

Then Angelo turned to Serafina, "*Nonna mia,* now the don got a question for you. Remember when we first come to the monastery we meet Holy Carlo and a big deer on the road. When we come back we see deer tracks in the snow goin' up to the road and deer tracks goin' away into the woods. But Carlo is gone and we don't see his tracks goin' away."

Serafina wagged a finger under his nose.

"Before *la nonna* answers, *la nonna* reminds *il nipote* he still keeps talkin' about himself like he's some other people. Lighten up!"

"*Scusi* Grandma. I am the don but I am still Angelo."

She hugged him. "Another miracle!" she said. "Because I am country girl I understand when I see that deer tracks goin' away is deeper in the snow than deer tracks comin'."

"So *nonna mia?*"

"So Carlo Peccato rode away on the deer's back."

"It figures. Why walk when you can hitch?"

But Serafina shook her head and opened a tiny drawstring bag from which she carefully shook a few corn kernels into her palm.

"Is not wild deer. Is tame. While you see only tracks in snow, I see corn left there too."

"So?"

"So Carlo feeds deer from hand and I get this corn blessed and keep as holy *reliquia.* And now I go to feed holy deer too."

"It's a long walk down the road, Grandma."

As she left she jerked her thumb at him, "Not if you got this."

A few espressos later Angelo beckoned Benny Deuce. "*Per favore* maybe you drive down our road and give *nonna mia* a lift back."

But Benny Deuce who was near the window beckoned Angelo. "With all due respect maybe the don shouldn't underestimate a little old lady," Benny Deuce said.

Angelo's mouth dropped open. Ambling up the monastery road was the deer with Serafina on his back. "Another fuckin' miracle!" Angelo said.

When he returned to the table he opened Carlo's small metal box which rasped on rusty hinges. Angelo smiled, displayed the currency and told the company, "Rabbi Raphael gave the don—I mean me—Holy Carlo's will. Carlo says he buried this box out in the woods and that I gotta dig it up and use the dough for a special purpose."

"Brother Angelo, how much was in the box?" Raphael said.

"Exactly $100,000 in these 10 packs of $100 bills, $10,000 to a pack."

Mordecai skeptically looked at the opened box. "Those packs fill only half the box."

"Shrinkage."

"What was the purpose of Carlo Peccato's bequest?"

"Blow it all on one *meraviglioso* weekend in Las Vegas for the brothers and sisters and everybody else who helped us fight them Chicago punks."

"Even my Brownies?" Yvonne said.

"Them too with their folks. I got *un cugino* who's an importer and runs an air charter service between Brooklyn and Bogotá. But he repays the don with a favor and will fly us to Vegas and back this weekend free."

"Just what does your cousin import from Colombia?" Mordecai said.

"What else—coffee."

"By any chance do you have another cousin in Las Vegas who manages a hotel and casino?" Mordecai said.

"You got it."

"Then why do we have to spend all of the bequest in one weekend?"

Angelo sighed. "Brother Mordecai, *un consigliere* is supposed to give answers, not questions. So let's everybody start packin'."

"Saint Peccato didn't leave nothin' to the church for good works?" Raphael said.

"Carlo says you only live once."

Reilly raised his hand and Angelo nodded. "I've been baking bagels a long time but never have I tasted a bagel with the unique flavor ours has."

Angelo smiled and said, "A panel of rabbis just voted Rabbi Raphael's Classic Bagels No. 1 in a taste test. Brother Goldbach who does the testing conjectures we're a long way ahead of second best."

"Mazel tov!" Reilly said. "As head baker I know all our ingredients except the secret additive you keep in a brown bottle, an additive you alone put in the dough."

"*Si.*"

"For our guests here who are not into bagel baking, I'd like to explain something with your permission, Don Angelo."

"Shoot."

"If a packaged product is kosher it can indicate this in one of several ways. For example, the package could simply say kosher or abbreviate this with a K."

"*Si.*"

Reilly displayed a package of Rabbi Raphael's Classic Bagels. "Then with all due respect how come our symbol is L?"

"Brother Reilly, you is my special *compagno* from the days when I was a poor kid workin' at Reilly's Bagels. So I feel now is the right time to put the secret ingredient on the agenda."

Angelo nodded to Benny Deuce. "Lock the door."

Before Benny Deuce could comply there was a polite tap on the door and the motel manager stuck his head in.

"Excuse the interruption Don Angelo, but I couldn't help eavesdropping since the secret ingredient has intrigued me ever since I saw your bagel package."

"You wish to stay?" Angelo said.

"Thanks but the constable and our first pilgrim are waiting for me. Could you just confirm this: The L on the package is the clue for an Italian word?"

"*Si.*"

"Five letters?"

"*Si.*"

"English equivalent also five letters starting with—"

Angelo put his fingers to his lips. "Enough! You already know. So I recommend you keep your mouth zipped."

"Of course. Brother Benedetto discussed silence with me when we first met. That word was six letters—"

"*Arrivederci!*" Angelo commanded.

Benny Deuce ushered the manager out and locked the door. Then Angelo looked around the table. "Everybody raise their right hand even the lefties."

When they complied he said, "You now take the oath of *omertà* which means what I tell you in this room stays in this room. *Capite?*"

When everyone nodded, he produced a brown paper bag and removed a half-gallon brown glass jar. "After Claudio got whacked and I took over as prior, I had a food chemist analyze Claudio's secret ingredient." Angelo pulled the bottle's cork, inhaled, smiled and poured a small quantity of granules into Rabbi Raphael's palm. "Taste and see," Angelo said.

Raphael cautiously took a pinch of the granules and chewed slowly.

"Manna like the children of Israel ate in the wilderness,"

"*Bene,*" Angelo said.

Then he beckoned the company and when they leaned toward him he cupped his hand near his mouth and whispered, "The L stands for *il lardo* which means bacon. So the secret ingredient is finely ground bacon bits which is why my favorite nosh is ham on bagel."

Rabbi Raphael coughed, spat into his napkin, adjusted his yarmulke and cried, *"Oy Gottenyul"*

-Finish-

Loving Wife and Mother Winnie Knoll

Loving Daughter and Sister Margaret Knoll

Loving Husband and Father Harold Knoll

This book is dedicated to the memory of my generous and loving father, Harold Knoll, my mother Winnie Knoll, and my precious sister, Margaret Knoll.

Daniel Knoll, son and brother